SEDUCING
the BRIDE

Brides of Mayfair series – Book 1

MICHELLE McMASTER

Published by Michelle Killen
ISBN-13: 978-0-9947817-1-0

Cover Art by The Killion Group, Inc.
Interior Formatting by Author E.M.S.

OTHER BOOKS BY
MICHELLE McMASTER

THE BRIDES OF MAYFAIR SERIES

Seducing the Bride

Taming the Bride

His Courtesan Bride

REGENCY SHORT STORY COLLECTIONS

Summer Passions

Autumn Desires

PROLOGUE

Isobel stepped back into the dark hallway of Hampton House, her family's London home, and covered her mouth with her hand.

The shock and fear of what she'd just witnessed made her dizzy...

Her guardian, Mr. Langley, lay dead on the floor of the library.

Sir Harry Lennox—her father's distant cousin—stood over him with a blood-stained knife.

Her worst nightmares were coming true.

Sir Harry had sworn he would have both her and the Hampton fortune eventually. Since her parents' deaths a year ago, Langley had looked after Isobel's affairs—protecting her from gold diggers, swindlers and worse.

Now the poor man was murdered...all because of her.

Her eyes watered with hot tears of grief, but she kept her head. She dared not make a sound. But Sir Harry couldn't kill her—not now. He would want her alive, at least until he forced her into marriage. After that, who knew what her fate would be? Once he gained control of the estate as her husband, Sir Harry could keep Isobel a virtual prisoner.

She'd be damned if she spent the rest of her days as Sir Harry's plaything, and she'd be damned if she allowed him to get his greasy fingers all over the Hampton estate.

There had to be a way to outwit him. But right now, she had to stay alive. Isobel stepped backward gingerly, her slippered feet as silent as a cat's. But in the dark hallway of the townhouse, she bumped into a potted fern on a stand. It knocked softly against the wall, but it was enough to turn Sir Harry's attention from the knife he wiped down with a handkerchief.

Fear spiked in Isobel's gut as he moved toward the library door.

Then her feet froze in place to the floor as Sir Harry's taunting voice called out, "Isobel, my darling girl. So happy you could join me, though it is quite late for you to be up."

She glanced at the clock on the wall and saw that it was near to three in the morning.

"Happy?" she demanded, incredulously. "You've just killed a man...and you dare to say you're happy?"

Sir Harry shrugged, seemingly unconcerned. His tall figure, dark hair and eyes would have made him handsome if not for the black heart that matched his looks. "I am happy, Darling."

"Don't call me that," Isobel spat.

"Come now," he warned, "we're not even married yet and you're already acting like a shrew. But I shall soon cure you of such disobedience."

"We shall never be married, Sir Harry," she insisted. "That I can promise you. Nor shall you ever have control of my family's estate."

"Don't be too sure of that, my dear," he said, slowly walking toward her. "Langley can't protect you anymore. Your father never should have inherited the estate anyway. It should have gone to my father, and then to me. But as you can see, I'm in the process of fixing all that. Hampton Park will be mine, the London townhouse will be mine, and and so will you—one way or another. Now, Isobel, you should be getting back to bed. I urge you to forget whatever it is you think you saw tonight."

Sir Harry came to stand before her, still holding the knife in his hand. Dark, penetrating eyes bored down into hers, with all the malice of the devil himself. His free hand snaked around Isobel's waist and pulled her roughly against him. "But first, I should like a taste of what's to come," he said, lowering his mouth to hover dangerously over hers. "*You will learn to please me....*"

Revulsion, anger and hate burned in the pit of Isobel's stomach. Using all the strength her body possessed, she kneed him hard in the groin.

Sir Harry's eyes nearly popped out of his head and he doubled over, bellowing like an angry bear. He fell to his knees in agony.

It was just the chance Isobel needed.

She ran to the front door, unconcerned at her state of dress. She would take her chances out on the dark streets of London, no matter if she only had a nightdress, housecoat, and slippers to keep her warm.

As she flew down the steps toward the cobblestone street, she heard Sir Harry call out through the open door of the townhouse. "*I'll find you, Isobel! And when I do, I shall make you pay.*"

Isobel refused to look back. Instead she ran as fast as her legs could carry her, and disappeared into the night.

CHAPTER ONE

L ord Beckett Thornby looked down at his cards, hoping that somehow they had changed into a winning hand. Alas, they hadn't.

He sat at a table in London's newest gaming hell, Mrs. Barbary's at No. 16 King Street, St. James. The establishment had no sign hanging outside, or anything else to indicate the type of business, just a brightly painted green door, and was known among the ton simply as 'Barbary's.'

Everyone who was anyone could be seen there, laughing, drinking, and betting til the wee hours of the morning.

For Beckett, this was his last chance. His solicitor had recently informed him that the family funds—what little there was left after his father's disastrous investments— had finally run dry. Beckett would soon have to put the Covington Place townhouse up for sale. His mother would be crushed.

The Dowager Viscountess Thornby was currently visiting her sister, Petunia, and her husband, Sir Charles Bampfylde at their home on Gloucester Street. He only hoped Aunt Petunia would take his mother in and let her live with them after he broke the news. Beckett could look after himself. He could always stay with his friend Alfred, Lord Weston, at his townhouse in Warwick Square.

Beckett glanced across the room and saw Alfred at the Hazard table, which made his mood even darker. Damnation, why couldn't Alfred stick to cards like he was doing? At least you had more of a chance at winning something.

Of course he was losing badly right now, so perhaps Alfred had the right idea.

One of the ladies of the house slowly sauntered by his table. She wore a daring gown of lavender silk with a low bust line which left little to the imagination, but then again, that was the whole point for the girls at Barbary's. Augusta—that was her name—gazed at him with heated green eyes and flirtatiously twirled a tendril of auburn hair around her finger. Damn, but she reminded him of Cordelia...yet another thing to solidify his bad mood.

Augusta ran a gloved hand across Beckett's shoulder, lingering beside him. "If you win," she said seductively, "will you buy me a new bauble?"

"Of course," Beckett replied, though after tonight he doubted he'd be able to afford the price of a ribbon to tie up her stocking.

He supposed he should get used to women like Augusta, as no woman of good breeding would have him now. An impoverished viscount wasn't much of a catch in London's Marriage Mart.

Cordelia—his former fiancée—had opened his eyes to that unwelcome fact.

"Damn," Beckett said under his breath, tossing his losing hand on the table. Meanwhile, Sir Benjamin Danvers looked quite pleased with himself, and why wouldn't he be? He'd just won a large sum of money.

Beckett wasn't surprised to see Augusta now hanging off Sir Benjamin's arm, looking up at him adoringly, and flattering him with compliments.

"How fickle is woman," Beckett muttered to himself as he crossed the room to join Alfred at the Hazard table.

They watched with the rest of the crowd as Lord Cranford cast the dice and rolled the same number he'd rolled just previous to that—which was known as the *chance*. The spectators around the table erupted in cheers as Lord Cranford won the round.

"Damn!" Alfred said. "He'll be at it all night, now. I'll never get the dice back."

"It's probably for the best," Beckett replied. "Seems luck has run out for both of us tonight, Alfred. Though I hope we still have funds to hire a cab, otherwise we shall have to walk home."

They retrieved their hats and coats and headed out the door. King Street was fairly quiet at this hour of the night, but for a carriage or two passing by. A fine mist dampened the air.

"I lost almost everything I came in with," Alfred said. "But I think I still have enough for that. Don't tell Great Aunt Withypoll I've been gambling again—she'll cut me off, and we'll both be paupers."

"About Aunt Withypoll," Beckett said, "do you think she'd mind if I came to stay with you for a little while?"

They walked to the corner and stopped beneath a streetlamp, waiting for a cab to come by.

"I don't see why not," Alfred replied. He was his great-aunt's favorite nephew, and she allowed him to use her London townhouse as his main residence. "Is there something wrong with your house?"

"Yes," Beckett said flatly. "It shan't be mine much longer. I shall be forced to sell, I'm afraid. I'm hoping Mother will be able to go and live with Aunt Petunia and Sir Charles until I get things sorted out."

"It's that bad, is it?' Alfred asked.

"Unfortunately, yes," Beckett said. "My funds are all but exhausted. I was hoping to win something tonight to get me through the month, but we know how that turned out."

"Damn, Beckett—how are you going to find a wealthy bride now?" Alfred said. "When word gets out that Lord Beckett Thornby is poorer than a church mouse, the Mad Mamas of the Marriage Mart won't let you anywhere near their daughters. After Cordelia broke your engagement, you should have accepted Aunt Withypoll's offer to find you a wealthy bride. You could be married now with a baby on the way."

"Married—to Lady Hortense Higginbotham?" Beckett said, wincing. "I tell you, I did not know it was possible for a woman to giggle uninterrupted for almost an entire day—without hurting herself."

"I'm sure you could have gotten used to it," Alfred said.

"I didn't see you offering for her hand."

"Well, I am not desperate for a rich wife, as you are," Alfred pointed out.

Beckett said, "*Yet*. You may well end up in my shoes one day, trying to sell yourself to the highest bidder in order to survive."

He leaned up against the cold lamppost as the mist dampened his coat, marveling how the weather matched the mood of the evening perfectly.

He heard a strange sound and cocked his head to listen.

Was someone moaning?

"There it is again," he said.

"There what is again?" Alfred asked.

"Shh!" Beckett hissed.

The two men listened intently as the sound seemed to emanate from a pile of rubbish alongside the gutter. It sounded like an animal in distress. Beckett crept toward the source of the sound, and in the dim lamplight, he saw a bedraggled cat hunching over a pile of fish heads in the trash-strewn alley.

Beckett held out his hand to the animal, carefully moving closer to it. But as he neared, the skittish cat sprang away, revealing a sight that made Beckett stumble backward in surprise.

He saw the face of a young woman lying motionless, surrounded by a stinking pile of rubbish that covered her like a vile blanket. Her eyelids were closed and dirt smeared her cheek...but even in such a condition, she possessed an ethereal beauty that made his gut tighten.

A small bare foot stuck out from under a ripped sack. The girl's only clothing was a dirty, damp nightdress, which was molded like a second skin to her body beneath. She looked like a doll that had been thrown away by a careless child.

A surge of protectiveness rushed through Beckett's veins, and he fought against it. He didn't want to feel anything for any woman, least of all this mysterious girl. And yet the urge to take her into his arms, to shield her from whatever had brought her here lingered. Unable to stop himself, he reached out to touch her face.

"It looks like some unfortunate trollop has been thrown out for the night," said Alfred. "Cover her back up and let's go."

"What?" Beckett demanded.

"You heard me." Alfred stepped back and crossed his

arms. "Let's go. I'm tired and I'm wet, now leave the wench where she belongs, in the gutter."

"Alfred, are you blind?" Beckett asked. "She's not from the gutter. Look at her nightdress. It is exquisitely made. And besides, streetwalkers usually don't ply their trade wearing only a nightgown and no shoes."

He checked her pulse and found it strong.

"Perhaps, but what would you have us do, Beckett?"

"We can't leave her here. God knows what might happen to her if we did," Beckett said.

"Try to wake her and see if she's alright. If she is, we'll go on our way," Alfred suggested.

Beckett touched her shoulder and gave her a little shake. "Miss? Miss—are you alright?" She gave no response. He checked her breathing and found it unencumbered.

Looking up at his friend he said, "She is unconscious, but I don't see any other signs of injury. Perhaps she fell and hit her head. We must get her home. I'd call the doctor, but I don't have any money to pay him. Now, you lift her shoulders and I'll take her feet."

Alfred groaned, putting his hands under the girl's arms and lifting her upper body. Beckett took her ankles.

"This is a bad idea, old man," Alfred warned.

"Your problem is—you never want to do anything heroic," Beckett said.

"No," Alfred corrected, "I never want to do anything utterly stupid, that's all. I still remember how you insisted it was our duty as officers to save those kittens from Napoleon's guns in Salamanca. It wasn't enough that you'd rescued a convent full of virgins, oh no! You had to save their cats, too. I still have the scars from that little escapade. And then there was the cow that we helped to give birth—a very messy episode, as I recall." Alfred shifted the girl's weight and added, "And need I mention the irate goose who tried to peck us to death when we rescued its eggs from being Wellington's breakfast?"

"Quit complaining," Beckett said. "You couldn't turn your back on any of those creatures any more than I could—just as you can't turn your back on this poor girl now."

The girl's head drooped to the side. A mass of damp honey-blond curls fell away from her face and revealed a nasty bruise near her hairline.

The thin nightdress clung wetly to her body, so that it was almost invisible. Beckett wanted to be a gentleman and avert his eyes from this involuntary display of her charms. He wanted to ignore the effect such sweetness was having on his own body. He wanted to tell himself she was just another stray, like the swan he had found walking down the middle of the Strand, or the sick, weakened puppy he had nursed back to health. But she wasn't.

Her innocent beauty had quiet an effect on him.

A coach turned the corner onto King Street and Beckett said, "Flag it down, quick."

The vehicle slowed beside the curb and stopped, the black horse stomping its hoof impatiently. Steam blew from its nostrils into the cold, damp night. The two men gingerly placed their silent cargo inside, under the driver's suspicious gaze.

"My dear cousin is ill," Beckett lied. "Please take us to Number Ten, Covington Place. There we can properly look after the young lady."

As the vehicle rumbled down the street, Beckett gazed at the girl across from him. What was he doing rescuing this strange girl in the middle of the night? This was no stray kitten he was bringing into his home. She could be anything from an innocent lost lady to a dangerous murderer, for heaven's sake. And yet, he'd never been able to turn away a creature in need. But would he later regret this penchant for rescuing strays?

He wanted to laugh at himself. He already had so many regrets, what was one more?

CHAPTER TWO

As the coach turned onto Covington Place, Beckett ran his hands over his face, trying to wake himself up. The coach came to a jolting halt in front of the townhouse, and Beckett stepped out. He reached back in to receive the girl's feet as Alfred lifted her shoulders. Finally, they managed to get her out and into Beckett's arms. Alfred paid the coachman while Beckett headed up the walk.

The ornately carved door of the townhouse opened silently, as if by magic. Beckett's valet, Hartley, stood behind it as they entered the foyer. Since Beckett could only afford one manservant, the long-suffering Hartley assumed the duties of butler, as well. Sitting on the man's shoulder was Beckett's African gray parrot, Caesar. Both looked at Beckett with interest.

"Who is the lady, sir?" Hartley asked.

"A poor woman in distress. Let's get her upstairs." With a nod to the valet, Beckett commanded him to light their way.

"Hello. You're a pretty bird," said Caesar.

"Hello, Caesar," Beckett replied as they trudged up the

staircase. He said to Hartley, "What's he still doing awake?"

"*Still awake*," said Caesar.

"I put him to bed, sir," Hartley explained, "along with Master Monty, Miss Cleo and the puppies—as you instructed. But Master Caesar simply would not keep quiet. He kept screeching and jabbering until I could take no more. I'm afraid he does that when you are out late at night, sir."

The familiar clicking of twenty toenails accompanied them on the stairs, and Beckett glanced down to see his mongrel, Monty, bounding up beside them onto the landing. "Come to see the new addition, eh, Monty?"

The big brown dog panted up at him in response, his thick, pink tongue hanging out of his mouth.

"What luck, Monty," Alfred whispered. "Your master has found you another playmate!"

"Hartley, we'll need fresh linens for our wayward miss. She'll sleep in my room tonight," Beckett ordered.

"Your room, my lord?" Hartley asked, an eye-brow raised.

"Yes, my room," Beckett said. "And don't look at me like that. I'll sleep next door in the sitting room. I want to keep an ear open if she awakens. She may be frightened by the unfamiliar surroundings."

Hartley nodded and said, "This must certainly be the most interesting stray you've rescued, my lord. But I'm afraid she smells as bad as the rest of them put together." He walked down the dark hall with Caesar still on his shoulder.

Beckett looked at the unconscious girl in his arms and took another whiff, turning up his nose. "My word, I think he's right."

Alfred nodded, stifling a yawn. "Why can't you rescue sweet-smelling females?"

"I'll try harder next time," Beckett replied, adjusting the girl's weight in his arms.

With Monty at his side, he walked down the short hallway to his bedchamber. Once inside, he carefully laid the girl's limp body on the huge bed, while Alfred followed him and lit the candles.

The girl's hair spread around her shoulders like a halo on the pillow. Beckett pulled the covers around her and watched her for a moment. No, she certainly wasn't a trollop, so what was she? Who was she?

Hartley hurried into the room carrying linens, towels and blankets, then returned again with a pitcher of warm water. Crossing the room to the washstand, he poured the water into a blue porcelain basin.

"Thank you, Hartley. That is all," Beckett said, and the valet took his leave.

Beckett set the linens on the edge of the bed. "She may not awaken this evening—we shall try to solve the mystery tomorrow."

"Well, Beckett, I shall leave you to it," Alfred said. "Alas, I'm not interested in playing nursemaid this evening. I'll just have a look at her tomorrow when she's cleaned up."

Beckett felt his eyes grow heavy as he stared at Alfred. "I wonder who she is, really...."

"You always did love a good mystery, old man." Alfred started for the door. "I'm going downstairs and have myself another drink. Then I am going to sleep in my usual spot: The Blue Room." Alfred chuckled, saying over his shoulder, "You know, I just thought of something—if you ever call her 'my pet,' it won't be the least bit of a lie."

The door closed and Beckett turned his attention to the unconscious girl lying in his bed. Normally he might have been more excited at the prospect of seeing a beautiful woman in his bed, but he was so tired, he just wanted to go to sleep.

Monty scooted himself closer to the bed and put his chin on it, his big, black nose sniffing energetically at the myriad smells covering the unconscious girl. His tongue snaked out and licked her hand.

"Monty, no!" Beckett said, frowning. "I need you to act as chaperon. It is your duty to make sure nothing untoward happens to our guest, understand?" The dog continued to look at the girl as if she were the sweetest-smelling thing he'd ever encountered.

Beckett tapped his chin and surveyed the situation. The fact remained that someone needed to get her out of that damp, soiled nightdress and dry her off. There were no female servants to ask for assistance. The cook wouldn't arrive for a few hours yet, and even so, would balk at such a request.

There was nothing for it—he would have to do it himself.

It wouldn't be the first time he'd undressed a woman with his eyes closed, Beckett told himself, though he'd usually be kissing the woman at the same time.

He felt his way to the buttons down the front of her dress. There were so many of them, and the damn things were as tiny as pebbles. This was not going to be a quick job....

When he was finally through them all, he eased the garment from her shoulders. It would be all he'd need for her to awaken right now, while a strange man was undressing her. How on earth would he explain that?

He worked as quickly as he could, peeling the dress off her warm, wet torso and down around her legs. Beckett reached for one of the blankets Hartley had brought to the room and covered the girl with it. He opened his eyes, sighing with relief that he'd managed to complete such a sensitive task while behaving as properly as he could.

She moaned and turned her head on the pillow.

Beckett leaned over to check her pulse and found it still strong. There seemed to be no problem with her breathing, and now that she was out of the cold, her color was improving.

He wondered what had happened to her. Had some dastardly man drugged her...? He'd heard of such things before, though the thought of it disgusted him. Hopefully, the morning would find her in a better way.

He had known other women before...hell, he'd even fancied himself in love with Cordelia. And yet there was something about this mysterious girl which got under his skin.

He yawned again and crossed the chamber toward the adjoining sitting room. The sofa there would suffice. He beckoned to Monty. "Come on, boy."

Panting calmly, the dog showed no signs of movement.

"Monty, come," Beckett commanded. In response, the dog moved to the foot of the bed and flopped down on the floor.

"You're right, Monty," Beckett said. "You should stay here and protect her. Good boy."

Beckett made his way toward the sitting room sofa, weariness dragging at him like a clinging child. Resting the candle on the table, he struggled to remove his boots, which hit the floor with a dull thud.

Finally stretching out on the firm sofa, Beckett let sleep take him where it would.

CHAPTER THREE

Beckett rolled over, his eyes still closed. Half-awake, he flung his arm out and it landed on something soft and warm. It felt like a...

Please, please don't let that be what I think it is.

Beckett opened his eyes.

It was what he thought it was.

A warm, naked breast. And attached to the warm, naked breast was a warm, naked woman.

It quickly all came back to him—he'd fallen asleep on the sofa in the next room as planned, but had must have wandered back to his own bed while half-asleep. Now he was in a very compromising position with the mysterious girl he and Alfred rescued from the street the night before.

Gingerly, he removed his hand from the girl's chest but it was too late.

She opened her eyes, a look of terror in their golden-brown depths. Then she screamed.

Beckett sprang from the bed like a cat. The girl jumped up as well, not realizing her nakedness until she was standing. She screamed again, grabbing the blanket and wrapping it hurriedly around herself. She stared at Beckett as if he was the devil himself.

Monty skittered up, and tail wagging, barked at all the commotion.

"Who are you?" she shrieked, grabbing a nearby candlestick. "Stay away from me—or I swear I'll bash your head in!"

"Please refrain, madam," Beckett said. "You will ruin my coiffure, not to mention my health."

"I said, stay away!" she yelled, brandishing the candlestick when he took a step closer.

"I'm staying away" Beckett answered. "Far, far away over here. Now, be a good girl and put that thing down."

"Why? So you can ravish me again?" she shrieked incredulously, pulling the blanket closer around her naked body.

"Ravish you? No, no—you misunderstand. I can explain everything, but you must be quiet!" He half-shouted, half-whispered his words, not wanting to wake the household.

"I will not be quiet until you explain who you are and why you've brought me here! And what have you done with my clothes?" she demanded.

"Ah, yes," Beckett replied. "Your clothes... I'm afraid they're not here at the moment."

"Not here?" she said. "I suppose they grew tired of my company and simply walked away?"

Beckett tried not to laugh, but the effort seemed to rile the girl's anger even more. She grabbed a little clock and launched it at his head. Beckett ducked, and just missed having his face rearranged by the marble timepiece.

He stood straight again and whistled. The girl had an impressive aim.

"So you intend to keep me prisoner like this?" she

asked heatedly. "Am I to spend the rest of my days naked in your rooms?"

"Don't put ideas into my head," he answered smoothly.

Hartley's voice echoed in the hallway, "No, no, Lady Thornby, don't go in there!"

The door creaked open. In his strangest nightmare, Beckett could not have imagined what he would see there, standing in the hall behind his worried valet.

His mother and his solicitor.

They stared with pale, bloodless faces at the scene before them. Beckett realized what it must look like, standing there with a beautiful, half-naked woman in his bedchamber. Of course, that fact that he was bare-chested himself wouldn't help, either.

"Oh,..." his mother cried, her hand to her mouth. Her eyes rolled back in her head and she fainted in a heap of ribbons and lace.

As Hartley quickly attended to Lady Thornby, Mr. Livingston of Livingston, Farraday & Peel stared at the shocking scene with bulging eyes, and Martha, the portly cook, covered her mouth with a flour-stained hand.

Alfred appeared in the hallway as well, and seemed quite amused by the scene.

Monty skittered around the room, still wagging his tail and barking at the girl in the blanket. She fearlessly brandished the heavy candlestick, sizing up the new arrivals as if to choose who first to clobber.

"Monty, quiet!" Beckett said.

The dog hushed, but everyone else seemed to take it as a cue to pelt Beckett with questions, though Lady Thornby was still out cold.

"—What is going on, sir?" said Livingston.

"—Oh, m'lord, who is that lady? What shall we do?" said Martha.

"—I demand to know who all of you people are!" shrieked the girl.

"I said, quiet, all of you!" Beckett commanded. "Martha, would you take the young miss into my chamber and try to quiet her nerves?"

"My nerves don't need quieting," the girl retorted, eyeing the cook distrustfully.

"Come on, now, miss," Martha said. "Just do what the master asks."

"He's not my master," she said haughtily. "He hasn't even told me who he is."

"Lord Beckett Thornby, at your service," Beckett said, and made a grand, sweeping bow.

"That name means nothing to me," she replied, hotly. The blanket slipped farther down her shoulder, and she fought to pull it up. "How do I even know that you are who you say you are?"

"I can vouch for Lord Thornby's identity, madam," Mr. Livingston said. "I am his solicitor, and have been for many years. He is of the utmost character and breeding, I assure you."

"I don't care if he's the regent himself," the girl replied. "He has brought me here against my wishes, and now I want to leave."

"No one is stopping you, Miss..." Beckett prodded.

She sidestepped the question. "You know I can't leave. I haven't any clothes—thanks to you, Lord Thornby."

"We shall procure you some clothes, then," Beckett assured. "And you may do as you wish. But I insist that you stay for breakfast. My reputation would be ruined if it became known I didn't properly entertain my guests."

She seemed to weigh her options, then nodded her agreement.

"A pot of strong tea for our guest, then, Martha," Beckett said.

Still clutching the candlestick, the girl followed Martha from the room.

"And you thought bringing her home was a good idea," Alfred whispered into Beckett's ear.

"It seems I've made nothing but a mess of this," Beckett observed.

"I did try to warn you," Alfred said, grinning/

Beckett glared at his friend. "I'm glad you find this amusing." Then he asked his solicitor, "Livingston, what exactly are you doing here, at this hour of the morning?"

"My lord," offered Mr. Livingston. "It is well past noon. I met Lady Thornby as she was coming to your door. It was then that I was able to share with her the good news."

"What good news is that, Livingston?" Beckett asked, thinking he was due for some.

"Why, of your inheritance, my lord," the solicitor replied.

"I haven't got an inheritance, man. That's my whole problem."

"Oh, but you do, sir," Livingston said. "Your mother's cousin, the Earl of Ravenwood, has died without any heirs of his body, leaving you the next in line."

Beckett shook his head. "Lord Ravenwood has both a son and a grandson, Livingston. You are terribly misinformed."

"Actually, my lord, I am very well-informed," Livingston said, unfazed. "The earl's son, Lord Haughton, was killed in a boating accident only days before Lord Ravenwood's own death. Unfortunately, Lord Haughton's only son was with him and also perished in the accident. I have the honor, my lord, of naming you heir to the sixth earl of Ravenwood."

Beckett stood back on his heels. "Is this some kind of joke? Alfred, did you put him up to this?"

"I assure you, it is not," the solicitor replied.

"Oh... I have swooned..." Lady Thornby murmured, regaining consciousness.

Beckett crouched down beside her, assisting Hartley as he struggled to raise Lady Thornby to a sitting position.

"Mother, are you alright?" Beckett asked, daintily adjusting her lace cap from where it had fallen over her eye.

He was rewarded with a hearty slap across the cheek. Well, he thought, as he rubbed the stinging flesh, at least his mother was feeling better.

"I am not alright, Beckett," Lady Thornby said haughtily. "Thanks to you and your disgraceful shenanigans."

The portly lady rose to her feet with much grunting and groaning, pushing away those who tried to help her.

Lady Thornby pointed an accusing finger at her son. "I want to know one thing. Who is that disgraceful woman?"

"How do you know she's disgraceful?' he asked, purposely trying to irritate his mother.

"Because she was not wearing any clothes, Beckett. She was clad in only a bed sheet!" Lady Thornby retorted.

Beckett shrugged. "Newborn babies arrive into the world unclothed. If your theory is correct, then babies are also disgraceful, simply because they do not yet possess a wardrobe."

Lady Thornby's eyes narrowed. "This is no time for your silly games, my boy. You are trying to distract me from the problem at hand. I saw a half-dressed hussy in your bedchamber. What in the world should I think?"

"The opposite of what you are thinking," Beckett said dryly.

Lady Thornby huffed, saying, "You have not yet answered my question, Beckett. Who is that woman, and how did she end up in this house?"

"The girl was unconscious when we found her," Beckett explained. "Alfred and I brought her home and we took her straight to bed—I mean, *put* her straight to bed. I went to sleep in the sitting room, but I must have returned to my own bed without realizing."

"You expect me to believe that?" his mother asked.

Beckett continued, "I expect you to trust me, yes. I don't know who she is, but I'm sure of one thing—she's no strumpet. She obviously doesn't live in the street, or she would have been in much worse shape. Her dress was not in tatters, but looked quite finely made. It was merely soiled."

"That only proves that she's new at the profession and she has a skilled seamstress," Lady Thornby replied peevishly.

"You're wrong, Mother," Beckett said "and I won't apologize for my actions. She may have died if we had left her in the street. You know I can't abandon a creature in need."

"You want me to believe she's another one of your strays?" Lady Thornby shrieked, disbelief in her eyes. "I am getting old, but my brain is far from addled. I saw what I saw. And what's worse, Mr. Livingston saw it as well."

"Well, I'm sure Livingston can be trusted to keep this quiet." Beckett gave a pointed look to the solicitor. "And now that I'm the earl of Ravenwood, what does it matter how many strays I take in—or if they happen to be animal or human?"

"Actually, my lord, you aren't the earl quite yet," Livingston said.

"But you said that I was the heir," Beckett replied.

"So you are, my lord, but there is a stipulation in the sixth earl's will, which is quite standard," Livingston explained. "The will specifies that the heir must be married in order to inherit, or the estate will immediately pass to your cousin, Mr. Coles of Dorsetshire. In fact, I have already received a letter from his solicitor regarding execution of the earl's will. Since Mr. Coles is already married, my lord, I would hasten to find yourself a bride."

Lady Thornby grabbed her son's arm. "I'm sure the Honorable Miss Cordelia Haversham will take you back, under the circumstances."

"Mother, I will choose my own bride, if you please," Beckett said stiffly. "Cordelia Haversham is the last woman in the world that I'd marry. And you well know the reason why."

"But that dreadful business is all behind us now," Lady Thornby said, waving her hand in dismissal. "If only I had known that your father had less sense for numbers than a chicken, I could have stopped him from investing in his reckless schemes. But once Cordelia learns that our fortunes have been restored, I'm sure she'll reinstate your engagement. Her mother has been like a sister to me—we are such close friends. And Cordelia would make a wonderful countess!"

"Mother, I would sooner marry that girl in there!" Beckett pointed at the closed door of his bedchamber.

"Oh, don't talk flummery, Beckett," Lady Thornby admonished.

"Perhaps it's not flummery," Beckett said, enjoying the look of horror that had crossed his mother's face. "Perhaps I am quite serious about the idea."

"Fuddle-duddle!" she replied. "It is not your place to choose a bride, especially when that bride will be the next countess of Ravenwood."

"But it is my place to be led to the altar in a yoke and put to stud, I suppose," he retorted.

"Beckett...remember yourself!" she sputtered.

"I should be so lucky as to forget," Beckett said, folding his arms across his chest. "It will be up to me to decide, Mother, not you, or the ton, or anyone else. But mark me well, whichever bride I choose, it will certainly not be the Honorable Miss Cordelia Haversham."

His mother's eyes flashed. "I've always known you'd be a disappointment to me, Beckett. And now, you've ruined the one thing that would have made me happy—to bring Cordelia into the family where she belongs. But if you're as intent on ruining your life as your father was, well then, I wish you luck."

"Father did the best he could for us, Mother," Beckett said. "He was a kind-hearted man who made the mistake of trusting a swindler. He didn't mean to leave us penniless."

"Well, you certainly are your father's son," Lady Thornby said coldly. "You've done nothing but embarrass me from the time you could crawl. Always courting trouble, with complete disregard for the scandals you've caused. Well, now you're going to create a real sensation, aren't you? Go on, marry that little trollop in there, or any other hussy you like. It's none of my concern."

With a toss of her head Lady Thornby swept down the hall, stopping at the end of it, dramatically. "I will see myself out," she said, chin high, and disappeared down the staircase.

"I don't know why I bother going to the theater," Alfred said. "I see more drama under your roof than I ever do at Drury Lane."

"So do I," Beckett said flatly.

Mr. Livingston donned his hat. "I'll be going then as

well, my lord. I advise you to find a bride as soon as possible, so that we may proceed with the details of the inheritance. Considering the uncertain state of your finances at present, I should think you'll be anxious to take your new title." The solicitor made a quick bow and left.

Moments later, Martha emerged from the bed-chamber and closed the door quietly behind her.

"How is our guest, Martha?" Beckett asked.

"Restin', m'lord. She took some laudanum with her tea. She'll sleep for a bit, I expect."

Beckett nodded. "Let's leave her until she awakens. Then she and I shall have a little chat."

The men sauntered down the hallway and entered the drawing room, Monty following. Beckett flopped down on the sofa and looked at his dog, who sat near him, his tongue hanging out of the side of his mouth and dangling in rhythm with his panting breaths. He looked as if he hadn't a care in the world. Beckett reached out a hand and rubbed Monty's head, bringing an expression of pure ecstasy to the mongrel's face.

Alfred brought a bottle of brandy and two glasses out of one of the cupboards. He poured the brandy and handed one of the snifters to Beckett.

"Brandy for breakfast?" Beckett asked. "I suppose it wouldn't be the first time."

"A Livingston said, it's well past noon, so this can be considered luncheon," Alfred said. "Are you going to marry her, then?"

"I said that to give Mother a shock," Beckett replied, "but given my urgent need for a wife, I'm starting to warm to the idea."

"Your mother's right about Cordelia," Alfred pointed out. "Now that you stand to inherit a fortune, she would take you back—but I know you don't want to fall in love with her again. In fact, I remember you swearing you'd never fall in love with any woman again as long as you lived."

"And I never shall," Beckett stated firmly. "Just because I must take a bride doesn't mean I'm going to fall in love with her. In fact, the perfect bride for any man is one that he is not in love with. Love just spoils things, in the end."

"Exactly," Alfred agreed. "Which is why our mystery girl would be perfect. You don't know her from Eve., and if you don't know her, you can't possibly be in love with her, can you?"

"No." Beckett had an image of her naked covered in nothing but the sheet from his bed.

"Alright," Alfred continued. "Let's review your options. I think I'm right in saying you'd rather have your teeth pulled out by an angry barber than ask Cordelia to take you back. And I think that goes for the other ladies of the ton, who, due to your previous lack of funds, have scorned your recent proposals; though they would surely now be yours for the asking."

Beckett sipped his brandy. "You're right about that. I'd sooner wed a goat than take my suit to any of them."

"I am also assuming you've ruled out Martha, your cook, whom—though she is a lovely woman and makes a delicious 'canard l'orange'—I doubt you would want to kiss, let alone take to your bed."

Beckett frowned.

"Right. Which leaves our girl," Alfred said. "Her voice and manner show her to be cultured—"

"She tried to brain me with a candlestick," Beckett interjected, "and she threw a clock at my head."

Alfred grinned. "So, she's spirited. It'll keep the

27

marriage interesting. She obviously doesn't have any family or she would have asked after them. And as for money, she seems woefully without. So you see, she will probably be more than agreeable—and she's here now, which will save you a lot of time. Not to mention that in the light of day, she is quite an eyeful."

Beckett gave his friend a look of warning. "Watch it—that's my future wife you're talking about."

Alfred ignored the comment and continued, "It's a brilliant scheme, Beck. Marry her, inherit the estate, stick her off on one of your properties—as you would do with any wife—then visit her from time to time to make a baby or two, and you and I go traveling about the continent spending your money and having fun."

"Your reasoning is not without merit," Beckett agreed. "Certainly I never want to fall in love again, with any woman. I've learned that lesson. Love is nothing more than a disease that infects your heart and makes you delusional, leaving you wasted and empty when it has run its course."

"You make it sound so dreary." Alfred made a face. "But then again, you'd know. I've certainly never fallen in love."

"It is dreary. It's worse than dreary," Beckett asserted. "Love is an illusion, old chum. Cordelia taught me that. I can still see the look in her eyes when I told her my father had lost most of my inheritance in bad investments. She told me everything had changed. I realized then that the only thing that had changed was my eyesight. For the first time, I was seeing things as they really were."

"Well, you wouldn't have to worry about that with our mystery girl," Alfred argued. "Marry her, and you're the next earl of Ravenwood. You'll have money, power and position. What's not to like about that?"

Beckett swished the last of his brandy around in his glass, and then downed it. The fact remained that he had to marry somebody, or risk losing his inheritance. There was no doubt—he was attracted to the girl. The golden hair, the challenging eyes, the perfection of a body he shouldn't have lay next to in bed, not to mention her spirited nature.

The decision was made, then.

"Alright, Alfred. You win. I shall make her my bride," Beckett said, standing. "I only hope I can convince her."

As Beckett shook his friend's proffered congratulatory hand, he found himself smiling. It was the perfect plan. A marriage of convenience would keep his life just as he liked it. Simple and uncomplicated.

And what could be more simple and uncomplicated than marriage to a beautiful, golden-haired goddess he'd found in the gutter?

CHAPTER FOUR

The pale yellow light of late afternoon crept through the window, filling the bedchamber with a warm, golden glow. Isobel lay on her side in the huge bed, wondering what time it was. She surveyed the room groggily, studying the dark mahogany furniture and the heavy brocade draperies.

There was a distinct smell in this chamber. It smelled faintly of cigar smoke and leather and horse. In short, it smelled like a man.

A knock sounded on the door, startling her. She sat up in bed and brushed the hair away from her face.

Was it Sir Harry, come to take her away? Was she in the house of his minions?

Another knock came, only a little louder.

She grabbed the candlestick and leapt from the bed, now clad in one of the cook's dressing gowns. If it was Sir Harry, he wasn't leaving this house without a nice big hole in his head.

The knob turned slowly, and Isobel watched, readying herself to spring into action. As the door opened, she braced herself for the worst.

It was the man who had lain in bed with her. He looked to be in his late twenties, tall and muscular, with a handsome face to match his sparkling blue eyes. His wavy, tawny-brown hair gave him a mischievous air, and when he looked at her, he smiled.

"I should like to come in for a chat, if you promise not to brain me with that," he said.

Isobel nodded warily, lowering her weapon. She kept it at her side as she sat on the edge of the bed.

He entered smoothly and brought a chair from his desk, moving it and sitting down at an acceptable distance away from her.

"Feeling better?" he asked. "You've been resting for a few hours, now."

Isobel felt herself relax a little, and wondered at it. "Yes, thank you."

"I am glad to hear it. I've managed to arrange some clothes for you, so you can leave at any time."

"Thank you," she replied. "That is very kind."

"Not at all," he said. "Of course, you are invited to stay for supper before you go. But before you leave, I wish to make you a proposition. I wish to make you my wife."

The viscount waited for her response. Isobel stared at him silently as a maelstrom of thoughts whirled through her head.

Finally she asked, "I beg your pardon?"

"I wish to marry you," he said.

"And why should you want to do that, my lord?"

"That is a long story, only some of which you know," Lord Thornby replied, rising and walking about the room. "I shall give you the condensed version. You see, last night, my friend Lord Weston and I stumbled upon you unconscious, under a heap of refuse on King Street. We decided that we could not leave you there in good conscience, so we brought you here, to my home."

He ran a hand through his wavy hair. "We put you to bed and I retired to the adjoining room. Unfortunately, I awoke in the night and through habit made my way back here, unwittingly falling asleep beside you. For which I now offer my deepest apologies. You may remember the fiasco that followed with my mother fainting and screaming in shock. While Martha attended to you, I had the most amazing news from my solicitor. News which also concerns you, my dear."

"Me?" Isobel asked, her pulse quickening. Was Sir Harry involved in this somehow? Had he found her, as he'd promised?

"Yes," Lord Thornby answered. "You see, it appears that I am the sole heir to the sixth earl of Ravenwood. In order to claim my inheritance, I must have a bride."

Isobel stared at him. "A bride?" What did any of this have to do with her?

He continued, "Yes, my dear. And I feel that you would be perfect. Considering the circumstances—you and I caught sharing a bed together—I would presume an offer of marriage to be most acceptable to you. In truth, I offer a business arrangement, one that would be very advantageous to both parties. Of course, it would be a marriage of convenience—a union in name only. We would have to make the usual appearances before the ton—a few balls, the theater and whatnot, then we could go our separate ways. I would provide a handsome allowance, a nice little property of some sort, and you would be, after all, a countess. That is, assuming that you are not already married."

"No," she replied, "I am not married."

"And you have no other family to look after you, or who might object to the match?" he asked.

"No." If she had, she wouldn't be in this mess, she thought.

"Good," he said. "It's settled, then. We can be married by special license."

"One moment, my lord," she said. "I have not yet consented to your proposal."

Lord Thornby paused, piercing her with his dynamic blue eyes. "But I pray that you will."

"You do not even know my name," she pointed out.

"Details," he said, waving a hand in dismissal. "We'll get to your name, eventually."

Why was she even entertaining the idea? Her life had been turned upside down and this man was only making it worse. "My name is Isobel Hampton."

"A perfectly good name," he said. "You see? Isobel, Countess of Ravenwood. It has a ring to it."

"But you don't even know me, my lord," she pointed out.

"Then tell me about yourself," he countered. "How did you come to be in that alley all alone? Where is your family?"

Isobel had never lied to anyone before, never had the need. But she found how quickly one could acquire new skills when it was a matter of survival. She would lie to this man. She would accept his generous offer and gain back her life.

The sad truth was, she would do anything to escape life with Sir Harry Lennox. Anything at all....

"I have no home, Lord Thornby, nor any family." That wasn't completely untrue. "My guardian recently died. He had accumulated a vast debt. The barristers sold everything, and I had nowhere to go." Her lies and the truth were all mixing together now like knotted embroidery floss.

"I am terribly sorry to hear that, Miss Hampton," he said. "Do not trouble yourself further with those awful memories. You needn't tell me everything now. There will be plenty of time for that, if you consent to marry me."

"But why me, my lord?" she asked. "Surely someone of your rank could have any bride he chose."

"That's true, now that I stand to inherit an earldom. And I choose you, Isobel Hampton."

"But why?" she demanded. "I must know."

"I could say all number of things to you," Lord Thornby continued. "I could confess to being overwhelmed by your ethereal beauty, or to feelings of undying love for you. I have my reasons for wanting a marriage of this kind, and part of it has to do with love. You see, I have no interest in it."

He studied her with those blue eyes that seemed to look straight into her very soul. "If you agree to this 'marriage bargain,' you must know that love will never have a place in our union," he said. "What I propose is not so unusual, after all. Most of the marriages in London fare the same, I'd wager. Hopefully, we will enjoy an amiable friendship. Hopefully, there will be children. I must know as soon as possible if you accept. Because if you don't, I'll need to start looking for another bride before the day is out. And I must remind you that although it was an innocent mistake, you have, in fact, been quite decidedly compromised. Of course, the decision is entirely yours."

Isobel twisted her fingers around the candlestick in her hands. The urge to trust him grew stronger. Something in his voice made her feel strangely comfortable in his presence, though she knew she should be wary.

But if his proposal was serious, it could be the answer to her prayers.

Awful memories spun in her head. Even now, a part of

her hoped that what she had seen before her flight from Hampton House had been some sort of nightmare, but the hard knot of fear in her gut meant it had been all too real.

She'd witnessed the murder of her beloved guardian, and the man responsible—Sir Harry Lennox—had sworn to find her. No one could know the depths of the man's depravity. He was determined to possess both Isobel and the Hampton estate, no matter what the cost.

Something had guided her out of that strange hell and led her here—an instinct to survive. She refused to give up now.

This was a golden opportunity. What other option did she have? She had nowhere to go. Marriage to this newly minted earl would offer her valuable protection. She would be safe. Hampton Park would be safe. The price would be a loveless marriage.

Compared to the alternative, it was an attractive offer.

Isobel cleared her throat and leveled her eyes at him. "I accept your proposal, Lord Thornby. I will be your bride. And I understand the terms of our agreement. Completely."

He reached for her hand, and brought it to his lips. A sizzling tingle whispered up her spine as his mouth pressed against her skin. She wanted to lower her eyes to hide her reaction, but found that she couldn't. This man, this handsome stranger with the enigmatic blue eyes, would be her husband.

In name only.

"We shall be married as soon as possible," he said, standing. "Please join me in the salon. We must discuss details about the wedding." He closed the door behind him.

Isobel looked at a crumpled handkerchief that Martha had given her earlier and smoothed it, fingering the pale-blue stitching of his initials. God in Heaven, had she done the right thing? Was a marriage of convenience to this Lord Thornby the only way to remain safe from the fiend who haunted her nightmares, and threatened her body and soul?

Soon she would be Lord Thornby's wife. He needn't know about Hampton Park just yet. He would inherit substantial property with the earldom. When the time came for her to assume her new residence, she would merely state her preference for her ancestral home.

It was dishonest, what she was doing. But given the circumstances, it was clearly her only choice.

Another knock sounded at the door. It opened and Martha came bustling in with a gleaming silver tray carrying steaming tea, mouthwatering scones and pastries, and bowl of fresh, fragrant strawberries with Devonshire cream.

"The master said I was to bring ye a breakfast tray, Miss, even though it is almost time for luncheon," Martha said with a warm smile. She placed the tray over Isobel's lap, then poured the tea. "I hear there's to be a weddin'! And so much to be done. Cakes and pastries to be made. I'll need eggs and kidneys for the breakfast. And ham... Lord Thornby likes ham, so he does..." The cook muttered the last to herself as she waddled out the door.

Isobel raised the cup to her nose and breathed in its warm, earthy scent. She sipped the drink and took a bite of buttered scone, thinking of her wedding. She would need more than tea to get her through that.

As she devoured the contents of the breakfast tray with unladylike speed, Isobel's thoughts centered around the man who would shortly become her husband. Could a man as handsome as Lord Beckett Thornby really be so desperate for a bride that he'd marry a girl he found in a rubbish heap?

Lord Thornby's secrets were none of her concern. Perhaps he wanted to continue with a carefree life, as most noblemen did. Perhaps he already had a mistress. Perhaps he had children with her.

She should consider herself lucky that Lord Thornby had chosen her to be his bride, whatever his reasons.

Suddenly, the memory of waking up next to him sent strange shivers down Isobel's spine. She'd been naked in that bed...and he'd been half-naked, for his part. What exactly had happened between them?

He'd apologized, but he hadn't explained the full truth of the matter. Who exactly had undressed her? The answer hit her with a horrible certainty. It had been *him.*

Isobel felt her blood heat with anger, and something else she couldn't name.

Excitement?

Lord Thornby had taken off her clothes with those strong-looking hands of his. What happened after that?

Still, if Lord Thornby had wanted to take advantage of her, wouldn't he have done so, and tossed her right back onto the street? He certainly wouldn't have felt obliged to offer for her hand in marriage.

A quick knock sounded at the door and Martha appeared, bringing clothes, along with warm water for the wash-basin.

Finished with her breakfast, Isobel completed her toilette and Martha assisted her with dressing.

She donned a fine muslin day dress, with a sprigged pattern of clover green. She couldn't help but wonder where the garment had come from. It was certainly not the portly cook's. Perhaps it belonged to one of Lord Thornby's mistresses. Absently, Isobel thought how she missed her own clothes, her own bed, and her own house.

If she played her cards right, they would be hers again before long.

Isobel pinned up her long blond curls and arranged them as fetchingly as she could. The state of her hair was the least of her concerns.

The heavy door creaked as she opened it, and Isobel almost tripped over the dog lying in the doorway. The shaggy brown shepherd bounded to his feet, tail wagging furiously, and turned around to pant up at her.

"I remember you," she said, patting his big furry head. "You certainly gave me a fright when we first met. But now I see you're really a pussycat. Pardon the comparison."

The dog didn't seem to mind. He regarded her through half-lidded eyes, his pink tongue hanging from the side of his mouth.

"Where's your master?" she asked. "Can you take me to him, boy?"

The dog barked, then trotted down the hallway to the top of the staircase. He stopped to look back at Isobel, then headed down.

As Isobel tried to keep up, she heard loud male voices coming from one of the front rooms. Her heart beat a little nervously at the laughter and scandalous cursing. As the dog led her to a doorway, Isobel heard more of what seemed to be a strange conversation between three people.

"*Caesar want treat. Caesar want treat,*" a strange, high-pitched voice said.

"No, Caesar. No treat," Lord Thornby replied.

"*Caesar good boy. Caesar want treat.*"

"I said no, Caesar."

Did Lord Thornby have a child he hadn't mentioned?

"*Caesar want treat. Caesar want treat. Ahhkk!*"

A loud flapping sound filled the air, and curiosity made

Isobel rush around the doorframe. Her eyes widened as she saw a large gray bird sitting on Lord Thornby's head, flapping its wings and screeching like a banshee.

Thornby turned, the bird still on his head. When he saw her, he grinned mischievously. A dark-haired man stood beside him and chuckled at the scene.

Isobel covered fought to stifle a giggle.

"*Pretty bird. Ahhkk! Pretty bird,*" squawked Caesar.

"That's right, Caesar. She is a pretty bird," Lord Thornby said, grinning wickedly.

Caesar took flight in a flurry of pale gray wings. Isobel squealed in shock as the creature landed on her shoulder and fluffed its feathers.

"Oh!" she sputtered, fearfully looking sideways at the big parrot who studied her with a penetrating yellow eye.

"*Hello. Ahhkk! Hello*" the bird said.

"Caesar! Get off Miss Hampton's shoulder at once, you silly bird! My apologies, Miss Hampton," Lord Thornby said, putting the loudly protesting bird back in its cage. "Caesar becomes excited when he meets new people."

"Oh, no harm done," she replied. "What kind of bird is he?"

"An African Gray parrot," he replied. "I found him sitting in a tree in Hyde Park one morning. He flew down to see me, and I brought him home to join the menagerie."

"You mean there are more?" Isobel asked.

"Beckett's been taking in stray animals since we were boys," the man next to her fiancé answered.

"Do forgive me, Miss Hampton," Lord Thornby said. "Allow me to introduce Lord Weston, who assisted me in bringing you home. Alfred, Miss Isobel Hampton, soon to be the Viscountess Thornby and Countess of Ravenwood."

Lord Weston took her hand and gallantly pressed it to

his lips. His dark, coffee-brown eyes bored into hers with a smoldering look. "I am honored to make your acquaintance, Miss Hampton, and very pleased to see you have recovered from your ordeal."

"I owe you a great debt, Lord Weston," Isobel said. "I can only thank you and Lord Thornby for helping me. I'm afraid most people would have left such a bedraggled-looking creature to her fate."

"It is the duty of all gentlemen to protect the fairer sex," he insisted. "I am only thankful that we happened along when we did."

"I am glad to see that the gown fits you," Lord Thornby said. "We borrowed it from Alfred's sister-in-law until I could properly fit you with your own trousseau."

Isobel replied, "You are very generous, my lord—"

"Nonsense, Miss Hampton," Beckett insisted. "I have Madame de Florette coming within the hour. She'll bring a selection of ready-made dresses that she and her seamstresses will alter for you here. They will have to do for the time being, I'm afraid."

"Really, there is no need."

Lord Thornby quirked a brow. "You intend to marry me in that, then?"

Isobel looked down at her borrowed dress. It was totally unsuitable for a wedding. But it wasn't as if this would be a real wedding, anyway. How extravagant could the ceremony be with such short notice?

Why was it so impossible to look away from this man's gaze, she wondered?

He took her hand in his and kissed it, saying, "It is my wish that you be beautifully dressed for our wedding, my dear."

Isobel felt tingles skip over her skin at his touch, his words, and the intensity of his eyes.

This man would be her husband. And she would be his wife, for better or for worse.

As Beckett had promised, Madame de Florette arrived not thirty minutes later. The diminutive, dark-haired Frenchwoman hurried Isobel into Lord Thornby's chamber and began flinging dresses out of a trunk and onto the bed. Her two assistants stood with needles poised, like soldiers ready for battle.

The women spoke in rapid French as Isobel was fitted for a multitude of dresses. And though Isobel spoke the language fluently, Madame de Florette never asked for Isobel's opinion on any of the gowns—in English or in French.

But when Madame de Florette presented the last dress, she gave Isobel a brilliant smile. "Your wedding dress, ma belle. I had been making it for the Marquess of Salisbury's daughter, but apparently, she has called it off. The groom was caught with not one but *two* other women in zee Marquess's own bed." She wagged a finger and said, "Tsk, tsk tsk! But zis dress should not go to waste. For you, ma chere, I'll put more bagatelles, a different trim, and no one will know ze difference!"

Isobel held her arms out as Madame de Florette slipped the dress over her shoulders. The women fluttered around her like sparrows—pinning, stitching bows and trims, and Isobel felt a huge sadness wash over her like a cold ocean wave.

This was her wedding dress. So many times as a girl, she had dreamed of her wedding. Of marrying a dashing, gallant man—a handsome hero who had won her heart. She had never dreamed of a marriage of convenience to a man she barely knew. Obviously, such girlish wishes of love no longer had a place in her life. Not with Sir Harry as such a threat.

Now, there was only duty—to her future husband. And to Hampton Park. If Isobel didn't become Lord Thornby's bride, Hampton Park would be lost forever.

The thought of Sir Harry clouded her vision and made her stomach swirl with loathing. After tomorrow, she would be safe from the foul monster. He would never put his threatening hands on her again. He would never take such liberties with a countess.

"There, ma petite. C'est finil" Madame de Florette waved her hand dramatically. Her assistants agreed, making last-minute adjustments to the flounces and bows.

The dress was beautiful, but Isobel felt nothing for it. She forced herself to smile as Madame de Florette placed the veil on her head.

Isobel just wanted the ceremony to be over. Then she would feel safe. And she would be that much closer to starting her new life alone at Hampton Park as the Countess of Ravenwood.

The dressmaker and her assistants spent the rest of the day taking measurements, and showing her fabrics and patterns. Isobel's arms ached from being held out straight and her eyes itched with tiredness.

When Madame de Florette and her assistants finally took their leave, Isobel found herself alone in the grand townhouse. It seemed that her husband-to-be and his friend Lord Weston had gone to their club for the evening and were not expected to return for some hours. Isobel took her supper alone, then retired early, exhausted from the day's preparations.

In the days before the wedding, Isobel stayed at the London townhouse alone. Beckett had gone to Kent, looking after the business of the Ravenwood estate.

On the morning of their wedding, Isobel was helped to dress by Martha, who, though she undoubtedly knew how to dress a turkey, proved to be all thumbs with a woman and a wedding gown. Still, together Martha and Isobel managed to secure all the buttons and affix the veil to her hair with some semblance of style.

As Isobel descended the townhouse staircase, Lord Thornby waited for her at the bottom. He leaned against the banister with one foot crossed over the other, looking for all the world as if he were about to go and play at cards. He was impeccably dressed, with a dark blue superfine coat making his eyes glow like sapphires.

Suddenly, Isobel's knees seemed made of apple jelly.

As she placed her hand in his, Isobel realized that as his bride, she would have to do whatever this man wanted. Wasn't that what all women had to do when they married? Why should her marriage be any different?

If he wanted to exercise his rights as a husband, she would have to surrender. Isobel wished she had a mother to advise her. Still, whatever Lord Thornby would do to her couldn't possibly be as vile as being touched by Sir Harry Lennox.

She struggled to shut the images from her mind. Her skin crawled as she felt Sir Harry's hard hand circling her waist and pulling her body against his.

It was no matter if she'd sold herself into a marriage of convenience for protection. She would be safe now. Everything had its price.

The carriage ride to the little church in Carberry Lane took only fifteen minutes, and it seemed to take less time than that for Lord Thornby to slip a ring onto her finger and for the rector to pronounce them man and wife.

Isobel looked up at Beckett's face as he leaned down to kiss her. She'd been quite unprepared for the heat of her husband's mouth, for the heady, male scent of his skin, and for the thrill that shot down her spine to the tips of her toes.

If her knees had felt like apple jelly before, they were now no more substantial than clotted cream.

Beckett broke the kiss and she looked up into fathomless eyes.

The rector spoke again, though what it was exactly that he said, Isobel didn't quite know. She was too busy staring at the man she had just bound herself to for life, as his friend Lord Weston shook his hand and gave him a beaming smile.

As they descended the church steps, a beautiful woman with rich auburn hair walked toward the bridal party. The woman's emerald-green eyes flashed up at her. An unbridled hostility glowed there, and seemed to be directed squarely at Isobel.

Who was this woman? And what did she want with them on their wedding day?

"So, Beckett," the flame-haired woman said. "This is the woman you dared to marry instead of me."

CHAPTER FIVE

Beckett kept his expression impassive. It would do no good to give Cordelia any satisfaction. This was his wedding day. And it might have been hers, too, if she'd been interested in more than just his inheritance. It stung to think of how blind he'd been.

"Miss Haversham," he said. "You're looking well."

"I wish I could say the same for you, Beckett," she replied. "You seem a trifle out of sorts. Of course, the stress of such hasty wedding plans would give anyone a turn, wouldn't it?"

"Strange how you found out about them so quickly," he noted.

Cordelia smiled, but there was no warmth in it. "Thankfully, your mother called upon me and told me of this ridiculous notion. Did you think I was going to let you make both of us the laughingstock of London?"

"Meaning?" Beckett asked.

"All of the *ton* knows about this girl you found in the gutter, Beckett," Cordelia said, as though Isobel were not standing right there beside him. "But I want you to know that I'm willing to overlook this bit of madness. You can have the marriage annulled immediately and we will have a proper wedding, not some farcical ceremony in a rundown church in the most unfashionable part of London."

Cordelia adjusted her gloves and looked at Beckett as if all were decided. "I must say, Beckett, I had no idea what lengths you'd go to in order to win me back. Truthfully, I am flattered. But it really was a bit much, don't you think, darling?" She glanced at Isobel. "A fine countess she'd make."

"My wife and I thank you for the compliment, Miss Haversham," Beckett said. "You are right, of course. Isobel is now Viscountess Thornby, and will soon be the Countess of Ravenwood. My lovely wife will undoubtedly make me the envy of the ton."

Damn, but he was enjoying this.

"You can't be serious, Beckett," Cordelia snapped, vainly trying to regain her composure. "You and I were to be married. We had an understanding."

"Until we didn't," he said. "You broke with me, Cordelia. You have no claim."

"Be assured—I won't be put aside so easily," she warned.

"I'm afraid you already have been," Beckett replied, turning to look at his bride

Cordelia's green eyes shot sparks at him. "You can't do this to me, Beckett. You made me promises. And I intend to have what is rightfully mine."

"Nothing of mine ever was or will be yours, Cordelia," he said. "You were quite willing to break our engagement when you found my inheritance to be no more than a few shillings. And your feelings on the matter are worth less than that to me now."

"But surely you knew that I wasn't serious about

breaking our engagement, Beckett," Cordelia replied. "A woman never is."

"So I mistook your intentions when you threw the ring in my face?" he asked.

"A lovers' quarrel, nothing more," she said. "We can put that nonsense behind us, and I will be your wife, as you've always wanted."

"It is strange to think it, Miss Haversham," Beckett said. "I did want that once. But I have chosen my bride, and I intend to keep her."

"But—" Cordelia looked disbelievingly at Isobel and then back at Beckett. "But, I must be your wife. I must be the Countess of Ravenwood!"

"I have my countess. Good day, Cordelia," Beckett said, touching the brim of his hat and leading Isobel toward their waiting coach.

Beckett handed his wife into the plush interior and stepped in beside her, sitting on the burgundy velvet seat. He felt a wave of relief. A chapter of his life finally had been closed, and another one was just beginning.

Isobel's intelligent brown eyes studied him as the coach jerked forward.

"My apologies for that dreadful scene, my dear," he said. "What is it they say—hell hath no fury like a woman scorned?"

"But I thought it was she who had scorned you," Isobel said.

"Cordelia was only interested in my money—" Beckett stated, "until it turned out I had none. Now that I am to become an earl, she has changed her mind once again."

"But you have not?"

"No," he said stiffly.

"I thought her quite beautiful," Isobel commented.

"As beautiful as a rose—with rather vicious little

thorns," Beckett said cynically. "If one gets too close, you end up bleeding."

"Is that why you have chosen me for a bride, my lord?" Isobel asked. "Because thorns pricked you last time, and you've sworn to give up gardening?"

"I was never much for roses," he said, adjusting his cuffs. "They make me sneeze."

Isobel closed the heavy book and rested it in her lap. Somehow, reading The Taming of the Shrew again had failed to lighten her mood as it usually did. Instead, it made her feel like Katharina, suddenly wed to a stranger—her world irrevocably changed.

The play had a happy ending.

Would her marriage turn out as well?

She had spent the afternoon and evening alone. After the wedding breakfast, Beckett had gone to complete the business of his inheritance with Lord Weston in tow. He had assured her that he would be home by six o'clock. It was now half-past nine.

Oh, she wanted to kick herself! Not even married a full day, and she was already acting like a shrew. Her husband's affairs were none of her concern. What did it matter when he came home, if at all? For if he did, it would bring up the question of the wedding night.

Lord Ravenwood—for Beckett was the earl now—had said the marriage was no more than a business transaction. But would he want a wedding night, with all the trimmings? What man wouldn't?

Perhaps if she retired now to her chamber, he would be reluctant to disturb her when and if

opened the door into the hallway, another door

opened, and accompanied by a draft of cool night air, her husband walked into the foyer.

Isobel felt a heated thrill move through her.

"Good evening, Isobel," Beckett said, taking off his hat and passing it to Hartley he came home. Yes, that was a good plan. And besides that, it was the only plan she could come up with at the moment.

Isobel rose from the library sofa and replaced the heavy volume on the shelf. Just as she, who quickly left them alone.

"I was just going up to bed," she blurted.

"To bed?" he asked. "That sounds like a wonderful idea."

"It does?" she stammered.

"Quite decidely."

"Oh, no," she replied. "In this case, it doesn't."

"Why not, darling?" He regarded her seriously, but Isobel could have sworn there was the hint of a smile on his lips.

"Because—I am very tired," she said. "And... I'm not feeling well at all. In fact, I am quite ill."

It was true. Her stomach churned dreadfully at the thought of a wedding night. Truly, she felt she must be turning green.

"Really?" he asked. "That is unfortunate."

"Yes—I am very, very ill indeed," Isobel said flatly. "In fact, I may faint."

"Then I must carry you up to your chamber, before you do," he said.

"There is no need—ooh!"

In one swift motion, Beckett swept her into his strong arms and held her as if she weighed no more than a feather.

"Really, I can walk." Isobel pushed against his broad chest, but to no avail. Her husband carried her aloft in his arms, and she was helpless to escape.

Worst of all, the sensation was anything but unpleasant.

Was he holding her tighter?

Whatever he was doing, he was taking his time!

The moments seemed to pass with agonizing slowness as Beckett carried her up the staircase. Funny, but Isobel had never noticed there were so many steps, or that the hallway was so long, or that her husband could set her pulse to racing so quickly.

Beckett entered in the Blue Room, and carried her to the huge, soft bed. Isobel's pulse quickened as he gently lay her down upon it. She half-feared, half-hoped he would join her there.

He looked down into her eyes, reaching out to lift an errant curl from her forehead. The back of his hand brushed against her skin, leaving a trial of tingles dancing over it. "I do hope you are feeling better," he said. "You've had a busy day, my dear. I bid you goodnight."

Isobel closed her eyes and waited for his lips to claim hers, but was surprised when he placed a chaste kiss on her forehead.

She opened her eyes to see him quietly leaving the room, as a knot formed in her heart. He was leaving her alone for the night.

Wasn't that what she'd wanted?

As Isobel lay there alone on the big, empty bed, she realized that it wasn't what she wanted at all.

"Good morning, Hartley," Beckett said, pouring himself a cup of hot black coffee. "Have you seen my wife about? I was told she came down before me."

"Lady Ravenwood is in the garden, my lord," Hartley replied.

"And how did she seem?" Beckett asked. "Did she look to be in good health this morning?"

"She seemed in excellent health, my lord."

Beckett popped a strawberry in his mouth. "Good. I am afraid the excitement of yesterday's events made the countess somewhat ill."

Hartley nodded sagely. "It is often the case with new wives, my lord. But these wedding-day illnesses are quickly cured."

"Undoubtedly," Beckett agreed. He took a linen napkin and placed a handful of strawberries in it, bundling it up and heading down the hallway.

He opened the French doors and walked out into the bright morning. Quickly, he spied her. She faced away from him, but he could see her profile in the warm yellow light.

He watched as the sunlight played upon her golden curls, and made them glint as if they were crowned with fairy dust.

Gadzooks, but she was beautiful.

Where Cordelia's beauty was almost blinding, Isobel's was soft as a rose petal. Cordelia's eyes burned with heat, but Isobel's glowed with warmth, like the play of firelight through a whiskey glass. Where Cordelia was statuesque and voluptuous, Isobel was dainty and petite.

And while Cordelia's voice was deep and throaty, Isobel's was soft and sweet. Beckett watched her as she sketched. She seemed so innocent, so unaware of her own loveliness. The realization stirred something powerful within him.

Damnation, he didn't have time for such nonsense. He would not start mooning over his new wife like a bloody schoolboy. Wasn't that why he'd married Isobel? To keep things simple?

He'd been glad she feigned illness last night.

For he had been so tempted to take her to his bed and bury himself in the perfection of her body...

Theirs was the perfect marriage: one of convenience. He would not let his base needs play havoc with his plans. It would be no use discovering any charms of Isobel's that might reduce him once again to a love-sick idiot. He had played that role once for Cordelia, and found it quite tiresome.

Certainly, he would be polite, and treat Isobel with the utmost respect.

But one thing was certain—no woman would ever sink her claws into him again.

Isobel sat on the marble bench beside the little pond and watched the fish swim up to the surface, then flip their tails as they headed back down toward the dark, soft bottom. This place was not unlike her own garden at home.

She had spent another restless night filled with terrible dreams of Sir Harry and Hampton House. She'd awakened to find her nightdress soaked through, her hands shaking in terror. Seeking to banish the fears of the night, Isobel had come out to the garden this morning with pencils and paper in order to sketch.

A bee buzzed past her on its way to some sweet-smelling roses. She watched the insect fly into the center of a delicate pink blossom, and gather its nectar to bring back to the hive.

She thought of Beckett's talk of roses yesterday in the coach. There were indeed many sharp, wicked-looking thorns adorning the flower's stem, a potent protection from anyone trying to possess its delicate beauty.

The confrontation with Cordelia Haversham had been unsettling. Isobel knew she had no reason to be jealous of Beckett's previous fiancee. After all, their marriage was purely a business arrangement.

Hadn't last night's events, or lack thereof, proven that?

Yet she couldn't help but be curious about her husband's former love. From what she'd seen, the woman was as spoiled as a wicked child. And though extremely beautiful, her personality was anything but.

Isobel had been trying to sketch all morning, but the face that flashed before her eyes clouded her vision. Dark, glittering eyes stared up at her from the blank paper and mocked her.

She tried to concentrate on her view of the pink rose and the yellow-striped bee that flew happily around it. Forcing her hand to the paper, she slowly sketched the rose on the sheet in front of her. As the picture took shape, the fluid lines and shadows drew her problems into the folds of the petals. Her artwork had always soothed her mind and spirit.

Taking a new sheet of paper, Isobel thought of Cordelia, of her rich red hair, porcelain complexion and bright green eyes. Though Isobel had no love for the woman, she would be a superb subject.

She moved the lead quickly this time, her soft lines becoming Cordelia's cheekbone, the regal nose, the coy eyes. Isobel worked methodically, the action blotting out the whirlwind in her mind. Using her fingertip, she smudged some lines to make them softer. Isobel looked down at Cordelia's likeness with a bit of shock.

There were the woman's calculating eyes and cold, thin smile. She was beautiful, yes, but had the hard beauty of a marble statue whose eyes appeared sightless, whose mouth would remain frozen for eternity.

"I didn't know you were an artist," a voice said from behind her, breaking the silence of the garden.

Isobel looked up to see her husband's face shaded by the branches of the oak tree. She felt a thrill of surprise, then self-consciousness. Usually, she didn't show her drawings to anyone, let alone the subject's former love.

"May I?" Beckett asked, his hand outstretched.

Reluctantly, Isobel gave him the drawing. "I hope it doesn't offend you, my lord."

"Why would it offend me? It is merely a piece of paper," Beckett replied. Abruptly, he held the picture toward Isobel. "You've captured her, my dear."

She retrieved it and stared at him for a moment, taking in his relaxed attire. The white shirt he wore was not buttoned to the top, and showed the soft, cinnamon-colored hair of his chest.

She had never been this close to a man who wasn't fully dressed before. No—she corrected herself. There had been that morning in his bedchamber. Of course, she had been unconscious for most of that. He'd been entirely without his shirt, but she'd been so concerned with her own state of undress that she hadn't really looked at him very closely.

But now she could see the texture of his skin in the sunlight. Isobel wanted to shake the thoughts from her head. She shouldn't be thinking about his skin, she should be thinking about her own. Isobel forced her eyes back to his roguish expression and took a deep breath.

A faint hint of his cologne drifted toward Isobel on the soft breeze, tantalizing her senses just as it had done yesterday when he'd held her close and carried her upstairs.

"I trust you slept well last night," he said.

"Yes, my lord. I slept quite well." It was a lie. She hadn't slept well, at all.

He made a face, waving his hand in annoyance. "And let us dispense with you calling me 'my lord.' We are husband and wife now, Isobel. I insist that you call me by my Christian name."

"Of course... Beckett," she replied.

"I am glad that your health has improved since last night," he continued. "Too much excitement, I expect. You had a very full day, as did I. Alfred took me to White's after I officially became Lord Ravenwood. We had supper, played at cards, and found I had all manner of new friends crawling out of the woodwork to congratulate me. Comes with being a wealthy earl, I suppose, because none of them was the least concerned with me when I was an impoverished viscount. What did you do, Isobel?"

"After supper I retired to the library and read Mr. Shakespeare's The Taming of the Shrew," she said.

"The Taming of the Shrew?" he asked. "Is there something I should know about? Am I to play Petruchio to your Katharina? Or Lucentio to your Bianca?"

"I cannot say," Isobel replied, "for those that you mention are both pairs of lovers. And as you have said, ours is a marriage only of convenience."

He stepped closer to her, his penetrating blue eyes holding her gaze. "You are right, of course. That is what we both wanted. Is it not?"

"It is what we agreed upon."

"So it is," Beckett replied, finally. "I shall be off to the solicitors' again this afternoon. Don't wait up for me, hmm?"

Isobel watched him walk across the lawn to the doorway without so much as a look back at her. Slowly, she packed up her drawing leads and papers, trying to quiet the thudding of her heart. She wanted nothing more than to retire to her room where she could be alone.

Doubts swirled in her head, as dark and brittle as a whirlwind of autumn leaves.

Who was this man that she'd married so hastily? He seemed such a contradiction—one day insisting that he wanted a marriage of convenience, and the next, teasing her about lovers and wedding nights.

But as strange as this marriage was, it was necessary for her survival. She would make sense of it somehow. If Katharina and Petruchio could make their marriage work, then so could she and Beckett.

Surely most of the women in London would trade their best bonnet for a true marriage with a man who was so attractive. And he was an earl, to boot. A very wealthy earl.

As she entered her room, Isobel found herself remembering the softness of Beckett's lips on hers yesterday in the church, and then last night so chastely upon her forehead.

She sighed and plopped herself down on the bed, lying upon her back and staring up at the ceiling.

Did he intend to honor their arrangement? His behavior in the garden had been most puzzling. She could have sworn he'd been flirting with her.

If Beckett decided he wanted her in his bed, she would have no right to refuse him. And what was more worrisome, she knew she would have no intention of doing so.

CHAPTER SIX

Beckett stood in front of the mirror and arranged his ivory silk neck cloth. Unfortunately, Hartley's talents in this regard were sorely lacking, and Beckett himself had been forced to learn how to tie a proper knot or risk looking like an uncultured oaf. He pulled on the bow to make it puff. There. Much better.

Tonight he and his wife were making their first public appearance since their wedding two days ago. By all accounts, their attendance at the Whitcomb Ball was the talk of London. It seemed everyone wanted a glimpse of the new Earl and Countess of Ravenwood.

Word was that Cordelia would be there, presumably with talons sharpened. According to Alfred, Cordelia had been campaigning to win support from some of the old guard—the Marchioness of Colborne, the Countess of Linfield and last but not least, the Duchess of Rowley.

No doubt, Cordelia was trying to discredit Beckett and his new bride, not that he cared what any of those old crones thought. He adjusted his cuffs and took one last look in the glass. It would do.

He trotted down the staircase with Monty on his heels,

then stood near the bottom to await his wife. He felt the dog's hot breath on his pant leg and moved away. The beast scooted closer, so that he was exactly the same distance from Beckett's leg as he had been before.

"Monty, I've already applied my cologne for the evening, thank you very much. Go on, now," Beckett said, pointing.

Monty looked up at him with happy brown eyes and continued to steam Beckett's trousers.

"Monty, go lay down," he said firmly.

The dog raised sad eyes to his master and obeyed.

A flapping of feathers whooshed through the air and Caesar flew out of the salon, landing on his favorite perch: Beckett's head.

"Oh, Caesar—get off!" Beckett reached up to disengage the parrot from his head.

"*Get off...get off, ahhkk!*" The bird flapped its wings enthusiastically, and flew up just out of Beckett's reach, then landed on his head again. They repeated this process until Beckett finally gave up, and stood with his hands on his hips.

"Caesar, I believe you have ruined my hair," Beckett said.

Light feminine laughter trickled down the staircase.

Beckett looked up to see Isobel standing at the top, covering her mouth with a dainty gloved hand as she giggled.

"You think this quite funny, do you?" Beckett asked.

Isobel appeared to be swallowing her smirk as she descended the stairs and stopped at the bottom.

"Hmph." Beckett reached up and grabbed the bird before he could flap his gray wings and escape. "Caesar, I'm afraid that your career as a hat is over. Back in your cage, now."

"*Ahhkk! Bye-bye. Bye-bye,*" the bird squawked as his owner placed him back in his big brass cage.

Beckett returned to Isobel's side. For some reason, she kept putting her hand to her lips and looking at the floor, or the door, or anywhere but directly at him.

"What is it?" he inquired.

"Your hair, I'm afraid."

"Damnation," He said, crossing over to the glass in the hallway. Beckett laughed himself when he saw the strange coiffure the bird had wrought upon his head. His hair stuck out in every direction. He turned back to Isobel, and with as serious a face as he could muster, said, "You mean you don't like it? But I hear it's quite the dash."

Isobel seemed unconvinced.

Beckett ran his hands through his hair and fluffed it forward, then checked in the mirror. It would have to do.

It seemed that only then did he notice her gown, a stunning creation of amber silk with a daring neckline. Well, he supposed it was respectable enough for a married woman. But the thought niggled at him that she was *his* married woman, and perhaps he didn't want all of society looking at her breasts all night long. He offered his arm and felt her little hand tuck into the crook of his elbow.

"You know what to do?" he asked.

"Yes," Isobel replied. "If anyone says anything out of turn, I am to bat my eyelashes, laugh as charmingly as possible, and perhaps sigh rather whimsically."

"Exactly," he said. "And if that doesn't win them over, be sure to swoon. Most people love a good swoon."

"Will Miss Haversham be there?"

Beckett nodded. "Like Napoleon, itching for battle. And you must be like Wellington. Stand your ground, and you'll see the enemy run."

"Will there be time to dance, in between dodging enemy volleys?" Isobel asked.

Beckett laughed, admiring Isobel's spirit. "I will make certain you do more dancing than dodging, my dear. This is our first ball as the Earl and Countess of Ravenwood. Let us enjoy ourselves, and in doing so, set all of London on its ear."

Beckett led his wife out the door and helped her into the waiting carriage. As they pulled away and drove down the street, he hoped for Isobel's sake that this evening would not be the disaster Cordelia would surely try to make it.

The carriage rolled into the long torchlit drive of Whitcomb Park and stopped as they waited for a space. Carriages lined the circular drive from end to end. In the flickering light, a steady flow of guests promenaded up the wide staircase and through the main doors.

As they waited to pull up beside the steps, Isobel looked across at Beckett, who sat back leisurely as if this were a simple soiree they were attending. The flames from the torches lit the inside of the cab, flickering over his face in the dark.

Beckett was an incredibly handsome man. The thought that he was her husband and would be squiring her around the ball gave her a heated thrill.

The door opened and a footman appeared, reaching his hand in to help Isobel out of the carriage. She gathered up her skirts and put her hand in the footman's as he helped her to the ground. Beckett quickly followed, offering his arm to Isobel.

"We must keep watch for Alfred," Beckett said. "It's always good to have him around once the quips start flying."

Through the massive front doors, Isobel could see the

dancers swirling around the ballroom. Music drifted out to greet them on the soft evening breeze. The orchestra played a sprightly waltz, which sang over the sounds of conversation and pattering feet.

The women floated in beautiful concoctions of diaphanous fabric, their jewelry glittering in the golden light of the candelabras. A heady mixture of flowers, food, and brandy perfumed the air.

Isobel looked down at her gown of amber silk and hoped she looked like a countess. She touched the emerald and diamond necklace that her husband had given her, and took a deep breath.

"The Earl and Countess of Ravenwood," the butler announced, holding his arm out and motioning them ahead.

"My dear," Beckett said, "may I present the Earl and Countess of Whitcomb."

Her husband's hand touched her lower back, steering her toward their hostess and her spouse.

"She's lovely, Beckett," the aged noblewoman said, smiling. "Wherever did you find such a treasure?"

"You know what they say about treasure, Lady Whitcomb," Beckett replied. "One always comes across it buried in the most unusual places."

Their hosts eyed each other, shaking their heads.

"Beckett, you are still the charmer, I see." The countess laughed, then whispered to Isobel, "I hope you can handle him, my dear."

"I will certainly try, Lady Whitcomb," Isobel replied.

They passed through the outer doors and into the ballroom. "There," Beckett said, "you're through the first assault of this ballroom battle. Stay sharp, Lady Ravenwood. This is where it gets interesting."

He led her through the crowd, introducing her to so

many viscounts, marquesses, earls, and even a few dukes, she knew she'd never remember all their names. Finally, he turned away from her to speak to a round little admiral with enough medals on his chest that it was a surprise he didn't topple over.

Isobel felt a man's hand on her arm. Startled, she whirled around to find Alfred close beside her. "Lady Ravenwood, you look absolutely beautiful." Languidly, he brought her hand to his lips and gently kissed it.

"What do you think you're doing?" Beckett demanded good-naturedly. "Trying to woo my wife, are you?"

"Why, yes, actually," Alfred replied. "She is the prettiest woman here."

"You'd better watch your tongue, Alfred. If you insist upon shamelessly flirting with my wife in such a manner, I may have to box your ears," Beckett warned.

"Hah!" Alfred scoffed. "I'd like to see you try, old man. Until then, I shall admire Lady Ravenwood's stunning beauty to my heart's content."

Alfred performed an elaborate bow for Isobel's benefit, his mischievous dark eyes shining up at her. "Lady Ravenwood, would you do me the honor of accepting my request for a dance?"

"I'm afraid I am not a very good dancer, Alfred," she said.

"Wonderful. Neither am I!"

But he was a good dancer. The room spun around her as Alfred expertly maneuvered them through the crowd. Isobel felt weightless as she danced in the glow of the candlelight, but Alfred's touch didn't make her skin tingle as Beckett's did. She glanced over at her husband.

For a moment she forgot everything. For a moment, as she met her husband's eyes across the room, and felt the heat of attraction quicken her blood.

Less than a week ago, she would have thought it impossible to feel anything but fear. Right now, in this ballroom, the memory of Sir Harry and her flight from her home seemed only a bad dream.

She would not think of it. She was safe now, surely. Sir Harry Lennox would never possess her or Hampton Park. He would never be able to make her his bride, now that she was another man's wife.

Isobel stole another glance at Beckett and saw his gaze upon her—a penetrating mixture of ice and fire. Instantly, the memory of their wedding-day kiss flooded her senses.

Isobel would fulfill her part of the marriage bargain by appearing publicly united with her new husband. Then she would retire to Hampton Park as the true mistress of the estate. And she would rid herself of Lennox once and for all. It was a perfect arrangement.

At least that's what she kept telling herself.

CHAPTER SEVEN

"So," the woman said, "you actually had the audacity to attend Lady Whitcomb's ball. How very provincial."

Isobel turned around slowly, as befitting a countess, and met the icy green stare of Cordelia Haversham.

Where was Beckett? He was nowhere in sight. She would have to do battle with this harpy alone.

"My husband and I were invited by Lady Whitcomb," Isobel replied. "I am sorry if our presence distresses you, Miss Haversham."

"Distresses me?" Cordelia gave a brittle laugh. "Oh, I assure you, I am not in the least bit distressed. It is you, my dear, who should be so. You have quite the nerve."

"That is precisely what I was going to say about you," Isobel said, smoothly.

Cordelia's eyes blazed as she replied, "You are deceiving yourself if you think Beckett married you for any other reason than to get back at me. You are a joke, my dear. A little trollop from the gutter, masquerading in a countess's clothing. Everyone knows what you really are."

"You mean the Countess of Ravenwood?" Isobel asked.

"Why, considering that you might have been Beckett's countess, it really is so very kind of you to call attention to my good fortune."

If steam had risen from Cordelia's ears, Isobel would not have been the least bit surprised. As it was, the woman's face contorted with rage and turned a very unbecoming color.

"Are you ill, Miss Haversham?" Isobel asked, innocently. "You look as if you've swallowed a large fruit."

"If there were any large fruit near at hand, I would most likely stuff it down your throat!" Cordelia said, seething.

"There is a pineapple across the room, there," Isobel said, pointing. "I would dearly love to see you attempt it. Shall we give everyone a good show?"

"Do you think me stupid enough to cause a scene?" Cordelia scoffed. "There's no use in trying to make me look a fool."

"You don't need my help in that regard, Miss Haversham, as you are doing quite well on your own."

Cordelia looked around quickly and grabbed Isobel's arm, jerking her close. "Look, you little harlot," she hissed. "You may be the Countess of Ravenwood right now, but who knows—you might get sick. You might die. People have accidents. I had Beckett wrapped around my little finger before, and I can do it again. I could have any man in this room, but I want Beckett and I want the Ravenwood estate. No one casts me off, do you hear?"

Isobel yanked her arm back and met Cordelia's venomous glare. "If you'll be so kind as to remember, Miss Haversham, it was you who put Beckett aside when you learned that he had no fortune."

"Well, now he has one, doesn't he?" Cordelia replied. "That was the only reason I broke the engagement. And don't try telling me you married him for love. I know very well why you married Beckett, and so does everyone else in this room."

"For his fortune and title?" Isobel asked. "Those were your reasons. Not mine."

Cordelia stood tall. "Whatever the reason, be warned. I shall not rest until I am the Countess of Ravenwood."

"Then you shall become quite tired, indeed," Isobel said. "And now, I must return to my husband."

Isobel turned slowly, as she had before, and walked away as if she hadn't a care in the world. Moving through the crowd, Isobel saw Beckett near the refreshment table. As she drew close to him he handed her a glass. She brought it to her lips and tasted the raspberry punch, its welcome sweetness filling her mouth.

"Are you enjoying the evening, Isobel?" her husband asked.

"Very much so. Though I was unable to use your advice about swooning while conversing with the Honorable Miss Haversham."

"Cordelia?' Beckett asked. "What did she say? What did you say?"

Isobel pondered thoughtfully, then replied, "At one moment she looked unwell and I remarked that she resembled someone who had swallowed an oversized fruit. To which she replied that if there was one available, she would take great pleasure in stuffing it down my throat. I pointed out the pineapple, but she abandoned the notion."

Beckett stared at her, seemingly dumbfounded. Then his face lit up, and he chuckled. "A pineapple? You don't say."

Isobel smirked and surrendered to her own laughter. "Do you think the story will get 'round?"

"I wouldn't completely rule it out," he replied. "We shall have to check the Times tomorrow morning."

"Oh dear," she said. "I shall cause a scandal."

"I don't care if you do, Isobel. And neither should you. I shall be quite happy being husband to the "Lady of Large Fruit.""

"Of large what?" Alfred said, popping up beside Beckett. "I say, is that any way to speak to your wife?"

Beckett took Isobel's hand. "They are beginning another waltz, my dear. Would you do me the honor?"

Isobel felt a thrill of excitement at his touch. "I would be most pleased."

Beckett led her onto the dance floor and curved an arm about her waist, his hand flat against the small of her back. She looked up into his face and saw the laughter was gone from his expression. He stared down at her with heated eyes, and all at once Isobel knew why moths flew into the flame.

Isobel felt herself becoming terribly warm all over. The memory of his lips on hers kept returning, and suddenly, unexpectedly, she wanted him to kiss her.

"What are you thinking?" he asked, his voice like velvet. "You're flushed, Isobel. Is it from your thoughts, or is it from the dancing?"

"I'm sure it is from neither," she said weakly.

"Are you? Well, I am not so convinced," he replied. "Let us do an experiment. What would you say, Isobel, if I pulled you close and kissed you here in front of this whole room?"

Isobel's head jerked up as she met his demanding expression. "You wouldn't." A cascade of hot tingles spilled down her back.

"You see, I was right," he said. "You blushed because of your thoughts. And right now I would give anything to know what they were."

Feeling suddenly daring, Isobel answered, "If you must

know, I was thinking about when you kissed me on our wedding day. I imagine you must be quite shocked by my forwardness. I admit, I am feeling very bold tonight. Becoming a countess must be going to my head."

"Then, it agrees with you. I like a woman who can speak plainly." He pulled her closer and they suddenly stopped swirling. "And I like a woman who thinks about kissing. Especially about kissing me."

Isobel stared transfixed. Was he really going to kiss her in front of all these people?

"Perhaps we should take a turn out in the gardens," he said, finally. "It is a lovely night."

Isobel nodded silently. Beckett was her husband. If he wanted to push her up against a tree and kiss her senseless, it was his right to do so. And suddenly she knew that if he wanted more from her, she would not protest.

Beckett led her out onto the balcony. He nodded to the other guests and as they walked. They made their way down the steps and headed toward one of the torch-lit paths on the grounds.

Oh, why was her heart pounding, so?

Beckett looked down at her and placed his hand over hers where rested in the crook of his arm. "One of the benefits of marriage is being able to enjoy a walk in the gardens like this without causing a scandal. I daresay these gardens are as big as Vauxhall. And just as private."

They walked farther, and Isobel became aware of a number of couples embracing in the shadows. The muffled sound of their giggles and laughter floated on the still night air with forbidden promise.

Beckett stepped off the path and led her into the trees. In one swift movement he turned her around to face him. She could just make his features out in the dim torchlight that spilled from the pathway.

Beckett lowered his mouth and captured her quivering lips with his own. He pulled her close against his hard body as his tongue delved into her mouth.

Instantly, hot, dangerous sparks shot down her spine.

Beckett's powerful arms encircled her and brought her hips tight against his own. Isobel clung to him, not knowing whether it was uncertainty or pleasure that made her do so.

"Wait," she said, "I fear someone might see us."

"So what if they do?" He asked, teasing her with his tongue. "We can do this whenever we like."

"We can?" she whispered weakly.

"This...and much more," he replied heatedly.

"How much more?"

Beckett smiled and slid her dress down over her shoulder. "Let me show you."

Isobel gasped in shock as the cool night air touched the bare skin of her breast. Certainly, this must be terribly wicked. Even if he was her husband!

He lowered his head to her breast and brushing his lips against it.

Isobel gasped in pleasure and clung to him for balance. The mixture of the cool air and his hot breath on her skin threatened to drive her mad as he continued his torment. Her knees felt as if they would buckle.

He pulled the other side of her gown down, baring her naked breasts to his gaze. With his tongue, he teased the nipple of one, making deliciously maddening circles around the hard tip. With his hand, he pinched the other until it was just as hard, just as aroused.

Isobel arched her neck back and whispered his name. What was he doing to her? Her body tingled with hot desire, which pooled achingly between her legs. Whatever this was, she didn't want it to stop. She had never felt this maddening, torturous passion before. Her body had somehow become an instrument, and Beckett was a skilled musician. He knew how to make her blood sing. She wanted him to touch her—she wanted to be naked before him as he took his time pleasuring her.

He lifted his head again and pressed his forehead against her shoulder. Then he stepped back, drawing her gown up to cover her.

"Why are you stopping?" she asked, momentarily bewildered.

Beckett's eyes burned down at her, simmering with raw, dangerous passion. "I must stop now, Isobel—or not at all. And I do not want to take your virginity in Lord and Lady Whitcomb's garden."

Isobel tried to reply but could not form words.

"Unless you have a preference for gardens, of course," he added.

"No. No preference," she stammered. "I mean, I'm sure I have no preference at all where to do such a thing."

Goodness, had that really come out of her mouth?

"Well, we shall have to do something about that, now, shan't we?" He smoothed away some of the wayward curls around her face. "Your face is a trifle flushed, my dear. And we have been gone a decidedly decadent amount of time. Everyone will know what we have been doing, out here."

"They will?" she said, alarmed.

"Anyone who was paying any mind," he replied, "and trust me, many were. It will only serve to intrigue the ton down to the soles of their shoes."

Beckett led her back to the path and they strolled toward the huge manor house.

"I'm not sure I should want to intrigue the ton...or their shoes," Isobel remarked, still trying to get her bearings after such a passionate dalliance.

"Too late, my dear," Beckett said. "You did that when you walked through the door."

They ascended the steps and crossed the terrace, re-entering the ballroom as nonchalantly as possible. A curious couple nearby noticed their arrival, and a few ladies began commenting behind their fans. Isobel could almost hear the gossip-mill turning now.

"I must find Alfred," Beckett said. "He's in the card room, I think. Wait for me here, will you? I see Lady Whitcomb there. I'm sure she will keep you company until I return. I'll be back directly."

Isobel nodded and watched her husband round the corner and disappear down the hallway of the huge manor house. She glanced around and took a step toward Lady Whitcomb.

Isobel was totally unprepared for the firm, familiar grip which suddenly circled her wrist, but even as she turned to face him, she knew who it was.

Icy fear squeezed her heart as Isobel stared into the glittery dark eyes that had haunted her dreams since that terrible night at Hampton House.

It seemed a lifetime ago, and yet all too fresh in her mind. What had been happening in her absence? Had Sir Harry Lennox installed himself as master of the estate, as he'd promised he would? And now he was here, like a wolf at the door....

Sir Harry smiled, darkly. He pulled her close and brought his mouth to her ear.

"I've missed you, my darling," he whispered.

CHAPTER EIGHT

"Come with me out into the garden, Isobel," Sir Harry ordered in a calm voice that gave her chills. "Don't make a scene. We have much to discuss."

Isobel glanced around, but there was no one near. No one who could help her. Oh, where was Beckett?

As if reading her thoughts, Sir Harry said, "Your dear husband is searching out that dreary friend of his. Good of him, really—giving us time to be alone."

"What do you want?" she demanded.

Sir Harry dug his iron-hard fingers into her flesh and she struggled not to wince. She would give him no satisfaction. He couldn't hurt her now and she wanted to tell him so.

"What do I want?" Sir Harry asked. "Why, only what's mine of course. You remember what's mine, don't you, Isobel?"

Quickly he walked her down a deserted pathway dragging her deep into the trees. He spun her around and held her in front of him.

"Foolish, foolish girl," he said, almost sympathetically,

lifting her chin with his fingertips. "Whatever am I to do with you?"

Isobel stared into his black eyes and said, "I'm sure I don't know what you mean. I am the Countess of Ravenwood, now, and under my husband's protection."

"Yes, I know about your farce of a marriage to that fop," he said.

"It is not a farce," she countered.

"Does he know your story, Isobel?" Sir Harry asked. "From what I can tell, he knows nothing about the tragic events at Hampton House involving your deceased guardian, Mr. Langley. It was wise of you not to tell him, Isobel. Very wise, indeed."

No one frightened her as much as this man did, for she knew what he was capable of.

"I saw you out here with him," Sir Harry continued "I saw his hands touching your naked skin, and I heard you sighing and gasping like a little trollop. Naughty girl. I advise you not to make a sound, or I will be forced to hurt you. And I would rather save your punishment for later."

Suddenly, the scene of her guardian's murder flashed into her mind. She pushed it away, refusing to let the terror overtake her. She would not show fear to this man. That was what he wanted.

"You hold no power over me," she insisted.

"Oh, my dear, sweet Isobel—I hold every power over you," he replied. "I shall have both you and the Hampton estate before the season is out."

"And how do you propose that?" she asked. "As Lord Ravenwood's wife, my husband now has claim to my property."

"If you were his wife, yes," he agreed. "But if you were no longer his wife, what then?"

"What do you mean?" she demanded, a vein of fear snaking its way around her heart.

Sir Harry smiled calmly. "I wonder...would he care to tarnish his name by staying married to a murderess?"

Isobel was dumbstruck. "What are you talking about?"

"Do you know Lord Palmerston, the chief justice of the King's Bench?" He asked. "He's an old friend of mine. I explained it all to him, you see. After you are arrested for the rather grisly slaying of your late guardian, I'm certain Lord Ravenwood will arrange for an annulment with great haste. And Palmerston has agreed to hand you over to me. For a price, of course. So you see, Isobel, you will be mine, after all."

Isobel tried to swallow her fear.

Sir Harry reached out to stroke her face, but Isobel jerked away. He grabbed her jaw, and cruelly forced her to face him. "You have been missing for over fifteen minutes, now, Isobel. You were seen coming out here with me. How will you explain that? Do you think your new husband will believe in your innocence? Or will he believe me when I tell him I'm your lover and I've just enjoyed your favors?"

"No!" She bucked and struggled against him, but he held her fast.

"Yes, Isobel," he said, "keep this up. You'll only look exactly as you should from another passionate tryst in the garden."

She flailed in outrage and clipped his chin with her fist.

Quickly, Sir Harry blocked the next strike and pinned her arms to her sides. He smiled dangerously. "You'll pay for that later, my dear, along with your other transgressions."

With all her might, she pulled against Sir Harry's grip, throwing him off-balance. She brought her heel down sharply on top of his foot, and he groaned in pain, momentarily releasing his hold on her arms.

Isobel ran down the dark path as if wolves were chasing her, and she heard Sir Harry curse.

She reached the terrace steps and looked quickly over her shoulder. In the distance, she saw Sir Harry emerge from the darkened path. With a trembling hand, she smoothed her hair and tried to steady her breathing. She ascended the stairs with as much grace as she could muster. Coming around the corner and through the French doors, she almost slammed into her husband.

"Oh! —"

Beckett paused and took quick stock of her appearance, saying, "Where have you been, Isobel? I've been searching everywhere for you."

"I needed a bit of air," she replied, pointing toward the gardens. "I suddenly felt a bit ill."

That wasn't really a lie, for she'd felt dizzy with fear when she'd set eyes on Sir Harry.

"You're white as a sheet," Beckett said, touching a hand to her forehead. "And you're cold as ice."

She glanced behind her and felt her heart leap into her throat as Sir Harry entered the ballroom. His menacing eyes locked onto hers as he strode boldly toward her.

There was no other choice. Isobel let her knees go weak and gave a piteous little moan as she collapsed into Beckett's arms.

"Oh!" she heard someone exclaim beside her.

"My word, is the lady alright?" another asked.

She felt herself being hoisted into Beckett's arms, and let her body flop like a rag doll's.

Where was Sir Harry?

"Make way!" Beckett shouted as he moved through the crowd. "Lady Ravenwood has been taken ill. Alfred, run ahead and see that the coach is not blocked in. Hurry, man!"

In moments they were outside. Beckett carried her into the carriage and laid her down on the seat. He draped a cloak over her and took her hand in his, slapping it lightly.

"Isobel," he said. "Isobel, can you hear me?"

She waited a few moments, then slowly opened her eyes. There—she was safe, now. Safe with Beckett, for the time being. Immediately, he came to her side and helped her sit up.

"Oh, dear," she said. "I must have fainted."

"You most certainly did," he replied. "You finally took my advice about swooning, I see. How are you feeling now?"

"I'll be fine," she responded. "Too much excitement, I expect."

That was an understatement if ever there was one.

"It was the dancing, no doubt," Alfred remarked, sitting across from them in the carriage and looking quite concerned. "They say too much waltzing can cause terrible health problems. And you, my dear Lady Ravenwood, seem to be living proof."

"I am sure it was not the dancing that made me ill, Lord Weston," Isobel said.

No—it was coming face to face with her enemy.

Though she had feigned swooning in order to escape the ballroom, there was no doubt that she now felt as ill as she'd claimed. She could still feel the touch of Sir Harry's hands on her skin, and it made her want to retch.

Soon they were pulling up in front of the town-house at Covington Place. Beckett helped Isobel up the walk and into the foyer.

"I should like to retire, now," she said, desperately wanting to be alone to sort out her thoughts.

"Of course," Beckett answered. "Shall we fetch Doctor Pembleton?"

"Oh, no," Isobel protested. "It is not necessary. I need to rest, that is all."

Beckett hesitated. "But surely, a doctor must be called."

"No, no, I am feeling much better, now. Only tired," she insisted. "A good night's rest will cure me."

"If you are certain, my dear."

Isobel gave a weak smile, saying, "Yes, I just need to go to my chamber."

Beckett supported her arm as they mounted the stairs. "Hartley," he said over his shoulder. "Will you bring Lady Ravenwood a tonic to help her sleep?"

"Certainly, my lord," the butler replied from the bottom of the stairs. Beckett and Isobel continued up.

Finally, Isobel was alone in her room. She had ignored the sleeping tonic and lay on the bed still dressed in her ballgown. She stared up at the ceiling, vainly trying to calm the waves of fear that washed through her heart. The nightmare was upon her again, her enemy nipping at her heels like a hound from hell.

Sir Harry had found her. It was all over.

The reality of that thought made her eyes well with heavy tears. She closed them, feeling helpless as a rabbit in a trap.

Surely, it was only a matter of time before Beckett abandoned her and washed his hands of his new bride. What reason would he have to stand beside her? They had married for convenience, not love, and it was hardly convenient to be married to a woman accused of murder, no matter the passionate tryst they'd shared in the garden.

Sir Harry could be a very persuasive, charming man when he chose to be. She had no doubt that Sir Harry could make Beckett believe whatever he wanted.

Isobel thought she could escape Sir Harry, yet she'd been like a little mouse trying to outrun a tom cat—blindly running for her life, all the time within sight of the amused and capable predator.

She had to take action. She couldn't just sit here and wait for Sir Harry's men to come for her. Beckett might very well do as her enemy predicted. She couldn't blame him if he did. Worse, her very presence here might endanger the man who had saved her life.

She had to leave. She must run again. But she would wait until dawn. The London streets were dangerous at night.

Isobel turned onto her side and stared into the darkness of her chamber, knowing that sleep would be impossible for more reasons than one. Memories teased and swirled around her—of Beckett's hard body pressed against hers, creating intoxicating sensations which she'd never felt before. Sensations she would never feel again.

Banishing such pointless thoughts, she waited for the dawn to light her escape.

CHAPTER NINE

Beckett closed the ledger and pushed it across the oak desk.

It was official.

He was terribly, terribly rich.

Beckett hated to admit it, but he didn't feel much different from the impoverished viscount he'd been before. The only difference was that now he had bags of money and vast amounts of land.

Besides the Ravenwood estate in Kent, he now held property in Cumberland and Lancashire, as well as a large sugar plantation in Barbados. According to the ledgers, this plantation had enabled the previous earl to almost double the family fortune.

He would settle some property upon his mother, as well as a generous allowance and a fashionable London residence in which she could hold court. That ought to put him back in her good graces for awhile, at least.

He poured himself another cup of tea from the silver service and opened the second ledger. But as he tried to concentrate on the figures, his mind returned to Isobel once again.

He would have to arrange her settlement with the solicitors and install her in her own residence, as they'd agreed. But at some time, he supposed, there would have to be an heir.

Isobel understood that her matrimonial duty included producing an heir. They didn't have to live together to do that. They didn't have to be in love. They could stick to their agreement. Like many other men of his rank, he could visit his wife wherever she chose to live until she was with child. His child.

She had not been averse to his advances last night in the Whitcomb garden. In fact, there was no point denying the physical attraction between them, which was a good thing—until it was a bad thing.

The more attraction he felt for his bride, the more danger that he might develop feelings for her. Real feelings—not just sexual arousal.

It had taken a good deal of his strength not to lay her down in the grass last night and take her right then and there. Just thinking about it brought heat to his loins.

She had done battle with Cordelia and survived. Isobel had a sharp wit that he found admirable and an exquisite beauty that made him want to protect her and ravish her at the same time.

Yet, their marriage of convenience was a business arrangement, and he had to remember that. He would make sure that while he was kissing Isobel, and stroking her, and mounting her, and burying his face in her neck as he exploded within her—that it was purely business.

Unable to fix his attention on the figures before him, Beckett closed the ledger and looked at the clock. Quarter-past-ten.

He had thought it best to let Isobel sleep late this

morning. But he was curious as to her health after last night's excitement.

Beckett found Hartley in the salon, and asked, "Has Lady Ravenwood arisen yet?"

"She has, my lord," Hartley replied. "The countess went outside to the gardens to sketch earlier this morning. She must still be there, as I have not seen her since."

"Is she feeling better?" Beckett inquired.

"She looked well, my lord."

"Thank you, Hartley," he replied.

Beckett looked for her in the garden, but Isobel was nowhere in sight. He walked across the lawn, and peered around a rose-hedge.

No Isobel.

Monty, Beckett's big brown dog jumped to attention and barked happily when he saw his master. Beckett patted his companion's head. "Did Isobel bring you out, boy?"

He and Monty walked scoured the grounds, at one point, circling the oak tree.

"Isobel?"

The garden answered with silence. Perhaps she had gone into the townhouse again.

Beckett walked back inside. "Isobel?" he called. He trotted up the stairs and nearly bumped into Isobel's new maid.

"Oh, Katie, is Lady Ravenwood in her chamber? I should like to speak with her."

The dark-haired girl shook her head. "No, m'lord. I haven't seen m'lady since early this morning."

Beckett's brow furrowed. Obviously, misplacing one's spouse was one of the irritating aspects of marriage. Beckett hastily checked the upstairs, then descended to the first floor and took a quick look in all of the downstairs rooms.

But Isobel was nowhere to be found.

"Perhaps she has taken a walk, my lord," Hartley offered. "To the park?"

"It may be possible," Beckett replied. "Though I'd have thought she would have more sense than to go to Hyde Park alone. If she does not return soon, we shall go and look for her. She may have become lost."

The door-knocker sounded, and the two men looked at each other with knowing expressions.

"That must be Lady Ravenwood, now," Beckett said as Hartley went to answer the door. "Doesn't realize she needn't knock at her own door, I suppose."

Hartley opened the door, but instead of Isobel standing there, three gentlemen stared back.

"May I help you?" Hartley asked.

"I should like to know if Lady Ravenwood is at home, if you please," a distinguished-looking man said.

"She is not at home," Beckett said. "I am her husband."

"Then you are most unfortunate, my lord," the man replied.

"And who are you sir, to speak so?" Beckett demanded, though he couldn't ignore a sense of foreboding.

The man regarded Beckett with hard, flat eyes, saying, "I am Lord Palmerston, chief justice of the King's Bench."

"And what could you possibly want with my wife?" Beckett asked.

Lord Palmerston pulled a sheet of paper from his coat pocket.

"I am here to arrest her, sir."

"On what charge?" Beckett said, snatching the paper away.

Looking quite bored with the matter, the old man straightened his cuffs and answered, "Murder."

"I beg your pardon?"

The magistrate continued, "Your wife is accused of the murder of Mr. Edward Langley, her late guardian. Well, where is she, Lord Ravenwood? The constables will take her into custody until trial."

"Until trial?" Beckett said, trying to make sense of this. "Who is Edward Langley? And why would you think that Lady Ravenwood could be guilty of killing him?"

"We have witnesses, sir, who claim to have seen the former Miss Isobel Hampton stab her guardian to death at Hampton House, Cadogan Place, a week ago."

"You must be mistaken, Lord Palmerston," Beckett replied. "I know nothing of Hampton House. My wife has never mentioned such a place to me."

"I assure you," Lord Palmerston said, "she is Isobel Hampton, late of Hampton House, and soon to be of Newgate Prison."

"She is not here," Beckett said, folding his arms. "She has gone to visit a family friend."

Lord Palmerston did not look pleased at this news. "And what would be the name of this 'friend?'"

"Lady Withypoll Weston, of Broomely Park, Luton," Alfred's eccentric great aunt would be thrilled to have visitors.

"I shall send constables to fetch her then," Palmerston said, clearly perturbed that his quarry was not immediately at hand.

"You must know these charges are pure flummery," Beckett stated.

"That remains to be seen," Palmerston said. "You sound very confident about the character of a woman you've known only a week, Lord Ravenwood."

At the man's blunt words, Beckett felt uncertainty slowly spreading through his veins, dark and bitter as cold coffee. Alfred's warnings about taking Isobel home that night echoed in his head. Who was this mysterious girl he had married?

Beckett didn't know the answer.

"I shall ask you to leave now, Lord Palmerston," Beckett said, crossly.

The magistrate opened his mouth to say something, but before he could, Beckett's valet slammed the door in his face.

"Well done, Hartley," Beckett said.

"Shall we go and look for Lady Ravenwood, my lord?" Hartley asked.

"Yes, but first you must have a message sent to Lord Weston," Beckett said, quickly donning his jacket. "We shall need his help in this. If we find Lady Ravenwood, we must take her back to Lord Weston's townhouse. I'm sure Palmerston will have someone watching this place."

"Thank goodness Lady Ravenwood went out for a walk when she did," Hartley remarked.

"Yes," Beckett said, "very convenient of her to disappear just before a magistrate came to arrest her for murder, wasn't it?"

"You don't think—" the servant began, aghast.

"I have no idea what to think, Hartley, but we'd better find Lady Ravenwood before they do," Beckett replied. "I'd like to ask my wife a few questions of my own."

CHAPTER TEN

It was hopeless. She was completely lost.

Street after busy street seemed to be populated with the same people, the same carriages nearly running her over, and the same hawkers advertising their sweetbreads and pastries.

Isobel brushed aside a curl from her face and tried to look like she knew where she was going. All the while, she kept her eyes alert for Sir Harry. She didn't bother looking for Beckett. There was no chance her husband would pursue her. Surely Sir Harry's cronies had come to the house by now, telling their lies.

At times, Isobel would think she spotted Sir Harry moving in the crowd ahead of her. Hot fear would rip through her gut like a pistol ball. Then she'd see that it wasn't him at all, yet the whisper of terror would follow her like a ghost.

"Ow!" Isobel stumbled on a loose cobblestone and lost her shoe. Quickly, she placed it back on her foot before a hungry-looking dog could snatch it out of her hands. "Go away! Shoo!"

The dog snarled at her, then ran off after some other prize.

Isobel resumed walking, wondering where on earth she was going to spend the night. Perhaps a church would offer her shelter. At least she looked like a proper lady, although walking the streets of London by herself, even in daylight, was anything but.

Her feet began to ache. These shoes were not designed for anything more strenuous than sitting down with needlepoint in her lap. How long had she been walking? And how much farther would she have to go before she could stop?

She had no money and nothing of value to trade or pawn...except for herself.

Certainly, she could have taken the emerald jewelry Beckett had given her to wear to the ball. Or she could have ripped the expensive lace and pearl trimmings from some of her dresses and sold them to a dressmaker.

It was hard to know what to pack when you were fleeing for your life. Wasn't that how she'd ended up in the alley in nothing but her nightdress that horrible evening?

Taking the emeralds, or the expensive trimmings that Beckett had given her would have been theft. And though money would have been helpful, she could not steal from the man who had rescued her.

Somehow, she would manage.

Isobel stared at the busy street before her, hoping she could manage to get across it without getting herself killed.

A carriage charged in front of her, practically spinning her around like a child's top. When the dust settled, she turned to cross again, but stopped when a huge white stallion blocked her way. Could these Londoners be any more rude? Looking up, she shielded her eyes from the mid-day sun to see the rider.

Beckett.

His blue eyes flashed as he swung a leg over the saddle and hopped to the ground.

Isobel turned to run, but he was immediately upon her, strong hands grabbing her arms and jerking her out of the middle of the street.

"And just where do you think you're going, my charming little countess?" he asked, his face towering above her, blocking out the sun.

"I—I went for a walk and I became lost," she stammered, trying to free herself from his grip, but his powerful hands held her prisoner.

"Lost?" Beckett replied. "You managed to get yourself halfway across the city! Very conveniently, I might add. You had some callers this morning. Lord Palmerston and his constables."

Isobel felt the blood drain from her face. "Lord Palmerston—"

"He came to arrest you for murder," Beckett said gruffly. "Why would anyone suspect you of such a thing? And why didn't you tell me about Hampton House?"

Isobel struggled to break her husband's hold, but Beckett mercilessly tightened his grip.

"What are you hiding?" he demanded.

She squirmed and wrenched free, darting into the busy street. Would he turn her over to Palmerston, as Sir Harry had claimed?

"Isobel!" Beckett shouted from close behind her.

Fear pulsed through her blood as she dashed between carriages and horses, but it wasn't from the danger of the street traffic. It was her husband she feared.

It was all over, now. She had lied to the man who had saved her life. And now, he too, would abandon her.

She was almost across the street. Was he still behind

her? She dared a quick look over her shoulder and didn't see him.

As she turned her head to look forward, she saw the strangest sight. It seemed to be happening so slowly, yet she knew that the curricle bearing down on her was travelling terribly fast—so fast that she couldn't get out of the way in time.

She was going to die.

Merciful heavens, she was going to die!

Suddenly she was flying. The ground came up to meet her and she hit it with a breathtaking thud. A heavy weight pressed down on her and she tried vainly to get a breath, but the wind was knocked out of her.

Strong hands yanked her up and thumped upon her back. In a moment, her lungs found the breath they'd been struggling for, and she closed her eyes in relief.

"That was bloody stupid!"

She opened her eyes and she saw Beckett fuming down at her. Isobel fought against his grip but knew it was fruitless.

"Let go of me, you great oaf!" she cried.

"Oaf, you say?" he barked. "Well, if that's the thanks I get for saving your life, I should have let the blasted curricle run you down."

Beckett grabbed her shoulders and pulled her closer toward his hard, muscular chest, saying, "Call me 'touched-in-the-head,' but I have a strange aversion to becoming a widower in the same week that I was married. And I do not like to be lied to by my wife, do you understand?"

He continued, "To say I am curious to hear what possible explanation there could be for all this—starting with why you ran away this morning—is putting it mildly. Promise me you will never do anything so foolish as that again."

Momentarily silenced by his words, Isobel nodded. A faint glimmer of hope shone in her heart. Would he listen to her, then?

"Good," he said, finally. "Obeying your husband—very good. Yet, I think you need more improvement in that regard." He put his hand around her shoulder and steered her down the street. "I am taking you to Alfred's townhouse in Warwick Square."

"Lord Weston? But why?"

"They will be waiting for you at Covington Place," Beckett explained. "I told them you've gone visiting Alfred's Great Aunt Withypoll at her home in Luton, but I don't think they quite believed me. So we will stay at Alfred's until we sort out what to do. And I would like a quiet place in which to hear your answers to this murder charge. Just because I didn't wring your lovely little neck doesn't mean you are forgiven."

The ride to Alfred's townhouse was terribly quiet. Isobel stared out the window of the hired coach and tried to collect her thoughts. So much had happened today, it was difficult to make sense of it all. So instead, she watched the city go by as the coach rolled toward Lord Weston's home in Warwick Square.

What would Beckett do to her? Would he wash his hands of her, and turn her over to her enemies? Many men in his position would do exactly that.

But surely, Beckett was not a cruel man. He was angry with her, and would probably be even more so before she was through explaining the truth of the matter. But would he have come looking for her if he didn't care?

He must have felt the weight of her stare, because he glanced at her with eyes that seemed to pierce straight through her. Then he looked away, dismissively.

His indifference felt like a slap, but Isobel couldn't

blame him. He'd made it very clear how things stood between them. Beckett was her husband. She was his property in the eyes of the law, and therefore her life was very much in his hands.

Sir Harry's threat echoed in her ears. Would Beckett believe her story after he realized she'd been lying to him about everything? If he didn't, what would her fate be then?

Oh, this would not do. She had to get her head on straight before the carriage reached Lord Weston's home. She wanted to be calm when she told Beckett her story. She needed to be calm, because the truth would bring the horror of that night back to torment her.

In far too short a time, the coach stopped in front of an opulent townhouse. Beckett got out of the cab and handed her down onto the street.

He looked at her silently before mounting the steps to the great oak door. Before Beckett could knock, it opened, and a gray-haired butler ushered them in.

Beckett addressed the man. "Crandall, will you tell Lord Weston—"

"That you are here, yes, yes," Lord Weston finished, bounding down the staircase. He took Isobel's hand in his and kissed it. "Are you alright, my dear lady? We have been looking for hours. Beckett, is she alright?"

"Yes, Alfred, she is in perfectly good health," Beckett replied, darkly.

Isobel felt a wave of fear infuse her veins. She didn't think she could bear the ugly scene that was surely only minutes away. But she would have to, just as she had borne everything else.

"We have need of lodgings, Alfred," Beckett continued. "May we presume upon your hospitality?"

"Of course you shall stay here," Alfred replied. "Now

what's this about Hartley wanting to stash Isobel out of Lord Palmerston's clutches? Has your man been reading penny novels again?"

"Those questions will be answered in due time," Beckett said, glancing at Isobel. "But for now, may we use your library? I hate to be a boor, but I need to speak with my wife. Alone."

Isobel tried to calm her beating heart. It felt as if a bird were trapped inside, beating its wings furiously to escape.

Alfred guided them down the hall to a huge book-lined library. "I shall have Crandall bring some tea."

"Thank you, Alfred. My wife is in need of refreshment, I expect," Beckett said, opening a cupboard and brought out a decanter and crystal glass. "But I require something stronger."

Alfred gave a nod and left them alone.

Beckett lifted the glass of brandy to his lips and downed a mouthful.

"Shall we begin?" he asked, his eyebrows raised in question. "And I warn you, my good humor is back at my townhouse. I believe I left it in the front hall when Hartley opened the door for Lord Palmerston and his scandalous accusations about you. Perhaps you should start by telling me about Hampton House."

Isobel met his eyes and took a deep breath, saying "It is my family's London home, on Cadogan Place."

"Go on," he prodded.

"I told you that my parents died in a carriage accident a little over a year ago, and that is true. I was left in the care of Mr. Edward Langley, my guardian. He was a very kind man." At the memory, Isobel felt a lump forming in her throat.

"He was murdered?" Beckett said.

"Yes," Isobel answered.

"But not by you?"

In her mind's eye she could see the fondness that had always swept over Edward Langley's face at the sight of her, and her heart knotted painfully in her breast. She forced herself to continue, "I was there. I saw it happen."

A knock sounded at the door and Crandall brought in a gleaming silver tray. "Tea, m'lord," he said, then smoothly exited the room.

"Continue, my dear," Beckett said.

Isobel took a deep breath. "I'd heard an argument, so I came downstairs to see what was going on. I hid in the dark hallway, but when I heard him stab Mr. Langley, I screamed, and he saw me."

"Who saw you?"

"Sir Harry Lennox," she replied, her voice shaking.

"What reason would he have to kill your guardian?"

"He wants the Hampton estate, and he wants me," Isobel said. "Sir Harry is a distant cousin of my late father's, and insists that he is the true heir. But my father left the estate to me, as was his right. Sir Harry tried to strike a bargain with Mr. Langley to purchase my hand in marriage. If Langley helped him force me into marriage, Sir Harry promised to pay him a large sum once he got his hands on the Hampton fortune. But my dear guardian would have none of it. That's why Sir Harry killed him."

"Tell me more about this Lennox," Beckett commanded.

Isobel swallowed, trying to calm her nerves. But relating the tale to Beckett brought everything back regarding the horrible night Mr. Langley was killed...and she had tried so hard to forget.

She forced herself to continue, "As I said, he was a distant cousin of my father's. After my parents' funerals, he produced what he said was a valid will which was only recently discovered, saying my father had left the estate to him. But Mr. Langley confirmed with our lawyers that the document was a forgery. Yet this did not dissuade Sir Harry in the least. He swore he would be master of Hampton Park, and master of me as well."

Beckett asked, "Hampton Park is your family seat, I assume?"

Isobel nodded, the thought of her beloved family home almost bringing tears to her eyes. "Yes, in Hertfordshire. My father was William Hampton, 4th Baron Pomeroy."

Beckett continued, "Which makes you, as your father's sole heir, Baroness Pomeroy in your own right."

"Yes," Isobel answered. "That's why I ran. I had to protect the estate, and myself, from Sir Harry's clutches."

"And that's how you came to be on the street the night that I found you," Beckett said.

"I broke free from Sir Harry," she explained, "then I ran and ran until I had no more strength. The next thing I remember is waking in your bed."

"And this Palmerston fellow," Beckett continued. "What sort of evidence could he have against you?"

"Whatever Sir Harry presented to him. He's a very persuasive man," Isobel explained. She searched Beckett's eyes, but they gave away nothing. "Sir Harry found me at the Whitcomb ball. He took me out into the gardens—"

Beckett set the glass down on the desk and took a step toward her. "To the garden? You went with him willingly?"

"Certainly not! Have you heard nothing I've said?" she asked. "When he had me alone, he threatened me. He told me he would have no trouble convincing you that we were lovers—so that you would refuse to protect me."

"And how do I know you aren't lovers?" Beckett asked, darkly.

Isobel's temper flared. "How dare you say such a thing?"

"Forgive me, Isobel, but I've no experience in accusing a wife of being unfaithful. Is there a trick to it I don't know?" he said flippantly.

Before she knew what she was about, Isobel slapped him.

All the anguish and desperation of the past weeks erupted from her heart and found its target in the man before her. She beat her fists against his chest and flailed in his arms as Beckett struggled to hold her.

"Isobel!"

She struggled against him. "Get your hands off me!"

"Isobel, stop it!" Beckett shouted, quickly winning the physical battle and holding her immobile in his strong, unyielding arms.

"Let me go," she demanded, hotly.

He ignored her, holding her effortlessly against him.

"Surely you don't want to keep a murderess as a wife?" she said.

Beckett held her away front of him, so he could look at her. "I don't believe you are a murderess, Isobel."

She stared up into his eyes, unwilling to hope. "You don't?"

"No." Beckett touched his hand to the side of Isobel's face. His thumb rubbed against the soft line of her jaw. "I am your husband, and I will protect you."

Isobel closed her eyes against the burning heat of tears. A strong hand curled gently around her neck as Beckett pulled her close against his chest.

"I swore to honor and protect you all the days of my life, and all the days of yours," he said, looking down at her with a wary expression. "You should have told me before."

"I was afraid," she answered.

"I can imagine you were," Beckett replied, turning away from her. "This changes things, Isobel. I will have to take you away from London, certainly—someplace where you'll be safe from both Lennox and Lord Palmerston's arrest warrant. Until we can get these charges dropped and find some evidence against Lennox."

"What if we can't?"

Beckett faced her. "Then we shall have to live abroad."

Isobel studied him for a moment, shocked by her husband's decision to stand by her. "Why are you doing this? Most men in your position would think twice about giving up so much, especially to protect a woman who was a wife in name, only."

Beckett returned nonchalantly to his glass and downed the rest of the brandy. "I am not most men."

"You'll go to Barbados, then?" Alfred asked.

Beckett nodded. He, Alfred and Isobel sat at the long dining room table in Alfred's townhouse, breakfasting on braised ham, poached eggs, toast with blueberry compote, and fresh strawberries with clotted cream. There was nothing like an adventure to stir up a man's appetite.

"Barbados?" Isobel set down her teacup and looked at Beckett, her eyes wide with shock. "It's not a very civilized place, is it?"

"How civilized is it here in London with Sir Harry Lennox running about, trying to have you hung?" Beckett asked, swallowing some coffee. "I don't think it's safe to stay in England at all, not with Lord Palmerston on his side. I was planning to go to Barbados next month to visit the Ravenwood sugar plantation there. We could leave as soon as possible. Lord Palmerston thinks you've gone to Broomely Park. I'll have it put 'round that I've gone off to Ireland, or someplace that will take them awhile to get to. Before he and his men can get back to London, we'll be aboard a ship bound for the islands."

"Capital idea, Beckett," Alfred said. "I'll go along with you...make sure you don't get into trouble."

"But I need you to stay here and find proof of Isobel's innocence, and Sir Harry's guilt," Beckett replied.

Alfred gave a wicked grin. "Even better! I adore a good mystery. You know, if I didn't have to be a lord of the realm, I always thought I should make a dandy Bow Street runner."

"But Lord Weston," Isobel said, "you must be careful. I do not like to think of what might happen if Sir Harry gets wind of your plan. He is a very dangerous man."

"As am I, dear lady," Alfred said, kissing her hand.

Isobel looked imploringly at Beckett. "There must be another way."

"Lord Palmerston's men will be back from Broomely Park in a few days," Beckett explained. "We must be safely on our way before they return to London."

"But what if Alfred doesn't find any proof of my innocence?" Isobel asked.

"Fear not, dear lady," Alfred assured her. "I possess a wealth of scandalous skills. Isn't that right, Beckett?"

"Very true," Beckett replied, grinning. "Sir Harry will be no match for you, old friend."

He saw the worried look in Isobel's eyes, and took her hand, saying, "Isobel, you must obey me in this. We will be on the next ship bound for Barbados. It is the only choice we have. As for Alfred, he and I have been getting in and out of trouble together since we met at Oxford. And we always get out of it, don't we Alfred?"

"Yes," Alfred agreed, "but this raises the challenge to new heights. And as you know, Beckett, I simply adore a challenge. In fact, I should be thanking you. I was getting a bit bored, of late, and this dangerous mission should do nicely."

"Excellent, Alfred," Beckett said. "Here's the plan: Isobel and I will book passage to Barbados under assumed names. Alfred, I'll need you to spread the word that I've gone off to Dublin. I shall have to return to the house briefly to have a trunk packed for my phantom trip to Ireland. That will include a few dresses for you, Isobel. But we must both travel lightly. You won't be needing ball gowns where we're going."

Isobel said soberly, "You can be assured that fashionable dress is the furthest thing from my mind at the moment."

"Now remember, Alfred," Beckett continued, "I shan't tell the house staff anything. Sir Harry may find a way to bribe information out of them, and if he thinks they know more he's likely to use stronger methods. The less they know, the better. I shall have to tell Hartley, though, as you may need his assistance in your investigation. We'll spend at least a month or so in Barbados. When we return, hopefully you'll have gathered enough evidence to refute this ludicrous murder charge against Isobel. And do me another favor, look in on the pets from time to time, will you? I shouldn't want Hartley to get overrun. And most of all—be careful."

"Don't worry about me, old man," Alfred replied. "It is Sir Harry Lennox who should be careful."

CHAPTER ELEVEN

Isobel took a deep breath, inhaling the strong, briny smell of the sea. Overhead, the gulls' cries made an eerie music over the Portsmouth dock.

They boarded the ship, and Beckett introduced her to the captain, using their assumed names. They were travelling as Mr. and Mrs. Evans, a well-to-do merchant and his wife from London. She had still been trying to get used to being called the Countess of Ravenwood, and now she had another name to answer to.

At last, the ropes that moored the ship to the wharf were cast off and the vessel lumbered slowly through gray-blue waters. Isobel stood beside Beckett at the starboard side and waved goodbye to Alfred, who bid farewell from the dock.

So much of this plan rested on Lord Weston's shoulders. But Alfred, who always appeared so light-hearted and entertaining, had a mind as strong and sharp as a sword... Beckett had sworn to it.

Isobel would depend upon that sword to fight the battle for her here in England, while she was spirited safely away. It seemed strange that she no longer had to defend herself alone, and that others were willing to stand by her in this fight for justice.

The ship's captain, Mayfield, took them on a brief tour of the vessel and Isobel was glad for the distraction.

She found herself fascinated with the rhythm of the huge ship. Its sailors all seemed to work together effortlessly, as if they could hear each other without speaking. From time to time, the bosun would call out orders, and the sailors would respond with feline agility and grace. They flew up and down the rigging as if it were more natural to them than walking upright.

But more striking than the rhythm of the crew was something entirely different: a large black-and-white cat who appeared on deck. She supposed cats were common upon seagoing vessels, what with the mice, but this cat in particular seemed strange; it surveyed the crew as if he commanded them.

As she stood there, wondering about the feline, it met her eyes. The cat stared at her intently from across the deck, and Isobel felt strangely unnerved. She glanced away. Had that been intelligence she'd seen in its eyes? Obviously, her misadventures had to be taking their toll on her, if she were imagining such things.

When she looked back, the cat was gone.

Captain Mayfield returned to his duties, and Isobel looked up at her husband as he surveyed the ship. An uncomfortable silence thickened the air between them.

She wondered what would happen, now. Although he had assured her of his protection, she had sensed Beckett distancing himself from her since learning of Edward Langley's death.

He hadn't mentioned her guardian's name since then, or the other sordid circumstances leading to this impromptu journey. And yet the silent questions stood between them like a wall. The passionate flirting they had enjoyed at the Whitcomb ball was all but gone.

The wind lifted Beckett's hair with invisible fingers, taunting Isobel to reach out and do the same. But she knew that was impossible now. He'd stood by her out of duty, not because of any feeling he had for her. It would do no good to become sentimental about a relationship that would never be.

As the ship left Portsmouth harbor, they were shown to their quarters. Their cabin was spacious enough, though of course, it held only one bed. And though they had already shared a bed in one regard, it would be very different to sleep next to Beckett now that they were man and wife.

Dinner was brought to their quarters and they ate it without ceremony. Then Beckett produced a deck of cards, and enticed Isobel to play ecarte. Considering the maelstrom of thoughts that swirled in her head, she welcomed the diversion.

They played countless games, until Isobel found her eyes drooping as she tried fruitlessly to ward off the heaviness of sleep.

"You look tired, my dear," Beckett said, putting down his cards. "It has been a long day. Shall we go to bed?"

Isobel looked up at him, her blood suddenly racing. "To bed?"

"Yes," he said, standing. "I suppose it is a good thing that we are married—seeing as there is only one bed. We can sleep in it together with a clear conscience."

Isobel stared at the bunk they were to share as if it had burst into flame. Upon closer scrutiny, it appeared quite narrow. There would not be a lot of room between them....

Beckett pulled off his shirt, revealing his well-muscled chest. Isobel's breath caught in her throat as she stared at the dusky skin of his taut nipples. The lamplight gave his skin a golden glow, and accentuated the powerful lines of his arms and stomach. The sight of his body sent waves of heat dancing over her skin.

"Come here," he said, finally.

Unable or unwilling to refuse, Isobel obeyed. When she reached him, Beckett slowly turned her around, sliding his hands down to the little cluster of buttons that fastened the upper part of her dress. He began to undo them.

"I thought you might need help, without a maid to undress you," he said, easing the garment apart and sliding his warm hands in. The touch of his hands seemed to burn her skin. He slid the dress slowly down over her chemise, his hands lingering. Then he released her, saying, "I think you can manage the rest."

Confused, Isobel searched his eyes. He was holding something back, just behind the impenetrable walls of his stormy-blue eyes.

What did he want from her?

She searched for her night-dress, and hesitated once she found it, but there was nowhere to hide in such limited space. Reluctantly, Isobel faced the fact that she would have to disrobe in front of her husband.

As fast as she could, Isobel shimmied out of her dress and chemise and threw the night dress over her head. She glanced over her shoulder and saw that Beckett had climbed into bed. Gingerly, she turned down the lamp. Feeling much braver in the dark, Isobel pulled back the covers and slipped between them as if this were the most normal thing in the world. Then she lay on her back near the edge of the bed and waited.

And waited.

She listened to Beckett breathing. Soon, the sound took on a new tone. It was lower, deeper.

Devil take him, he was snoring!

Her husband, whose very presence made her tingle with feminine arousal, was snoring.

Well, if that didn't just take the flip.

Perhaps it was best to keep things uncomplicated between them. Yet as Isobel lay next to him in the dark night, she couldn't clear the image of his magnificent naked chest from her mind.

And worse than that, she couldn't ignore the heat that still lingered on every inch of her skin from the sight of it.

CHAPTER TWELVE

Beckett looked out over the railing, marveling at the beauty of the sea. It calmed him to watch the movement of the gray-blue water, whose only constant was its never-ceasing movement.

Like life itself, it made no promises to anyone.

He turned his head and saw Isobel approaching. The sight of her sent a disconcerting wave of desire through his veins.

Damn and blast.

This woman was his wife, a mysterious beauty who had been implicated in a murder, yet here he was mooning over her as if he were a youth and she a famous chorus girl.

She came to stand beside him, a warm smile curving her lips. She looked out over the beckoning sea, and let her arm brush against his as she leaned on the railing.

Beckett regarded her, so composed beside him. Was she indeed the innocent victim she appeared to be? Or was it all an act designed to save her own skin?

He felt his gut tighten at even the notion of abandoning her. He could never fully dampen the flame of passion that she stirred in him, or fight the powerful conviction that because he had found her, she now belonged totally to him.

He would protect her.

Or die trying.

"There is something you never told me, Beckett," Isobel asked. "Why did you take pity on me and bring me home that night?"

A knot formed in his heart.

Why had he helped her? He had asked himself the same question as he'd undressed her that night, as he'd ducked from the clock she'd thrown at him, and as he'd stood next to her at the altar and taken her as his wife.

The answer still eluded him.

Was it her beauty that had captured him and so easily taken him prisoner? It was more than his habit of helping strays, he knew.

He curved his arm around her narrow waist and pulled her close. Desire—dangerous and demanding—fired his blood. "Do I have to give you a reason?"

"Yes."

"Perhaps it was because I wanted to take you in my arms and do this." He covered her mouth with his own, and felt her lips tremble beneath his. Desire burned though his body. He imagined laying her down on a bed, spreading her legs, and plunging himself into her soft, warm depths.

Beckett deepened the kiss, and she tilted her head back, clutching onto him to keep her balance.

He could take her down to their cabin right now. She was his wife. He had every right to take her body with his own. Somehow he knew she would not protest.

He kissed her hungrily, as if she were the only nourishment his body would ever need.

Oh, how he wanted her beneath him, naked and open and weak with desire—desire for him.

She stirred powerful feelings in him—more powerful than he'd ever felt for any other woman. Even Cordeila. And he'd fancied himself in love with her.

If he fed those passions with the taste of Isobel, he might lose himself completely. He broke the kiss, but still held her close.

"There," he said, brushing away a silken curl from her cheek. "That is the only answer I can give you."

She studied him for a moment with eyes that seemed to see far too much for his liking.

"Your answer only raises more questions, Beckett," she replied. "For both of us."

Isobel's words were the only truth they could share at the moment. If Beckett allowed her to know the depth of his desire for her, it would put him at a disadvantage. He could not give her that power over him. She already had too much for his liking. He could not let his passions run unchecked. For if he did, there might be no turning back.

An uneasy silence remained between Beckett and Isobel for the remainder of the voyage.

As husband and wife, they maintained a cordial atmosphere that Isobel considered might be quite common to any marriage. But beneath that calm veneer lurked the shadows of the past, like a great whale that swims below a ship—far too deep to be seen—yet still posing a dangerous threat.

Every night Isobel found herself hoping Beckett would reach out and pull her to him, kiss her passionately as he had on the deck, and touch her in ways she could only imagine.

But he didn't.

To keep her mind off her husband during the day, Isobel observed ship-board life on deck, recording all she saw in her sketch-book.

She drew everyone, including Captain Mayfield and the large sailor with the black-and-white cat she'd seen curled on top of his shoulders. She'd had to make her observations from afar, as the mysterious cat always disappeared when she approached.

On a particularly breezy afternoon, while she was drawing a sailor who worked up in the rigging, the cat appeared beside her and sat still. It seemed to study what she was doing as it sat there, silent yet imposing.

Isobel reached out to stroke his soft, furry head in greeting. The cat's green eyes narrowed to slits, and he purred in pleasure. Reluctantly taking her hand away, Isobel flipped to the next blank sheet of paper and began to render the feline's image.

The cat was huge—not fat by any means, but with muscular shoulders and haunches. No doubt, he was well fed by keeping rats and mice out of the galley.

Isobel noticed that one of his black patches covered the side of his head and his left eye, looking remarkably like a pirate's lopsided kerchief and eye patch.

Captain Mayfield came to stand in front of her, but at his approach, the cat rose, stretched, and walked away.

"I wasn't finished," Isobel called out, but the cat simply walked haughtily across the deck and disappeared from sight.

Mayfield chuckled, saying, "I suppose I didn't mention that this ship has two captains, did I?"

Isobel shook her head. "Two captains? I've never heard of that. Who is the other?"

"You just met him."

Isobel put her pencil down and asked, "What do you mean?"

"That cat is more than he seems," Mayfield said, sitting down beside her. "His name is Captain Black. I first met him on one of my journeys in the Caribbean, which is swamped with pirates, as you well know."

Isobel smiled at the gray-haired man beside her. He was going to tell her a sea-faring yarn, she supposed. He was just having fun with a land-lubber. She would play along with the old soul.

"We were off the coast of Jamaica," he began, "carrying a heavy cargo of coffee beans, when we were attacked by a rather notorious pirate ship, the 'Midnight Star.' Its captain was named Worthington, a shrewd but fair man who was more famous for his cat companion. Legend has it that the beast was the ship's previous master, a man named Black, who had been transformed into the guise of a cat during an obeah ceremony in Jamaica."

"Obeah?" she asked. "What on earth is that?"

"The religion of the Haitians," Captain Mayfield explained, "also known as voodoo. Their ceremonies are filled with chanting, wild dancing, and other practices that are too indelicate to mention in mixed company."

Isobel was intrigued. "And they used it to put a spell on Captain Black? How?"

"Apparently this man Worthington had planned to mutiny against his captain and take over the ship himself," Mayfield said. "While in Jamaica, he discovered the powers of obeah and arranged to do away with his rival."

Silly or not, the tale was suitably unnerving. Isobel admired the old captain's story-telling ability.

"Members of the pirate crew swear they saw their captain changed into a cat during one of those frightening ceremonies."

"But how did Captain Black arrive on board your ship?" she asked.

"It was during the battle with the 'Midnight Star,' when the pirate ship caught fire," Mayfield explained. "We searched for survivors after she sank, but found no one except for a mysterious cat who appeared on our ship, as if out of thin air. The crew was naturally suspicious, but unwilling to dispose of the creature in fear of bad luck. They believe he possesses mystical powers."

The cat suddenly appeared again, as if he'd heard them talking. He leaped up onto the railing and landed solidly, turning to arrange himself into a comfortable position.

Captain Mayfield grinned and regarded the cat, who stared back at him with a penetrating gaze.

"Though we found no other survivors, there are rumors that Worthington is still alive, and even now searches the seas for his cat companion. As you can see, we gave Captain Black a position on our ship as chief mouse-catcher, one that he performs exceedingly well."

Isobel regarded the man with a wary smile. He'd almost had her believing the incredible tale. "You wouldn't be teasing me now, would you, Captain Mayfield?"

"That is Captain Black before you, Madam," he insisted, "in flesh and blood! He tries to steer the ship, you know."

Isobel laughed, and Captain Mayfield leaned toward her in a conspiratorial way.

"Sometimes, I let him," he whispered, then returned to his post.

Isobel regarded the cat, still sitting on the narrow railing in front of her. "Are you really a pirate, then?" she said.

The cat returned her gaze, then gave a long "meow."

"Perhaps you are," Isobel mused. Then Captain Black leaped down to the deck and strolled away from her, doubtless to resume his mouse-catching duties below.

An eerie moan broke the dark silence of the cabin. Beckett jumped up and hit his head on the low ceiling above the bunk. He was momentarily stunned, but quickly recovered as another hair-raising wail cut through the darkness from beside him.

Isobel.

She thrashed about on the bed, her breathing shallow and strained. He reached out to shake her awake.

"Isobel, you're dreaming," he said, pulling her into his arms. He touched her face and felt her cheek, hot and damp with tears. Her whole body was covered in perspiration, soaking her linen nightdress.

She stiffened and awakened then. Beckett loosened his hold on her, suddenly aware of how naked she was beneath the damp night dress.

"Are you alright?" he asked.

"Yes, I think so," Isobel whispered, her voice shaky.

"You were having a bad dream," he explained. "Lay down and try to go back to sleep."

"No—" She sprang up and clutched at his hand. "I don't want to go to sleep. I don't want to have that dream again."

Beckett propped himself up on one elbow. "Come, now. Lay down and go to sleep. There's no one to trouble you here."

Isobel exhaled slowly, and lay back down on the bed. She turned onto her side and her rose-water scent reached out to him, teasing his senses.

Beckett watched the moonlight spill through the window and play on Isobel's hair, like silvery fingers dancing across a river of gold. He reached out to stroke it. The texture of the silken strands running through his fingers sent a jolt of heat through him.

He continued to stroke her hair, not for his pleasure, but for hers. It seemed to relax her, and soon he heard her breathing regain a steady rhythm.

As he lay there beside her, he was glad Isobel was able to go back to sleep.

Damn, but he desired her.

Beckett doubted he'd be able to resist her next time. But he couldn't let his guard down—there was far too much at stake. He'd promised to protect her, and he would do exactly that.

He could not let himself become distracted by Isobel's charms.

Her very life depended on it.

Isobel opened her eyes slowly, peering at the dim morning light through squinting eyes. She had done it. She had fallen asleep and not dreamt the awful nightmare again. As she became more fully awake, she remembered what had made such tranquil sleep possible.

Beckett's arm lay curled about her waist, a bit of her nightdress bunched loosely in his fist. A thrill zoomed though her veins at the sweet heaviness of her husband's embrace. How wonderful it would be to wake like this every morning.

Her breathing quickened as the arm about her waist tightened and drew her closer.

Beckett's deep, steady breathing told her that he was

still asleep. Her back pressed against the hard wall of his chest as he held her firmly against him.

Then Isobel felt something else—something hard—pressing gently against her buttocks. It couldn't be his knee.

Good Lord, it was his—

She knew she should try to get up, but it clearly seemed impossible without waking him. And surely this situation would embarrass him as much as her. No, she would have to endure this wicked intimacy until she could unlock his arm from her waist and move safely away.

Gingerly, Isobel closed her hand around Beckett's wrist and tried to lift his arm. This was going to be more difficult than she'd thought. Although he was asleep, Beckett's muscles were anything but relaxed.

Isobel closed her eyes in shock as his hard manhood pressed against her bottom. She clamped her lips together to keep from making a sound as he ground himself quite brazenly against her.

The most exquisite sensations swept through her body. Her breasts throbbed with heat, aching to be touched. Desire teased between her legs, unnerving her with its intensity.

Oh, this was dreadful.

Wasn't it?

But if it was so dreadful, why did it feel so wickedly good?

Her body was weak with desire. A dangerous heat burned in her veins, making her almost light-headed. She had never wanted something as much as she did right now... Beckett's touch, his mouth, his hands. His body loving hers, making her his true wife.

Would he wake and make love to her?

She wanted him to.

Oh, how she wanted him to.

Every inch of her body begged for his touch. Beckett stirred a physical response in her she hadn't known possible.

Abruptly, Beckett released his hold on her waist and turned over, his breathing rhythmic and even.

Isobel lay in stunned silence, feeling an embarrassing sense of disappointment.

He was still asleep, thank the Lord.

She pulled back the covers and tiptoed across the room to the screen in the corner. Isobel pulled off her night dress, wet a cloth, and rubbed it over her hot skin, trying desperately to slow her racing pulse.

Isobel donned her underclothes and stockings, followed by a somber fawn-brown day dress. She hoped it would set the mood for the rest of the day. She picked up her paper and leads, but paused a moment before leaving.

Beckett was still asleep. She watched him in the pale morning light.

An uneasiness crept into Isobel's heart, like a soft-footed cat bent on mischief. She had been fooling herself to think she could make this marriage purely one of convenience. Their arrangement was doomed to be a dismal failure. Like it or not, Beckett stirred passionate feelings in her. And like unruly children, each day she found them harder to control.

CHAPTER THIRTEEN

Isobel watched as a dark shape grew along the horizon. She had dreamed with such longing of land beneath her feet again.

As they neared the island, she was entranced by the clear, turquoise waters. The sun shone high in the sky, and made the water sparkle as though covered in twinkling jewels.

The heat grew a little more intense as the ship neared the island. The wind had been constant out on the open water, and the temperature on deck had been warm but bearable. Now, she felt the sun beating down on her and she shaded herself with a parasol.

Isobel looked over the side of the boat into the depths of the blue-green ocean, and was startled as she saw a large, dark shape swimming through the water far below.

"Captain Mayfield, what is that down there?" Isobel asked, with some fear.

The captain looked over, but the shadow was no longer in sight.

"Most likely a dolphin," he replied. "Though to an untrained eye, a shark can easily appear to be a dolphin."

Isobel nodded, remembering the stories he'd told her during their voyage about life in the tropics. Aside from the assortment of poisonous plants and insects, and the wild animals, there was also the native religion of obeah to send shivers down her spine.

"I needn't remind you that this isn't England," Captain Mayfield warned. "But many Europeans enjoy living on these islands and have done so for years with no harm coming to them."

Isobel smiled and tried to reassure herself. After all, they had come here out of necessity—not to establish a home in a strange land.

"Still," Captain Mayfield said, "be sure your husband teaches you how to shoot a pistol." He turned and walked along the deck to join his first mate.

Isobel hoped the captain was poking fun at her. However, learning to shoot might be a good idea.

Beckett appeared beside her, looking quite startling handsome as he surveyed the approaching shoreline. "I hope you won't find life here on the island too uncomfortable, my dear. My experience in Wellington's army has prepared me for almost any kind of accommodation, no matter how rough. But a lady might find such a wild land to be an adjustment."

"I have been well prepared by Captain Mayfield for the way of life here in the tropics," Isobel said. "Perhaps I might even teach you a thing or two."

"I look forward to being your pupil," He replied with a playful look.

Isobel gulped. She did not want to think about what he might want her to teach him.

She stared at the long wooden dock and saw Europeans dressed as they might be in London, as well as native workers loading various cargo.

The ship docked smoothly, its sailors all working in tandem to tie the lines. Some of their cargo was unloaded at once before the passengers began to disembark.

Isobel lifted Captain Black into her arms to say her goodbyes. She'd become fond of the surly cat during the journey, as had Beckett, with his natural affinity for animals. She smiled as she thought of the lovely sketches she had made of both Beckett and the cat. Would she stare wistfully at them in years to come, when she and her husband were living out their separate lives?

Captain Mayfield approached from across the deck.

"My dear Mrs. Evans," the captain began, using the name she and Beckett were travelling under. "It seems that Captain Black has grown tired of a seafaring life and now seeks employment on land. Could you perhaps find a suitable position for him at your new residence?"

Isobel looked at Captain Mayfield and then Beckett, who said, "My wife and I would like nothing more."

"But Captain Mayfield," she asked, "how can you be sure that Captain Black has given up the sea?"

"Oh, I am quite sure of it," the old man replied. "You see, I just left him in my cabin, having locked the door but a moment ago. And now, here he is in your arms."

Everyone looked at Captain Black for some explanation, but the cat merely blinked at them.

"Apparently, he has grown quite attached to you, my dear," Mayfield said. "Considering his experience with obeah, he will no doubt be adept at protecting you from any island mischief."

Isobel nuzzled the cat before the captain gently placed him inside a carrying basket.

"Now, you must promise to stay in your basket, Captain Black. Please." Mayfield shook his finger at the cat inside and then fastened the lid.

Beckett shook hands with the man. "Thank you for delivering us so expertly, Captain."

"It has been a pleasure, sir."

Guided by Beckett, Isobel made her way down the boarding plank and onto the dock. She turned to wave, but Captain Mayfield was gone, doubtless seeing to some part of the ship's business.

"We'll miss Captain Mayfield, won't we, Captain Black?" she said to the feline in the basket, as she followed Beckett down the length of the dock.

Beckett looked back at her over his shoulder. "Quite an elaborate story just to get rid of a cat. I suppose he wouldn't have known we'd be happy to adopt the creature. I must say, I miss being away from Monty and Caesar. Captain Black shall be good company for us."

One of the men from the sugar plantation, Ravenwood Hall, stood beside the waiting coach, hat in hand.

"Lord Ravenwood," he said, bowing, "Hal Cobb, sir, at your service."

"Mr. Cobb, may I present my wife, Lady Ravenwood," Beckett said, taking her hand.

"M'lady."

Isobel fanned herself as the man made his bows to her. "I am pleased to make your acquaintance, Mr. Cobb," she said. "Tell me, is it always this hot on the island?"

"Oh, no, m'lady" he replied. "It gets much hotter."

Isobel glanced at Beckett and saw him grin.

"I told you Barbados was not for the faint of heart," was all he said.

"So you did." She purposely closed her fan. "I shall have no trouble at all, then."

Beckett chuckled and handed her up into the carriage. Soon the vehicle rolled into motion and started down the rough dirt road.

Her fan did not stay closed for long. Much to her dismay, Isobel's entire body quickly developed a sheen of perspiration. As soon as she discreetly wiped some away from her forehead, it was instantly replaced. Her light muslin dress stuck to her like glue and most likely showed off far too much of her body. Isobel fanned herself energetically. It gave some relief.

She noticed that Beckett was also covered in sweat, and wiping at his forehead from time to time with a handkerchief. At last, he caught her staring at him.

She quickly looked out the window. Captain Black meowed loudly, apparently not enjoying the carriage ride at all.

As they traveled down the road, Isobel tried to focus on the beautiful countryside to take her mind off the heat. They left St. Michael and Bridgetown, and entered the district of St. James, which would be her home for the next while.

Outside, all around them bloomed flowers in colors Isobel had never seen before, with trees and various plants in such strange sizes and shapes, she wondered at nature's handiwork.

Questions and observations tumbled out of her like rambunctious children.

"—What is that tree?"

"—That flower, do you know what is it called?"

"—What an odd looking fruit! Surely no one eats such a thing."

Beckett patiently pointed out banana and fig trees, but he was silently chuckling at her, she was quite sure. He also identified mangoes, sugar apples and hog plums—all hanging in the thick boughs like richly colored jewels. The smell of their sweet scents on the breeze made Isobel long to stop and pick some of the succulent fruit.

The sky above them was a bright, warm blue—the same color as Beckett's eyes, Isobel noticed. Huge puffy clouds decorated the expanse of sky like dollops of clotted cream. This mysterious place was like a spell cast to invade all the senses at once. The sights, sounds and smells were almost impossible to resist.

"Such untamed splendor often has an intense effect on the human heart, does it not?" he asked.

Isobel opened her mouth to reply, but squealed as something quite large flew by the window. "Oh my! Whatever was that?"

She leaned closer to the window and almost bumped heads with Beckett as he did the same. They laughed, and Beckett pointed through the open window to the treetops.

"You see up there, in the tree?" he said. "Those are wild macaws. A macaw is a rather colorful type of parrot."

Isobel gasped at the beautiful birds sitting high in the branches overhead. "Oh, Beckett. It's as though someone has painted them by hand! But Caesar is not colored so."

"He would surely have something quite nasty to say on the subject," Beckett chuckled, sitting back. "We can count our blessings that it's Captain Black we have with us instead."

The carriage turned down a long drive. In the distance, Isobel could see Ravenwood Hall. It was surrounded by a magnificent lawn and exotic gardens, with palm trees standing tall overhead. Behind it, the vast sugar fields stretched out of sight.

They pulled up in front of the large, two-story house, which was surrounded by a verandah on both levels. Constructed of an unusual pink-colored stone, the house was offset by bright white shutters that flanked its long windows. Though the architecture copied the English style, the house seemed far more exotic than anything found in the British Isles.

The house staff of Ravenwood Hall stood at attention beside the steps, waiting to greet the new earl and countess. Beckett handed Isobel out of the carriage as Mr. Cobb prepared to introduce them to the staff.

Various male and female servants peered at them curiously, all seeming to be native islanders. There was a mature butler with a white beard, beside him a substantial woman whom Isobel took to be the housekeeper, and a few young girls who made up the rest of the household staff.

Mr. Cobb introduced the butler first. "This is Isaac."

The man made his bows, and spoke in a raspy voice. "It is a pleasure to welcome the new lord and lady to Ravenwood Hall."

"It is a pleasure to be here, Isaac," Beckett replied.

"This is Josephine," Mr. Cobb said. "The house-keeper of Ravenwood Hall."

Beckett nodded at the woman. Her high cheek-bones and intimidating stare made Isobel feel as if she herself should be making a curtsy to Josephine, not the other way around.

"Welcome, m'lord," she said in a voice as dark and rich as coffee.

"Thank you, Josephine," Beckett replied. "I am sure our stay here will be very enjoyable now that we are in your capable hands."

The woman nodded silently.

"May I introduce my wife. Lady Ravenwood," Beckett said. "And this is her cat, Captain Black."

Isobel smiled as Josephine looked suspiciously at the basket she held.

"You 'ave Captain Black in dat basket?" Josephine asked, raising her eyebrows.

Surprised, Isobel nodded.

"Captain Black is famous in dese islands," she whispered to Isobel then pointed towards the door. "I will tell you all about him later. But come inside, now."

They followed Josephine into their new home. The interior was stylish but not ornate. It had been decorated in vibrant colors too outrageous for London, but perfectly suitable for this island manor house. There were the usual comforts of home—a salon, a dining room, a small library. In each room, lovely arrangements of native flowers and plants made the house look and smell like a garden.

"We should like some tea in the salon please, Josephine," Beckett said.

Josephine smiled and nodded. "Yes, m'lord."

"Well, what do you think of your new home, Isobel?" he asked.

She turned to look at Beckett as she lifted Captain Black out of the basket, and felt a wave of mixed feelings wash over her. The house was lovely. Barbados was a paradise on Earth. Beckett was a kind and dutiful husband. But the circumstances that had brought her here cast a dark shadow over the island's beauty, and over their marriage as well.

"I think it very beautiful, Beckett," she replied. "Very beautiful, indeed."

"That does not sound very convincing," he said. "Come, let there be no more secrets between us, Lady Ravenwood. We have surely had enough of those."

Isobel wondered if Beckett meant for his words to sting? He was acting like their marriage was all her fault, yet he had been the one keen to marry her so he could claim his inheritance.

"I meant what I said," she answered. "This island, this home is indeed beautiful. I was only saddened by the memory of what brought us here in the first place. And you are right, Beckett. Secrets have no place in a marriage—even a marriage such as ours. And yet I find it strange to hear you say such a thing, when you yourself do not practice what you preach."

Beckett's eyes blazed for a moment. Then a barrier went up, cloaking their fire from view.

"You see? Even now you keep your feelings hidden from me."

"Perhaps it is for your own good, my dear," he said.

"So you are a hypocrite, then," Isobel boldly replied. "You are allowed to keep secrets from me, and yet you are unable to forgive me for keeping those I did from you—even though I felt my life depended on it."

"I am doing my best to be a dutiful husband, Isobel," he said dangerously.

"Oh, yes. You are very dutiful indeed," she continued. "A perfect gentleman, in fact. You treat me more like a sister than a wife."

Beckett stepped closer to her. Strong hands curled around her arms and he pulled her close. "And what would you have me do, little wife? Hmm? You know not what you say."

Isobel opened her mouth to reply, but Beckett silenced her with his own. His arms circled her, imprisoning her hard against his strong, muscled body. He parted her lips with his tongue, deepening the kiss until Isobel felt her legs would no longer hold her upright. She grabbed onto him for balance.

He broke the kiss, looking down at her with an intensity that threatened to ignite her like kindling where she stood.

Then, without so much as a glance over his shoulder, he turned and stalked from the room.

Chapter Fourteen

Alone in his bed, Beckett was unable to sleep. His mind kept settling on Isobel. Every time he closed his eyes, it seemed he saw her with her hair spread out on a pillow, her body riding waves of pleasure as he made love to her.

He flipped over onto his side, punched the pillow to make it comfortable—though it was not in the least bit uncomfortable at all—and closed his eyes again.

Instantly, he imagined her again. She lay on her side with her back pressed against him, gasping as he entered her. His hands roamed over her breasts as he thrust into her, teasing their hard peaks, reaching down to stroke between her thighs as she moaned and—

Damnation! This would not do at all. Not at all. But the insistent hardness of his manhood would not go away.

He flipped over again onto his other side, determined to purge his mind of these tempting, vexing thoughts. But then the memory of kissing her so passionately in the salon jumped into his brain, along with the silken texture of her skin, the smell of her hair, and the maddening pleasure of her kiss.

It was no use. He was fighting a losing battle with his base desires. Determined to clear his mind, Beckett rose and lit a candle, electing to read Milton's Paradise Lost. Perhaps that distraction would cleanse the wicked thoughts from his head.

He read a few pages, and then felt his mind drift back to the woman who had been nothing but trouble since he'd found her that night in the rubbish heap.

Isobel.

The woman who plagued his thoughts day and night. The woman who ignited his desires and made them burn with blazing heat. The woman who had lied to him about everything in her past.

His wife.

Devil take it, he was trying to honor their agreement. And she did nothing but upset his plans at every turn. Didn't she know that it was all he could do to keep his hands from touching her, his lips from kissing her, and his body from taking her?

If he did that now, he might lose himself completely, and he could not risk that. He would not risk that. For the truth of the matter was that Beckett was harboring a secret.

He had a bad heart.

The blasted thing was always getting him into trouble, developing feelings for women who would only let him down in the end.

He couldn't let Isobel know the truth, for if he let her into his heart now, he knew he'd never get her out.

After a breakfast of pastries and delicious exotic fruit, Beckett decided to take Isobel on a small tour of the St. James district. After he swung himself up onto his mount, and she onto hers, they set off down the grassy tree-lined road.

He glanced over his shoulder to see her riding behind

him, the wind playing with the curly tendrils of her hair. Isobel had forgone a bonnet today, telling him that she preferred going without.

Beckett slowed his stallion and let Isobel's mare walk beside him. The two horses greeted each other, their noses nuzzling slightly whenever they could.

"They seem quite fond of each other, do they not?" he asked.

"They do, indeed." Isobel smiled.

They stopped and let the horses communicate in their secret way. "Do you think...." Isobel began.

"What?"

"It sounds silly," she continued, "but do you think these two could be in love?"

Beckett watched the horses' heads rub against each other and listened to their quiet whickering.

"I suppose anything is possible," he replied.

Isobel smiled and said, "Then they are fortunate creatures."

"Some might disagree with you," he observed.

"Like who?"

"Romeo and Juliet," he said, "Hamlet and Ophelia, and Othello and Desdemona, to name but a few. Love didn't make them very happy, did it?"

"No," Isobel agreed. "But it made Beatrice and Benedick happy. Not to mention Orsino and Viola, Orlando and Rosalind, and Titania and Oberon. So there."

Beckett found himself grinning. "It seems you are having the better of this argument, madam. Shall we let the lovers alone then, and go exploring on foot? Mr. Cobb told me there were some very interesting caves down there by the beach. What do you say? Are you game?"

"I am," she replied. "This island enthralls me. I want to learn all I can about it while we are here.

"As do I," he said, dismounting and tying his horse to a bush. He reached up to help Isobel down from her mare, then tied it next to his. Taking Isobel's hand, he led her through the tall grasses toward the full sound of crashing waves.

They came around a bend to see a white sandy beach that stretched from the nearby cove as far as the eye could see. The turquoise water caressed the sand in frothy white waves.

Beckett stopped near a jagged rock formation, resting his boot on the bottom of it. Above, the entrance of the cave gaped like an enormous mouth.

"Might you be brave enough to go in there with me, my dear?" he said, flashing her a challenging look.

Isobel met his gaze evenly. "Of course. After all, someone has to protect you. Lead the way."

Beckett started up over the rocky terrain to the entrance. He glanced back over his shoulder to make sure she was following, and was surprised to see her only a few steps behind him.

She was tougher than she looked.

As they reached the cave mouth, he noticed that the air coming from the opening smelled quite earthy and pungent. It was strong but somehow pleasant, too.

"I should warn you, Isobel," Beckett said as he helped her over the rocks. "Caverns can be treacherous places. So watch your footing and your head. Stay close to me and don't make any noise."

"Why should we not make noise?" she asked. "There is no one in there, surely."

"For all we know, this is a pirate lair," he pointed out. "They could be in there right now burying their treasure."

Isobel put her hands on her hips, looking unamused at his teasing.

Beckett laughed at her expression, saying, "I thought you said you weren't afraid."

"Nor am I," she replied.

"If you say so," he said, unconvinced.

Isobel huffed in exasperation and stepped away from him.

Beckett searched the ground. "Cobb said that he left a torch here. He told me these caves are sometimes used by the natives in those rituals they have. Perhaps we'll find a few skeletons. What do you think? Aha, here it is."

Beckett picked up a well-used torch and reached into his pocket for a match to light it. The acrid smell of the burning torch mixed with the cave's unusual odor.

"Shall we?" he held his hand out in invitation.

Isobel took a deep breath and lay her hand in his.

"I should like to see Miss Cordelia Haversham go into a cave like this," Isobel said, her eyes glittering with challenge. "I would wager she'd have none of it."

Beckett cocked an eyebrow. "May I remind you that you have yet to enter it yourself."

Isobel smiled back, calmly. "Quite right. I'll remember those words when I'm forced to drag you out bodily, when you yourself are undoubtedly overcome with an attack of nerves."

He grinned.

Slowly, they entered the mysterious cave. Beckett's torch cast shadows everywhere, but provided enough light to show the incredible interior.

Beckett had never seen anything like it. The whole of the cavern ceiling was comprised of what looked like huge, dripping icicles, which seemed to glitter and glow with unusual, other-worldly colors.

"What on earth are those?" Isobel asked.

"Stalagmites and stalactites, if I remember my lessons correctly," Beckett replied. "Look, over there."

He pointed toward an underground waterfall nearby, the torchlight illuminating it as they approached. Water flowed and bubbled over the odd-looking rocks, down to more of the formations which seemed to grow out of the cave's floor like strange mushrooms.

"My heavens, I've never seen anything like it," Isobel said.

"Apparently there are caves like these all over Barbados," Beckett said, peering into the darkness. "Who knows how deep this one goes?"

"Shall we keep going?" she asked.

"We may explore a bit farther, but not too much," Beckett cautioned. "As I said, caverns can be very unstable—"

His words were cut off as a huge stalagmite ripped away from the ceiling high above them with a resounding crack. Beckett's head jerked up to see it falling right toward them.

Seizing Isobel in his arms, he rolled them both out of the way. The stalagmite smashed into the floor, its sharp point piercing the muddy ground a few feet away from their faces.

An eerie, high pitched squeaking sound filled the air, from somewhere deep in the cave.

"I don't like the sound of that, Beckett," Isobel said. "What in God's name is it?"

"Bats!" Beckett yelled, and quickly shielded her body with his own. The deafening sound of flapping wings surrounded them.

The air compressed as a huge gust of wind blew overhead. A thundering clamor filled the air as thousands of bats swept through the cave. Isobel buried her face in Beckett's chest and clung tightly to his body.

Then, like a summer storm, the squeaking and flapping ceased as quickly as it had come. Slowly Beckett raised his head and looked around. Their torch lay flickering a few feet away.

He looked down at Isobel lying beneath him. They were molded together. "Are you alright?"

"Fine—I think," she answered.

"You're not hurt?" Beckett rolled off her and pulled her up beside him.

"No, just a little shaken. Was that your attempt at making me swoon?" Isobel brushed the dirt off her dress.

"Yes, but as you can see, I failed," he said. "Now I shall lose my chance to carry you out of this dangerous cave and look the hero."

"But you protected me from the bats—and the falling rock. That was very gallant," Isobel pointed out. "Have I thanked you, Beckett?"

"For throwing you to the ground just now?" he asked, wryly. "I do not think many ladies would."

"No," she said, staring up at him. "For all that you've done for me."

"A husband does not expect to be thanked, nor does he need to be," Beckett answered. "It is my duty to protect you."

"And it is my duty to do this." Isobel touched her lips to his, kissing him with maddening delicacy.

Beckett felt himself hardening instantly at Isobel's touch.

Devil take him, how he wanted her!

She broke the kiss and touched his face, her eyes glowing up at him in the flickering torchlight.

"Are you trying to give me that attack of nerves, wife?" he asked. "For I warn you, two can play at this game."

Beckett's mouth descended to claim hers and he deftly parted her lips with his tongue. He heard her quick intake of breath as he pressed her body tight against his and skillfully explored the secrets of her mouth.

Isobel trembled in his arms. Damn, but it felt as if she'd been made for his hands and mouth alone.

"Don't swoon, now, or I'll have to carry you out after all. Like this," he said, lifting her up into his arms.

Isobel squealed adorably as he carried her toward the mouth of the cave. "Put me down! I will not have you say that I have swooned when I have not."

"No," he answered, "but you soon would have, trembling and sighing as you were in my arms."

"I did no such things!" Isobel protested.

Beckett set her down at the entrance to the cave, saying, "Would you like me to demonstrate again, my dear?"

"It might be dangerous," she answered. "We would invariably be late for dinner, and Jospehine would have the whole house staff out looking for us."

"True," Beckett said, with a pang of disappointment. He offered his hand to help her down the rocky slope "Shall we go back to the house?"

Isobel nodded.

They made their way to the horses, who were still nuzzling each other amorously. Beckett helped Isobel up onto her saddle before mounting, himself.

As they trotted down the road, Beckett fought a war with himself.

His resolve was weakening. Each day it became more and more difficult to resist his wife's charms. Perhaps he was making too much of the whole thing. Where was the harm in consummating their marriage?

He wanted it.

He wanted *her*.

It didn't mean he was in love with Isobel.

Yet, he had sworn to himself not to take her to bed until he was certain she was innocent of the accusations against her. But what if that day never came?

How long could he resist the desire to claim Isobel, and make her his true wife?

CHAPTER FIFTEEN

Isobel lay in her bed gazing idly up at the ceiling. It was quite late in the morning, she knew. But she had been having such delicious dreams. Why couldn't she stay in bed and think about them for awhile?

She hadn't known what had come over her when she'd kissed Beckett so brazenly in the cave. But she didn't regret it. She'd wanted to thank him, and it seemed a perfectly natural thing for a wife to do to her husband. Besides—being in his arms was the most exciting feeling she had ever known.

Still, Beckett had made it perfectly clear to her that he would never have feelings for her or any other woman. Falling in love with him would be like stepping off a cliff to see if she could fly. While providing a unique experience, both would lead to her destruction.

And what of Sir Harry? If Alfred couldn't find evidence against him, the despicable man would be free to torment her for the rest of her life. It didn't bear thinking about.

Her cat meowed his morning greeting and came to sit near her. Isobel was glad for the distraction. When she made no motion to get out of bed, the beast reached over with his paw and softly batted her cheek.

"You've got quite the nerve, Captain Black, even if you are a heathen pirate," Isobel said, pushing away the feline playfully. He meowed in protest, jumping back and then trying to pounce on her hand. She hid her hands under the bedclothes and moved them as if there were a mouse scuttling beneath. The cat leapt about, his tail swishing back and forth as he stalked the mysterious lump beneath the covers.

Suddenly tired of Isobel's game, the haughty feline leaped off the bed and headed for the door, trotting quickly away.

"Oh, don't leave in a huff." Isobel stared after him, but he didn't respond with so much as a meow.

"Men!" Isobel scoffed, finally getting out of her comfortable bed and going to look out the French windows. She opened them and sighed with pleasure as she breathed in the unique scent that could only be called Barbados.

Throwing on her dressing gown, she went out onto the verandah and took a seat in one a white wicker chair. She let her eyes travel over the grounds, seeing the sugar fields rolling far off into the distance, speckled with men working under the bright morning sun.

She looked over the gardens, and wondered what her next drawing should be. She had done so many of the island's different flowers and plants. Perhaps she should try some human subjects.

Perhaps Beckett....

No, she told herself. You will not find an excuse to stare at his wickedly handsome face any more than you have to!

It was as if he had cast a spell on her.

Beckett plagued her when she was awake, as well as

asleep. And she highly doubted that he had spent any time dreaming about her.

Then, as if called up by her very thoughts, her husband appeared around the corner of the verandah and approached.

Isobel sat up straight in the chair, realizing too late how little clothing she had on. She had only meant to stay outside for a few minutes. Now she was trapped. Perhaps he would go quickly when he saw the state of her dress. Knowing her spouse, he would enjoy making her squirm, for a little while at least.

He strode leisurely across the verandah until he came near enough to notice her attire. Isobel saw his eyes travel over her body slowly, then rest on her face, an appreciative grin curving his lips.

"Good morning, Isobel. I see you couldn't wait to greet the day. It is a lovely one." To her, his voice was like a physical caress.

"Yes, I'm sure it is going to be a beautiful day," Isobel replied, trying to appear unaffected by his nearness.

"Did you sleep well?" He asked.

"Yes. And you?"

"I was restless," he answered, his gaze traveling over her body. "I had the most bothersome dreams. They kept me awake half the night."

Isobel felt her nipples harden beneath the thin fabric of her nightdress and wrap as if he had touched them. Knowing just how naked she was underneath these flimsy clothes made her heart beat like a hummingbird's wings.

"I should be going in, now," Isobel said, desperate to escape the heated look in Beckett's eyes.

"If you must," Beckett said, his eyes dancing with mischief.

He was going to enjoy every minute of watching her parade before him in such a scandalous state.

Well, if he was going to enjoy it, so was she.

Isobel met his teasing eyes, then turned. She walked slowly back to the open door, letting the gauzy fabric of her dressing gown show what it would to her husband's hungry stare.

Reaching the doorway, she paused to look back at his amused expression.

Watching him chuckle and walk away, Isobel wished he had followed her inside.

She closed the doors and tried to banish the infuriating man from her thoughts. Since her skin burned with the heat of Beckett's gaze, she searched her wardrobe for something prim and proper to wear. She donned a suitably somber dark blue day dress and headed downstairs for breakfast.

Isobel walked to the kitchen to inform Josephine that she would take her breakfast in the dining room, but was nearly bowled over by the woman as she stormed into the hallway. Josephine held Captain Black aloft as if he were a creature from hell itself.

"M'lady, you must keep dis cat away from my kitchen," Josephine insisted. "He's eaten two of my frogs. We need dose frogs in de house to keep away de insects. And de lizards! I found him hanging off de cabinet trying to get one on de ceiling."

Josephine deposited the animal in Isobel's arms and dusted off her hands. "And if I catch 'im at it again, I be making soup out of his sorry skin!"

Astonished, Isobel watched Josephine stomp angrily away. The woman had been so irate she hadn't even asked Isobel about breakfast.

Holding Captain Black up so she faced him directly,

Isobel scolded the cat. "I am afraid it's the barn for you, my dear man. You shall have to do your hunting elsewhere from now on. I'm sure Josephine has every intention of making soup out of you, too, so watch out."

The cat meowed and squirmed in her arms, and she let him down unceremoniously. It seemed the men in her life were more trouble than they were worth.

She finally convinced Josephine to feed her, and afterwards Isobel hung about the kitchen, which was buzzing with activity.

"Whatever is all the excitement?" Isobel asked, plopping a cube of pineapple into her mouth. "It looks as if the house is being laid out for a feast."

"It's Cropover, m'lady." Josephine smiled at her. "We will harvest de sugar soon, and we be needin' all dis food for de celebration."

"Oh, *do* tell me about that, Josephine," Isobel said. "It sounds intriguing."

"Well," Josephine replied, "dere's dancin' and singin', and a whole lot of eatin'! We be startin' dis evenin'."

"Are Lord Ravenwood and I to attend?" Isobel asked.

Jospehine let out a booming laugh. "Of course! You two are the guests of honor."

"How lovely," Isobel said. "But I'm afraid style of dance we practice in England is much different than it is here. Will you tell me what to do?"

Josephine smiled at her and reached for another passionfruit, saying, "You'll know what to do, m'lady."

Later that night, the Cropover feast began.

Torches burned in the gardens, and huge tables were laid out with a delicious array of roasted pig, beef, chicken, baked fish, rice, spiced vegetables, fruits, cheeses, puddings, sausages and a variety of hearty breads. To drink, there was a selection of ciders, ales, juices, port wines, and sherries.

Traditionally, Josephine explained, all the workers were invited, along with their families. Isobel watched them talking and laughing with each other, their lilting voices floating on the air like music. They were dressed in colorful native clothing with wild designs. Many wore beads in their hair and around their necks.

It was all so different and exotic, like something out of a novel. Isobel loved every moment of it.

She bit into a slice of mango and marveled at the strange, sweet taste. As Isobel wiped a bit of juice from her mouth, she looked up and saw Beckett walking across the grass. He wore his usual white shirt and tan buckskins, but had added a multicolored sash around his waist that made him look rather piratical. Isobel didn't even attempt to tear her gaze away from him. He looked like Adonis himself.

The tawny waves of Beckett's hair shone in the torchlight, as if daring Isobel's fingers to touch it. As he made his way around the garden, Beckett laughed and talked with the workers, who greeted him with warm smiles.

Every now and then he would catch Isobel looking at him, and his mouth would curve into a wicked grin.

Isobel had dressed in a decidedly native style as well, in a turquoise blue frock that shimmered like the sea. Her hair was wound into an exotic style and adorned with a string of tiny seashells. Josephine had arranged it for her beautifully.

The drums began to pound their wild rhythm in the hot Bajan night.

It was time for the dancing to begin. Isobel stood back

and watched, captivated, as the torchlit garden pulsed with writhing bodies.

The Bajans danced feverishly to a chorus of drums that was unlike anything Isobel had ever heard. The men and women swayed to the music, and through some sixth sense seemed to move perfectly in time with each other. It was like watching music in a physical form.

How she envied them.

Her body longed to be as free, as vibrantly alive.

Isobel saw Beckett being pulled into the crowd, led by a beautiful young Bajan woman with masses of curly black hair and a fetching smile.

Isobel's heart gave a surprising lurch. She could see primal sparks traveling between her husband's eyes and his partner's as they began to dance. Though she tried to fight it, she felt a stab of jealousy.

Isobel watched their bodies pulse and sway and felt an unbidden desire to dance like that with Beckett. She wanted to see his eyes glowing blue fire at her as he held her close and moved to the drums' driving rhythm.

She wanted to feel the heat of the music moving in her veins—close her eyes and throw her head back, and let the drums take her like a lover.

Suddenly Josephine grabbed Isobel's arm and pulled her into the middle of the pulsing throng. Isobel tried to protest, but her voice couldn't be heard over the drums and the screeching of the crowd. So she kept moving along, feeling out of place and awkward.

Comfort came slowly, bewitchingly as the music itself.

Isobel's body began to sway to the pulsing beat. Her mind seemed to be in another place as her body relaxed and flowed with the rhythm.

Then, she saw Beckett.

He no longer danced with the other young woman.

He stood alone in the pulsing crowd, with his eyes were locked on Isobel.

She feared she might really swoon.

If she were back in England it would have been a certainty, but she refused to do so here. She was going to let her pulse race, let her breathing become heavy, and let the drumbeat sing in her veins.

She was going to experience her body in a way a proper Englishwoman would never dream.

As Beckett moved toward her through the crowd, Isobel stood transfixed. She was in his spell as surely as if he'd used obeah.

He moved around her slowly, holding her gaze with his. She felt a heady thrill as he looked her up and down, realizing for the first time the power she also held.

It was new.

It was reckless.

And it was thrilling beyond words.

Beckett began to dance before her, his body surprisingly fluid, his strong arms reaching out to touch her. But Isobel side-stepped him and twirled around, just out of his reach. His eyes burned brighter as he watched her, and a wicked smile played upon his lips.

Again he tried to touch her.

Again she moved out of range.

Isobel relished the sensual power that flowed through her. She twirled around again, then abruptly found herself pressed up against Beckett's hard chest like a wet sheet.

He gripped her arms and held her to him, his eyes travelling brazenly over her body. His hips pressed against hers and for an awful moment she worried about such a forbidden exchange in public. But it seemed no one took any notice. They were all too involved with their own dancing.

The drums grew wilder, more insistent. Beckett pressed her against his thigh, and she couldn't stop herself from grinding against him. Her eyes closed in heated arousal. Beckett pressed harder against her, and she felt her skirts being raised, his hands on the bare skin of her thighs, running up towards—

Her eyes flew open, and she saw Beckett's face inches away from hers. Desire glowed hot in his eyes.

"Shall I make you burn for me, Isobel?" he asked, dangerously. "Shall I worship you with my body, the way a husband should? *Shall I finally make you my wife?*"

Isobel stared at him, speechless, held prisoner by Beckett's body, his words, his gaze.

Beckett seized her hand, pulling her back toward the house.

Soon they were in her chamber. Through the gauze draperies, the torches lit the room from outside with a warm glow. The sound of the drums continued their relentless rhythm in the night.

Isobel heard the door latch click into place. The finality of the sound made her pulse race faster. Beckett turned around and gazed at her as he began to unbutton his shirt, and the sight sent a thrill up her spine. He reached for her hand and brought it slowly to his naked chest, placing her delicate palm on his warm, masculine skin.

In one quick motion, Beckett pulled her body against his, his mouth possessing hers feverishly. Isobel tried to catch her breath, but his dizzying touch intoxicated her.

Beckett pulled her dress down over her shoulders, uncovering her breasts. Isobel shuddered as he lowered his head, kissing her neck lightly, teasingly. She could hear herself panting as if she'd just run a great distance.

Good Lord, what was he doing to her?

His lips closed around a hard nipple. He flicked his

tongue mercilessly back and forth across it, and her knees went weak at the exquisite agony.

As she clutched at him, he lifted his head and growled, "You like that, don't you, my sweet?"

Isobel whimpered as an almost painful desire teased the tips of her breasts and snaked down to curl between her legs.

"Should I continue?" He kissed her mouth hard, then turned his attention to her neck.

"Yes," she gasped, breathless and weak, though she would surely die if this torment did not stop. Suddenly, she was as wild and feverish as he was, her hands running over his bare back, down over his hips and over the buckskins that covered the round muscles of his buttocks.

Beckett groaned at her challenging touch, and responded in kind, gripping her bottom and pulling her to him. She felt his hard arousal through his buckskins.

His hands went under her dress, sliding over her bare thighs. Isobel's eyes flew open as his fingers stroked her in a place for which she didn't even have a name.

Her heart beat so fast she thought it would burst. All her muddled brain could think of was how terribly good it all felt, and how much she wanted to continue this mad, incredible game.

"I think it's time I took you to bed, wife," Beckett said, swinging her up into his arms and carrying her to the bed.

She wanted him to hurry, though she feared what that would mean. Had this island's powerful spell turned her into a wanton? However it had come to be, when Beckett put her down on the bed, she pulled him on top of her, wanting, *needing* to feel the weight of him.

"Soon, darling," he whispered, and she heard a hint of laughter in his voice.

Oh, how could he be laughing at a time like this—when she was dying?

"Let us dispense with this bothersome garment," Beckett said, quickly undoing her laces and sliding the dress over her head. "And this one, too."

She twined her fingers in his hair as he peeled away her underthings, her body wriggling shamelessly beneath him. His own clothes joined hers on the floor. Isobel felt the length and hardness of him, and her hands slid down to explore his body which was so different from her own.

Beckett hissed a breath inward, and she felt him shudder as she stroked his manhood. She marveled at how something could be so very hard, and yet silky-soft.

Beckett moaned and pulled her hands away, holding them above her head as he whispered, "Eager little vixen, aren't you? But I'm not done with you, yet."

Now it was Isobel's turn to moan, and she struggled to touch him again but he held her hands fast. She opened her eyes, imploring him.

Beckett took one hand away, but kept both of her wrists imprisoned in the other. With his free hand he teased her sensitive nipples and she arched her back. She heard her own short, desperate panting.

Dear God, she was losing her mind...

"What do you want, Isobel?"

She whispered feverishly, "Don't you know?"

"No, I don't," he taunted. "You'll have to tell me."

Oh, she would throttle him for this! But as she stared up into his heated blue eyes, she knew he was the master of this game. For now, anyway.

"Tell, me," he insisted.

She bit her lip. "I—I want this aching to stop."

"Aching. And where are you aching, my beauty?"

"Inside..."

"I can make that sweet ache go away, Isobel," he said. "I can make you feel better. If I do this." His fingers delved between her legs.

She gasped and closed her eyes as he stroked her.

"And this." He rolled on top of her and spread her legs with his knees. He released her hands and positioned himself above her, piercing her with the intensity of his gaze.

"And this."

Isobel gasped as the hard silk of him slid inside her. She closed her eyes in disbelief but gave herself over to the invasion of her body. Because she wanted it. More than anything else in the world, she wanted *him*.

Her back arched against the pain and she gasped and clutched at him, but as soon as it had come, it was gone. The only thing left was his delicious thickness inside her and the pulsing rhythm of the drums driving them on.

Her hands roamed over the straining muscles of his back and buttocks, his skin slick with sweat. She pulled him hard against her, trying to take in more of him. His tongue penetrated her mouth, mimicking his sex, and she thrilled at how completely he possessed her.

The burning that had tormented her for so long became hotter, but it also held a sweetness, like warm, sticky honey. The sensation traveled through her veins and warmed her whole body, all the while getting hotter at its core.

Then a thundering pleasure so elemental, so complete, burst outwards from her very soul and left her trembling in its wake.

Beckett groaned as he gave a final thrust. He buried his face in her neck, and his body relaxed on top of hers. He stayed there for a moment, panting.

With a soft kiss he rolled off her, pulling her close in

front of him. And though it had been the last thing she'd meant to do, Isobel fell asleep exhausted in her husband's arms.

Beckett lifted one of Isobel's golden curls in his fingers and watched the light from the window play upon it. It shone as bright as a moonbeam.

Pale moonbeams, that was the color of her hair.

It must be the middle of the night, he thought. They had both fallen asleep after—

He felt a smile come to his lips.

Her response to his lovemaking had been hotter and wilder than any husband had a right to dream. His little wife had been as uninhibited as one of the undulating Bajan dancers last night at Cropover. Her passion had excited him unbearably.

Now, she slept in his arms, her warm, naked body curved into his, her round little buttocks deliciously pressed against his hips. He felt himself getting hard just thinking about her, about what they'd done together in this bed.

Perhaps he would wake her.

No. A good husband would let her sleep.

As he played with her hair, he doubted he was anything resembling a good husband—though perhaps he was making too much of this. It would have only been a matter of time until he had given in to his desire for her. What difference did it make if it was sooner rather than later? He had warned her not to expect more from him.

Suddenly, his thoughts skipped to Cordelia.

During their engagement they had never made love, though it hadn't been for his lack of trying. But she had always turned prudish in his arms. He'd thought her to be just playing coy, protesting her virginity for form's sake. Now, he had the feeling that Cordelia would never have warmed to him as Isobel had done. It simply wasn't in her nature.

Oh, but these were preposterous thoughts.

He did not want to let any lustful feelings for Isobel trick him into thinking he was the slightest bit in love with her. Nothing would make the *ton* wag their tongues faster, than if he came back besotted with his new bride.

Though Isobel had proven a superb bedmate, it didn't mean she was any different from Cordelia, deep down. Certainly, Isobel was beautiful, but Cordelia also had been beautiful. He had fancied himself in love with Cordelia. Hell, he *had* been in love with her, with a woman who had never truly loved him. And he had been pitifully blind to the truth. He would not let that happen again.

Cordelia had lied to him, and so had Isobel. He mustn't let himself forget that.

In her sleep, Isobel squirmed her bottom against his hips, fully hardening his arousal. *Oh, damn.* How would he be able to get back to sleep now?

She did it again, and he decided to take it as an invitation. Perhaps she was dreaming about their lovemaking, and wanted nothing more than what he was about to do.

Beckett slid his hand down and tenderly touched her nipple.

She moaned.

Gently, he pressed his hardened sex against the softness of her buttocks.

She sighed.

Then he reached down and softly stroked the velvet flower between her legs.

She whimpered adorably.

He flicked his tongue out to tease the edge of her ear, and heard her intake of breath as she awoke.

"Hmmm... Beckett?"

He chuckled lightly. "Were you expecting someone else?"

She looked back at him, and he smiled at her sleepy face in the moonlight. "What are you doing?" she mumbled.

He resumed his caresses and she closed her eyes.

"*That* is what I am doing," he answered. "But only if you want me to. I'm afraid you've been wiggling your bottom against me in your sleep, and damned if it didn't harden me up like stone." He kissed the back of her neck. "Are you ready for more of your husband's loving?"

"I think so." She started to turn to face him.

"No, you can stay like this." He pressed his chest against her back. "I've had dreams about loving you this way, and I would dearly like to see them become reality."

He gently pinched her nipple between his thumb and forefinger and heard her gasp.

"You see," he said, "I can pay your lovely breasts all the attention they deserve this way, and I know how greedy those beautiful little darlings can be."

He snaked his other hand down to keep stroking between her legs, and she reached back and grabbed his hip, pulling him against her.

Beckett nuzzled the softness of her hair, caressing her neck with his cheek. She moaned as his fingers slipped into her. Damn if the feel of her so hot and wet didn't threaten to make him spill right now.

"I can't wait any longer. I've got to be inside you. I've got to—" He groaned as he slid from behind into the slick heat of her.

Then, thrusting with long hard strokes, he drew out his pleasure until it was an unbearable madness.

Oh God, she felt good.

He was near release, now, and he wanted her with him, wanted her breaking as he was going to, and he stroked her little pearl of pleasure until she cried out.

He groaned, then pushed himself deep inside her. As the wave of his own pleasure approached, he thrust powerfully, and Isobel cried out as she climaxed.

Beckett gave in to his own surrender, letting out a shuddering breath. He pulled her close, squeezing tightly and kissing her shoulder, whispering, "Isobel, you make a man lose his senses."

Sated, he settled against her. As he drifted off to sleep, he thought it was a good thing he'd promised himself that he wouldn't fall in love with Isobel.

A very good thing indeed.

CHAPTER SIXTEEN

Isobel curled up on her side, watching the sunlight stream through the ivory curtain and onto the floor of her room. She sighed, feeling as warm and weightless as the light itself.

Was this the way every woman felt after the first time?

Just saying his name in her head made Isobel thrill uncontrollably.

Beckett.

Her husband.

Last night he had taken her body with his own, truly making her his wife. And she had enjoyed every moment of it.

Her only regret was that she had awoken in this bed alone. How she had wanted his arms about her this morning, hugging her tightly. How she had wanted to feel his lips waking her with a kiss.

Well, it would not be the least good manners to be greedy, she admonished herself. Beckett did not have all day to lay in bed with her. Doubtless, he had to see to the business of the plantation.

There would be plenty of time for these wicked games between them.

Thoughts of Beckett danced in her head. The texture and warmth of his skin, the strength and thickness of his hands, the muscles in his forearms, the way his eyes held the light of the torches as he'd watched her dance—these were the things that made him so beautiful, so powerfully masculine.

Isobel sighed as she remembered his hard hands on her body, pressing her hips against his as they danced, and later as he had loved her here in this bed. Beckett had awakened something in her—something she had never known existed. It was mysterious and powerful and made her almost giddy.

Not like the distasteful business with Sir Harry at all.

The vile touch of Sir Harry had made her want to be sick.

She shuddered involuntarily.

Isobel rolled onto her side, clutching at the bed linen and pushing the memory away. She was safe from that blackguard, now. Safe with her husband, thousands of miles away. She would never be Sir Harry's wife, and he would never be able to do *that* to her. No matter what he had threatened.

With Beckett it had been like a dream. She had not been afraid. She had welcomed her husband's instruction in the art of physical love. And she had received him with an open heart.

Isobel pushed that thought away. It would not help matters and would only complicate things.

They had *made* love, not fallen in love.

They had not.

But had *she?*

Isobel recoiled from the answer to that question. Beckett

had warned her that love was not part of the bargain. For him it would undoubtedly be true. But for her?

The thought sobered Isobel quicker than a dousing of cold water.

Oh, this was a mistake!

To fall in love with Beckett would be a *terrible* mistake. She had agreed to the terms of the marriage. They were to lead separate lives—he in London and she at Hampton Park. After this was done, she would spend the rest of her years alone on her estate, pining for a husband who had sworn never to love her.

And yet, it was too late. Last night had simply revealed the awful truth to her, removing the last barricade from her defenses.

It was true.

She *was* in love with him.

Isobel had criticized Beckett for keeping secrets from her, and now she would have to keep the truth from him forever.

No one ever said marriage was easy

The warm wind lightly caressed Isobel's skin as she and Beckett rode on horseback down a quiet road that led to the beach. The smell of the sea floated on the breeze, and the sound of the gulls beckoned.

They ascended a rise and Isobel smiled as she beheld the breathtaking ocean beyond. The brilliant turquoise of the water held a vibrancy she had never before seen. The swirling colors reminded her of Beckett's eyes—their beauty could bewitch and their depths could swallow one whole.

Beckett stopped his horse near some swaying palm

trees and dismounted, reaching up to help Isobel off her mount. His hands on her waist felt firm and strong and made her stomach thrill.

"This seems a good spot." Beckett guided her toward a grove of trees.

"The view is magnificent," Isobel agreed, gazing at the white, sandy beach and at the water that stretched as far as she could see. This was a paradise.

Beckett took the horses to a nearby patch of grass and picketed them. With an unhurried air, he strolled back to the palm trees, spread out a blanket and plunked himself down.

Isobel joined him as he opened the basket that Josephine had prepared for them. A wonderful aroma drifted up from the delicious lunch of cheeses, roasted chicken and hearty brown bread. Beckett took a bite of cheddar and offered her some.

"No, thank you, I had a late breakfast," she said.

Beckett grinned. "A late breakfast? Why were you so late to rise this morning?"

Feeling herself blush, Isobel looked away.

"Was that husband of yours keeping you up 'til all hours?"

Isobel met his eyes and saw the playful light dancing in them. Her stomach did flip-flops. "Yes, my lord, he did. He even woke me in the middle of the night to—"

"To...." Beckett moved closer to her.

"To continue with his—"

"His...?"

"His husbandly rights."

"*Husbandly rights?*" Beckett scoffed, amused. "Is that what you call what I did to you? I thought I was making mad, passionate love to you, Isobel. And that does not even consider what you were doing to me."

"Me?" she said, taken off guard. "I did nothing to you."

"I beg to differ, my dear, you did quite a lot," he insisted. "Such wiggling and squirming. What is a poor husband to do when his wife insists on being serviced at all hours? Ignore her demands upon his person? I ask you."

Isobel gasped and felt her cheeks burning.

"Not very kind of me to tease you so, is it?" He leaned back and lifted a morsel of bread to his lips. "Is there much pain today?"

She paused, but answered truthfully, "A little."

He nodded, saying, "I'm sorry to say, nature is often cruel to the fairer sex. For isn't it the woman who must carry and bear the child that the coupling of the two sexes might create? You could be carrying my child right now, as we speak. Have you thought of that?"

Isobel's heart skipped a beat. Last night had happened so fast, had been so intoxicating, she truly hadn't considered it. She'd thought only of the pleasure, of the way he'd made her whole body hum with passion.

And now, she felt a primal rush of pride at the possibility of carrying her husband's child. Beckett's child.

"I see the idea sits well with you, and that pleases me," he said. "Because as the earl and countess of Ravenwood, we have a duty to perform, Isobel. You must conceive my child and heir. And that could take months. In fact, my friends Lord and Lady Secord had to engage in this type of behavior every day for almost a year until Letty conceived. And the whole time, both she and George wore the silliest smiles about town. Come to think of it, they're still wearing them. Well, that stands to reason, as they've had a child each year since their marriage four years ago. Would you object to doing our duty as devotedly?"

"I would not, my lord," she said, shocked at her own honesty.

Beckett lifted her hand to his lips and kissed it softly, gazing into her eyes. "Nor would I, my dear. But I shall be a good husband to you tonight, and let you recover from your first taste of the marriage bed. It would be rather boorish of me to insist on performing our marital duty so soon, with you still tender from last night's loving."

No, it wouldn't! she wanted to say.

All this talk was making her skin positively tingle. Oh, why was he teasing her so?

Beckett turned his attention back to the picnic lunch beside him and picked up a leg of chicken. "Now that we've got that settled, I think I shall eat my lunch. I'm famished. Are you sure you don't want to join me?"

"No, I'm fine," she replied. "I'll sit here and sketch."

Isobel arranged her pencils and paper in a bid to avoid watching Beckett lick the crumbs from his fingers. Oh, why hadn't she brought her fan? It was decidedly hotter than before.

Isobel concentrated on the white sheet of paper before her. She did not want to be seen staring at her husband like a love-sick cow. He must not see the raw desire in her eyes. Nor how easily he could arouse her passions.

She picked up her pencil and began to draw the face of this man who drove her to distraction. She glanced up at him occasionally, his features quickly appearing on the paper in front of her. There was the arch of the eyebrow that sometimes taunted her, the regal nose, the sensuous mouth in that wicked half-grin. But Beckett's eyes seemed far too intense to accurately transfer to paper.

Isobel completed the portrait, regarding the finished result with a mixture of satisfaction and embarrassment. The drawing of Beckett showed a man brimming with raw sexuality. A man who could fulfill any woman's desires. It looked positively indecent. She certainly didn't want to show it to him.

But her reservations came too late.

He was already reaching for it.

Beckett studied the portrait silently.

"Well, what do you think?" Isobel said, brushing a flyaway hair from her face.

"Is this how you see me, Isobel?" he asked, pointedly.

She swallowed. "I suppose it is."

"I look like a male courtesan!" he said, chuckling. "We should send it back to London and have it published in the Times. Imagine my reputation after the *ton* sees this, and learns my wife is the one who drew it"

Isobel snatched it back. "You will do no such thing."

"Quite right." Beckett agreed. "A full nude would cause a far greater scandal. We should get started on that directly."

"What?" she asked, horrified. "I most certainly will not draw you nude."

"That, Madam, is your loss," he said cheekily. "Shall we go down to the water? I'll bet it's warmer than the English Channel."

Isobel paused, then nodded in agreement as Beckett began removing his boots and stockings. She slipped off her shoes and silk stockings, picked up her skirts and trotted down to the beach, with Beckett following behind. It would be good to get her mind off her husband's teasing.

They splashed their legs into the warm, foamy water, and Isobel gloried in the refreshing feeling. The tropical breeze sighed against her bare legs as Isobel lifted her skirts to keep them out of the water. She turned to see Beckett staring at her.

"You're making it damned difficult for me to keep my word about leaving you alone tonight," he warned.

"Perhaps I don't wish you to keep your word," she replied, splashing through the water and back onto the sand.

Walking down the beach ahead of Beckett, Isobel felt deliciously light-hearted. She drank in the blue sky overhead with its white, puffy clouds. The heady scent of the island's exotic flowers floated on the breeze.

Rounding a curve in the shoreline, Beckett stopped and looked down at the sand, kicking it with his toes.

"Now, what have we here?" he asked. "Footprints? Must have been four or five men at least, and they lead down to the water. Perhaps Mr. Cobb's talk of pirates wasn't just flummery after all. There, you can see where their boat was dragged up onto the sand."

"Might it not be local fishermen?" Isobel said, seeing the marks in the sand. An unsettling shiver ran up her back.

"Mr. Cobb said the fishing is done farther down the coast, where the waters are calmer," Beckett answered. "Of course, I'm most likely assuming the worst. But you must promise never to come down here alone."

Isobel nodded. "I promise."

It was not a difficult one to make.

They turned back toward the grove of trees, and as they neared the horses, Isobel tried to silence her fears.

Surely, it wasn't possible.

It couldn't be Sir Harry. *Could it?*

She pushed the frightening thought from her mind.

They packed up the picnic basket and her drawings, and mounted the waiting horses.

As they neared Ravenwood Hall, Isobel noticed an oppressive smell in the air. Beckett seemed to notice it too and they stopped the horses. They heard shouts of alarm floating on the breeze.

Beckett's eyes suddenly turned deadly serious. He kicked his stallion into a gallop, and Isobel followed as closely as she could.

As they approached the plantation, they saw pandemonium.

"The fields are on fire!"

CHAPTER SEVENTEEN

Beckett jumped off his horse and ran toward the burning sugar cane fields. Isobel struggled to keep up with him. She and Beckett stopped short when they saw Mr. Cobb running toward them.

"What's happened, Cobb?" Beckett shouted. "You said the fields weren't supposed to be burned until next week!"

"Not sure, m'lord!" Cobb yelled, his face and clothes blackened by soot. "Started 'bout an hour ago down in the south field. No one's supposed to be down that way. Don't know what could have happened. I've got all the men out there, and some o' the women, too. We've got to put it out, or the house'll be next, sir."

Beckett ripped off his jacket and rolled up his sleeves. "Tell me what to do, Cobb. I'm not going to lose Ravenwood Hall!"

"We're digging ditches 'round the fields so the fire won't spread," Cobb explained. "The women are wetting down the sides and roof of the house and barn. Don't want flying sparks to ignite the buildings."

"I'll help Josephine and the others up here," Isobel said, squinting her eyes against the heat from the fire.

"Whatever you do, don't get too close to the flames," Beckett commanded.

"But you're going down there!" she protested.

"I have no choice, Isobel. And neither do you." Beckett turned and followed Cobb toward the heart of the burning fire.

Isobel coughed from the smoke in the air and looked for Josephine, who would most likely be in charge of the women.

She found her quickly; Josephine was already busy issuing orders.

"You girls go and get all de buckets you can find. *Big* ones!" Josephine shouted. When she saw Isobel, she said, "M'lady, come wit me."

She led Isobel over to the well as the other women ran back with the buckets.

"Make a line to de barn," she told the staff, coolly directing the panicking servants like an army colonel. "M'lady and I will pull de water up from de well."

Isobel and Josephine worked together to crank the water up, handing bucket after bucket to the first woman in line, while the ladies at the other end doused the barn.

They worked as fast as they could to wet down the structure and get to the house before floating sparks landed on the roof. Next they made a line toward the manor, and bucket after bucket passed down the line until the house was dampened, too.

Isobel had no idea how much time had passed since they began their back-breaking work, but she could see the fire still burning down in the fields. She turned to Josephine, panting and wiping the sweat from her brow.

"We must go down and help the men dig," she said.

"Dat would be a good idea, m'lady," Josephine agreed.

After assembling the other women and taking what

shovels remained, Isobel led the women down to the burning fields.

The men had split up into small groups, each group concentrating on one side of the field. But the flames were getting closer, and there weren't enough men to control the fire's progress.

Beckett looked up as Isobel and the rest of the women approached. He wiped his forehead, hands and face blackened by ash.

"Isobel, take the women away. I told you it was too dangerous down here!" Beckett yelled over the crackling of the flames.

"You need our help," Isobel insisted.

"Don't you be arguin' wit m'lady, now!" Josephine retorted. Her dark eyes flashed a warning.

Beckett paused and leaned on the handle of his shovel. "Alright—since I can't dissuade you—split your women up into four groups and join the men."

Isobel and Josephine quickly divided the women up, and Josephine took the others to where they were needed.

Isobel's group began to dig near Beckett's.

As she worked, Isobel was surprised to feel herself regaining her strength. At the start, she'd felt clumsy with the shovel. But after a short time she found her rhythm, enjoying a new sense of power.

Isobel had never had to apply herself in such a physical way before. Back in England, it was considered most unladylike to engage in any activity more strenuous than waving a fan. But this sort of physical exertion made her feel more alive, and more capable than ever.

Isobel glanced at Beckett and was unable to look away. He had taken off his shirt, and although covered in ash and dirt—his muscular chest streaked in sweat—her husband had never looked more capable or strong.

She watched his body as it worked. The muscles in his arms and shoulders flexed as he dug into the brown earth. His hard thighs and buttocks strained against his buckskins and made her catch her breath.

She kept digging, though her initial stamina was fading. It was fruitless to be vain at a time like this, but she wondered what she must look like as she wiped the perspiration from her brow, undoubtedly smearing dirt and ash all over her face.

Finally their efforts were rewarded when the fire, contained by the network of ditches, began to recede.

"Good work, everyone," Beckett called out, resting his elbow on the handle of his shovel. "Split yourselves up, and let's finish this."

As they walked past, he patted several workers on the back.

Beckett tossed his shovel on the ground and walked over to Isobel. He looked down at her, brushing the hair away from her face. "What would the *ton* say if they could see us now?"

"I'm sure I don't care a whit," she answered, enjoying the way he was looking at her. Though she knew she was anything but, Isobel felt like the most beautiful woman in the world.

Beckett nodded toward the smoldering field, and said, "We still have work to do. Are you up for it?"

"As long as I'm with you, Beckett, I'm up for anything," she answered.

He gave her a quick kiss and led her back to a section of the ditch.

Isobel wanted to laugh as she tried to picture any other countesses of the *ton* digging ditches alongside their husbands. She simply couldn't picture it.

As she scooped up a shovelful of earth and heaved it,

she saw some of the dirt land on Beckett's boot. She glanced at his face to see if he had noticed. Thankfully it seemed he hadn't.

She continued her work, but was startled when a flying clump of earth caught the edge of her skirt. Isobel slowly looked over to see Beckett continuing to dig.

Casually, she lifted her shovel, filled it with dirt, and sent the whole thing sailing over to strike Beckett's chest.

He stopped for a moment, looking down at himself. Dirt was stuck to every inch of him.

Isobel was suddenly afraid she had taken it too far. Beckett would be furious with her. Unsure of what to do, she bent to continue her digging.

A huge load of dirt hit the back of her head with so much force that it nearly knocked her off her feet. Isobel spun about to see Beckett grinning devilishly at her.

Bellowing in a terribly unladylike manner, Isobel threw down her shovel and charged. Beckett dropped his shovel and ran, laughing. He easily evaded her pursuit by changing directions and dashing around the edge of the ditch.

He stopped long enough to pick up a handful of dirt and throw it at her. It splattered across the front of her dress. She was now almost as dirty as he was.

Isobel quickly grabbed a handful of dirt and lobbed it at Beckett's head. She just missed. His return volley landed in her hair and she shrieked in protest.

Dirt kept flying in both directions, until they were out of breath from running, and merely stood hurling handfuls at each other.

Finally, Isobel stopped and pointed at Beckett, laughing uncontrollably. "You look as if you've been rolling in a pig sty!"

Beckett laughed too, saying, "They'll soon be calling us the earl and countess of Ravendirt."

Isobel laughed harder, attempting to catch her breath. She noticed Mr. Cobb, Josephine, and about twenty men and women staring at them completely dumbfounded.

"I daresay that's enough mudslinging for today," Beckett said, dusting off his hands. "Besides, we are attracting quite an audience."

Isobel made a feeble attempt to straighten her filthy dress. Thankfully, no one could see her blushing beneath all the dirt on her face.

Beckett took her hand and placed it in the crook of his arm, as if they were about to leave a dinner party.

Josephine's face broke into a smile that rivaled the sun's gleam on the ocean. Her booming laughter rang out over the field. The others joined in as well.

Soon Beckett, Isobel, Mr. Cobb, and all the other workers were laughing and pointing at each other's dirty clothes.

Josephine held her stomach and doubled over in laughter. "I'd be surprised if 'dere be any dirt left in the field, now!"

"I fear you are right, Josephine," Beckett said.

"By the way, m'lord," Mr. Cobb said, grinning. "The fire's put out."

At this the crowd erupted in hoots of wild laughter. Beckett and Isobel couldn't help but join in.

"You both be wantin' a nice bath, now," Josephine said, wagging her finger. "I'll run up to de house and get de water boilin'."

"That won't be necessary, Josephine." Beckett pulled Isobel close.

Josephine looked unconvinced. "It will be if you want to get dat dirt off yourself."

"Oh, we shall get ourselves clean, but with a little help from Mother Nature instead. I couldn't bear to have any of this tracked indoors. Have some soap, towels, and clean clothes brought down from the house. I think it's time Lady 'Ravendirt' became acquainted with our natural spring."

Isobel felt butterflies flit through her stomach. Was he suggesting what she thought? She looked up at him, and the twinkle in his eyes confirmed it.

Good Heavens, they were going to bathe together.

Soon, a girl from the house appeared with towels and clothes in her arms and a yellow cake of soap in her hand.

The servants and workers looked at each other sheepishly before being dismissed by Josephine: "What you all lookin' at, now? You go and clean yourselves up and let de lord and lady do what dey please."

Isobel watched their knowing smiles as they turned away, and wondered why she wasn't mortified. Strangely, there seemed no need for such worries here.

Beckett led Isobel across the lawn to the path, with the servant girl following behind at a respectful distance. Isobel's heart skipped with excitement and this decadent excursion. Beckett led her deeper and deeper into the dense greenery.

Soon, the spring appeared, encircled by a lush array of colorful flowers and shiny green leaves. A rock wall rose up on one side, and a glistening waterfall spilled down over it into the pool.

The young servant set down their clothes, made a curtsy and left.

"My, my, but you're filthy," Beckett said flirtatiously, looking Isobel up and down.

"The countess of Ravendirt must dress appropriately," she replied, as innocently as she could.

"Take off your clothes, then," he commanded, bending down to remove his boots.

Isobel felt gooseflesh cover her skin at Beckett's words, but found herself obeying as if she had no will of her own. Soon she was down to her sheer lawn undergarments.

"*Everything*, Isobel." Beckett gazed at her with heated eyes while he unfastened the buttons of his tight buckskins.

Isobel swallowed nervously. She had never stood naked in front of anyone before—and certainly not in broad daylight.

When she and Beckett had made love, it had been blissfully dark. But now it was anything but.

As Beckett peeled off his buckskins and drawers, he looked up at her. She watched the last stitch of clothing fall away, and her uncertainty faded—replaced by raw desire.

He stood proudly nude, watching her.

Isobel let her eyes feast on the wonderfully masculine body before her. She had never seen anything so impressive before.

Had God made man for the sole purpose of tempting woman?

Isobel's eyes traveled unashamedly over the body she'd explored with hungry hands the night before. Her gaze lingered over his muscular thighs, and up, and she saw that he was powerfully aroused.

"Come on," he growled. "Your turn."

As if under a spell, Isobel slowly removed the rest of her undergarments, and felt the warm air touch every part of her naked skin.

Beckett held his hand out to her. Silently, they entered the water and walked in until they were waist deep.

He dipped the soap in the water, bringing it up and lathering it between his hands. "Close your eyes, tight," he said.

Isobel did as he asked and felt his hands gently rubbing her face. The sensation was wonderfully soothing.

"Dunk your head, now, like a good girl," he said.

Isobel obeyed, sinking down into the water. She came up and wiped the water away from her eyes.

"Now, your hair." Beckett said.

He moved to stand behind her, and she closed her eyes again as he ran soapy fingers through her slick wet hair. He scrubbed her head gently, and it was so relaxing Isobel thought for a moment she might float away.

After she rinsed her hair, she felt Beckett's strong hands on her back, sliding through the suds and massaging her tired muscles. A sigh escaped her.

"Enjoying this, my sweet?" he asked.

"You know I am," she whispered.

Beckett chuckled, saying, "I'm sure there aren't many husbands who engage in personally bathing their wives as I do. The poor fools should know what they're missing."

Beckett turned her to face him. If it was possible, his ocean-blue eyes blazed even more intensely than before. He looked like a lion about to pounce upon his prey.

Taking her hands in his, he placed the slippery round soap in her palm.

"Will you do me the same for me?" he asked.

Isobel replied, "I think you know the answer to that."

She lathered the cake between her hands and felt a thrill as Beckett closed his eyes. Reaching up, she smoothed think white suds over his chest, reveling in the feeling of his wet skin, his hard muscles, and their latent power.

She washed his face and his hair, as tenderly as he had done hers. She felt possessive of him, of this body that he seemed to offer like a gift.

Isobel waited as Beckett dipped beneath the water to

rinse the suds away. When he stood again, water running down the firm lines of his body, she found herself looking up into eyes as dark and dangerous as the sky before a storm.

Beckett ran his fingers through his wet hair, saying, "Cobb said the fire looked suspicious. It may have been purposely set."

He held out his hand to Isobel and they headed out of the water. They stood on the grassy bank, dried themselves off and donned their dry clothes.

Though the sun warmed them, Isobel felt a chill move through her. "Those footprints we saw in the sand. Could Sir Harry have found us?"

"I suppose it is possible," he said seriously. "You must not venture about alone, not even on the grounds. Is that understood?"

Isobel nodded, unwilling to believe the serpent had found its way into their Eden. "If it *is* Sir Harry—"

"We don't know that yet," he countered.

"But if it is," she insisted, "what will we do, Beckett?"

"We'll do what we have to do," he answered. "*I'll* do what I have to do in order to keep you safe, Isobel. I promise."

As they headed up the grassy path back to Ravenwood Hall, Isobel tried to quell the uneasiness in her heart.

Could Sir Harry be here in Barbados?

Beckett seemed unconvinced, but of course, he did not know Sir Harry Lennox as she did. He reminded her of a mastiff that used to live on a property near Hampton Park. Once the dog caught the scent of his prey he would not give up until the creature he hunted lay limp and lifeless between his jaws.

Though she tried to convince herself otherwise, Isobel couldn't dismiss the feeling that Sir Harry had found her after all.

The footprints on the beach, so close to their estate; the suspicious fire shortly thereafter; were these just subtle calling cards her enemy was using to announce his presence?

If so, when and how would he pay her and Beckett a formal visit?

CHAPTER EIGHTEEN

Beckett leaned against a palm tree and stared out at the windswept ocean. The turquoise water crested into white foam and spread toward him on the sand, only to roll back and disappear from whence it came.

Looking at a sight of such awe-inspiring beauty, he knew his heart and mind should have been at peace.

But they were not.

He was about as far from peaceful as he was from England.

He had been happy these past weeks with Isobel. Far too happy for his own liking, and it unsettled him.

Each morning, he and Isobel awoke in each other's arms after a night of passionate lovemaking. They flirted and teased. They made each other laugh.

For all intents and purposes, one might think they were in love.

Except for the fact that Beckett knew it to be impossible.

Love was an illusion. He vowed never again to let Cupids arrow play havoc with his good sense. He had done it once. And he'd learned from his foolish mistake of loving Cordelia.

At least he'd thought he had.

But didn't his actions speak louder than words? If he continued acting as if he were in love with Isobel, he just might wake up one day to find that it was true.

When they returned to England, he would be sending her off to Hampton Park with a settlement and hopefully an heir to raise just as they'd agreed. Only now, to his surprise, that plan lacked its former luster. When he asked himself why, he refused to listen to the niggling voice in his head.

It simply would not do.

Especially now, with the possibility of Isobel's nemesis having followed her here. But surely there was only a slim chance of that.

Surely, Lennox couldn't have found out where they had gone.

The thought of Sir Harry Lennox only served to remind Beckett of the danger Isobel might be in—both here in Barbados, and back in England. There was still that murder charge to be taken care of. And if Alfred was unable to find proof of Lennox's guilt in the matter, there was a possibility that Isobel could be arrested upon their return.

It was his duty as a husband to protect Isobel. And the best way to do that was to distance himself from the dangerous feelings that were gaining a foothold in his heart.

For if Lennox ever put his filthy hands on Isobel, Beckett would never forgive himself. Just the thought of that blackguard touching her made his stomach harden into a dangerous knot.

Beckett turned and saw Isobel coming up over the rise, her golden hair blowing in the wind. She wore a simple gown of palest pink that only accentuated her extraordinary beauty.

Damnation! Why did his heart feel so confused? As she came closer, his mind bucked from the answer.

Isobel smiled brightly when she reached him, and pushed her windswept curls back from her face. "I've been looking for you everywhere."

"Have you?" he replied.

"I missed you at breakfast, and now it is past luncheon," she said. "Shall we go back? Josephine has made a lovely cucumber soup."

He stepped away from the tree and offered his arm to her.

Isobel curled her hand around his bicep. They strolled down the wind-swept beach in silence. From the corner of his eye, he noticed her looking up at him questioningly.

"You seem rather preoccupied," she said.

He kept staring at the sea, as if in its depths he would somehow find his answers. "You are most observant, my dear," he said, finally. "Being an artist, that is quite natural for you, I'm sure. I am indeed, preoccupied."

"What is it, Beckett?" she asked, touching his arm tenderly, just like a loving wife would.

"I expected to hear from Alfred by now," he explained. "I must confess, I am concerned for his safety, especially since we cannot rule out the possibility that Lennox could have learned our location."

He felt Isobel stiffen.

"And there is something else that I must speak to you about," He said, turning her to face him. "This has gone too far, Isobel. And we must put a stop to it."

"What has gone too far?" she asked. "I don't understand."

"*This*. This sham of a marriage that we are starting to pretend is real," he retorted. "And we must stop it, now, before one of us gets hurt."

She held him with a steady gaze, and said, "One of us? Oh. *Me,* you mean."

He swallowed. She was not going to make this easy, was she?

"Yes. I suppose I do," he said.

"Because you feel nothing," she asked, calmly. "That is why you make love to me every night with such passion it threatens to turn us both to cinders? Because you feel nothing."

"I didn't say that I felt nothing," he responded. "Only that we have been playing at a dangerous game. And we would be deluding ourselves if we continue."

He looked out over the water in a bid to escape Isobel's accusing expression.

"I've been looking ahead to our eventual return to England," he continued. "We shall have to discuss your settlement, as well as other matters. Depending on the situation at home—whether or not you'll be required for appearances at court or that sort of thing—you may accompany me or go to Hampton Park directly, as you like."

"Is that what you want?" she asked.

Beckett fought the tightness in his chest, replying, "Of course it's what I want. It is what we agreed upon. And though we have proven to be suitable bed-mates and do not lack for conversation, we must remember the terms of our arrangement. This is a marriage of convenience. It is not, and never shall be, a love-match. That is what I want."

Her eyes flashed with accusation. "I know why you never sought a career on the stage, my lord. You are a very poor actor."

Isobel turned on her heel, but Beckett seized her arm and spun her back to face him.

"What is that supposed to mean?" he demanded.

"I mean to say that you are liar, my lord," she said. "Yes, you heard me. A liar. It's obvious this marriage doesn't suit you. That is why you are trying to deny the truth of it."

"I am doing nothing of the sort," Beckett retorted. "I am merely trying to remind you of the arrangement we made—"

"What are you afraid of?"

"*Afraid?*" he said. "I am not afraid."

"Oh, yes you are," she replied. "It's a strange thing, Beckett, but in my experience, a man doesn't run away from something unless it's got him scared witless."

Anger puled through his veins.

Good God, but the little chit could irk him! Didn't she know that he was doing this for her own good? It seemed he would have to make it very clear to her.

"What do you want from me, Isobel?" he asked, gripping her shoulders and pulling her closer, as if that would make her understand. "You want me to profess my love to you? I gave you fair warning when we struck this bargain. Love would have no place in our marriage. I have held true to that. I have kept my promise. And I can't help it if you haven't."

"I know what you're trying to do, Beckett," she continued. "You're trying to push me away—to make it easier on yourself somehow. So you won't have to risk anything."

"Why would I do that when there is nothing to risk?" he said, coldly.

He saw the shock in her eyes—the hurt. But she did not look away. She took a deep breath, and went on.

"Of course, you are right," she replied. "There is nothing to risk for you. But for me, there is much more than you could know. I am not supposed to love you,

Beckett. It is regrettable—*but I do*. And though you have said you don't want my love, I cannot simply end such feelings. They live within me, like something we created together."

Beckett cleared his throat, as it had somehow become uncomfortably thick.

So, he had her love, did he?

He'd wanted her body, her passion, but never her heart. And yet somehow he had won it.

Beckett took a deep breath and said, "I am sorry if I gave you false hope that I might one day return the sentiment. Even if I could love a woman again—it could never be you, Isobel. How could I love someone who lied to me about your past, as you did?"

Isobel closed her eyes and stepped back as if he had struck her. She took a moment, then opened her eyes to look at him again.

"You have a right to say that," she said. "It's true, I did lie to you before. And perhaps that will always stand between us. But there is something I want you to know. I want you to understand that even now, hearing these hurtful words coming from your lips—lips which have kissed and loved me in the night—even now my feeling for you is still as strong. It is still there."

Her eyes burned brightly with emotion as she said, "You are in my heart. You are there *every moment*. I cannot get you out. Do you not think I have tried? But there is no cure. You *are* my heart."

Beckett fought the urge to take her into his arms and crush her to him. "Then I pity you," he said.

He thought she might have slapped him, then.

In fact, he wished that she would.

The hurt and anger he saw swirling in her eyes was more painful than any blow she could have given him.

Isobel turned to leave, but in her haste, she stumbled over a rock and almost lost her balance.

Beckett stepped quickly to help her, but she shook him off.

"Leave me alone!" she warned.

"Isobel—"

"Don't touch me," she said, icily.

She stalked up the hill, and Beckett followed behind.

Oh, why did his heart pound painfully in his chest—as if it were actually punching him from the inside out?

Isobel stopped short, turning to face him. "If you want to push me away, that is your choice. But make no mistake, Beckett. It is I who pity *you*."

He let her walk on alone.

Isobel's indomitable spirit astounded him. So, she would not be frightened off by his attempts to hurt her. If only she could understand that he was pushing her away for her own sake. Surely, she would come to see that.

He looked up ahead. Where was she? He couldn't see her anymore. Trying to catch up, he broke into a run and dashed down the path to the road. He came around the trees, and his heart froze at the sight before him.

There, in the middle of the road, Isobel stood surrounded by...*pirates*.

CHAPTER NINETEEN

Isobel ran down the path, eyeing the rocks upon it with the thought of stopping to hurl a few at Beckett. But that would only prove to him that he'd hurt her. And she would rather eat broken glass than embarrass herself further.

He had every right to say what he did. Love hadn't been part of their arrangement. But she had fallen in love with him, anyway. Though she'd known it was foolish, she'd nurtured the fragile seed of her love, hoping that one day Beckett would feel the same. But all hope was lost now.

He would never, ever love her.

Her heart burned with hurt and anger. She wanted to kick herself! How could she have let herself fall for a man who was nothing more than a good-looking block of ice?

She heard Beckett calling from somewhere behind her on the path, and picked up her pace. She didn't want him to catch up with her now, because if he put his arms around her and tried to comfort her she would let him.

Isobel turned onto the road and ran headfirst into someone rather tall.

She looked up and saw a huge man with shaggy red

hair and a beard that had been twisted into braids. He looked down at her and smiled. He was missing several teeth.

A thread of fear shot through her and she turned back toward the path, but it was blocked by three other men who looked just as scraggly and menacing as the one in the road.

Isobel's heart raced as the realization hit her.

Pirates!

"Hello, my dear," A silky voice said from behind her.

She knew that voice.

But it couldn't be!

Isobel turned and her stomach lurched.

Sir Harry Lennox walked toward her, looking for all the world like a gentleman just stepping out of a London club. His eyes were dark and glittery, and a smile snaked across his thin lips. "Happy to see me?"

"Can't you tell?" she retorted, trying to appear fearless.

"And after all the trouble I went to in order to find you," Sir Harry said, eyeing her reproachfully. He grabbed her arm and jerked her towards him. "You've led me a merry chase, my dear, and I intend to make you pay for such foolishness. In very interesting ways."

"You're a murdering swine," she said. "Let go of me!"

Annoyance flashed in Sir Harry's eyes. "I advise you to behave, my dear. We are, after all, in public."

"Isobel!" Beckett shouted.

She turned to see her husband at the end of the road being over-powered by Sir Harry's men.

"Ah, the dutiful husband has made an appearance, I see," Sir Harry said, smirking. "How considerate of him."

"No!" Isobel cried.

One of the pirates punched Beckett in the face and Isobel saw his head snap back. He staggered, but stayed on his feet, even broke free to land a punch of his own in the man's face. But then the others had him and the bellowing pirate struck Beckett over and over in the stomach.

"Please, don't hurt him," Isobel begged.

"Don't hurt him?" Sir Harry replied. "But my dear, I intend to kill him."

Isobel felt the color drain from her face and forced down the nausea that whirled in her stomach. She looked at Sir Harry, beseeching him with her eyes. All this time, she'd thought she had the courage to face this man when the moment came. But seeing Beckett being beaten made her courage drain away like blood from a wound. "Please... I'll do whatever you say."

"You'll do whatever I say anyway," Sir Harry said, looking quite unconcerned. "And when I do kill him, you will watch every moment of it. Bring him here, Fergus!"

Isobel stared helplessly as the men dragged Beckett toward them. He was hunched over, obviously in pain from the blows to his stomach, and Isobel had to struggle to remain in control as they approached. One of the other pirates held Isobel while Sir Harry stepped away from her.

The pirate named Fergus grabbed Beckett's hair and wrenched his head back. Isobel's hand flew to her mouth to stifle a cry.

Beckett's eye was already swelling, and blood dripped from his mouth.

He glared at Sir Harry and growled, "If you touch her, I'll—"

Sir Harry smashed his fist into Beckett's face, then hit him in the ribs. Isobel screamed as her husband finally crumpled to the ground. Sir Harry bent down toward Beckett and put his hand to his ear.

"Sorry—you'll what, old chap? I didn't quite catch

that," Sir Harry said, lifting Beckett's head, and seeing no response, let it drop. "The man's at a loss for words, it seems. Oh, and just so you know, I *do* plan on touching her."

"I'll kill you first!" Isobel spat, struggling hopelessly against the pirate who held her. She stared down at Beckett's lifeless form and felt her heart break.

"Still my little spitfire, I see," Sir Harry said, smirking. "Just as I like you."

Isobel lunged at him with an unknown strength, suddenly breaking free of her captor's grasp. She dug her fingernails into Sir Harry's face as they both toppled to the ground. Isobel yelled in rage, thrashing and clawing at him like a wildcat. Sir Harry let out a howl as Isobel drew blood.

Sir Harry struggled for breath as the men pried Isobel off him. He stood up unsteadily, trying to straighten his disheveled clothing. Reaching up to touch his face, he stared with disbelief at the blood that stained his fingers.

"I hope I've left you a nice scar, you loathsome blackguard," Isobel said.

"You will pay for that, as well," he warned. "Very dearly indeed."

"As you will pay for your crimes," she replied.

He glared at her, saying, "We'll see about that."

Motioning to the men, Sir Harry led them down the road and onto another path. Soon they reached a secluded cove that Isobel didn't recognize. A large rowboat waited for them in the turquoise water, its front pulled up onto the sand like the nose of a sleeping dog.

The pirates dumped Beckett into the end of the boat as if he were no more important than a sack of potatoes. Two of them lifted Isobel in and she decided not to struggle. There was no question now of attempting to escape.

Beckett was unconscious and she had to stay with him. Sir Harry climbed into the boat and the last pirate pushed them off, taking his place at one of the oars.

Isobel twisted around to watch Beckett, who lay unconscious at the back of the boat. The sight made her heart tighten with wretched pain.

She watched the shoreline recede and suddenly felt she was going to be sick.

This couldn't be happening!

Now, Beckett's life was in danger because of her. Perhaps there was a way to change Sir Harry's mind. Perhaps she could convince him that Beckett should live. She would do anything—submit to any vulgarity that Sir Harry wished to inflict upon her—if it would save her husband's life.

They neared the pirate ship, and Isobel felt the hopelessness of their fate like a stone sinking in her gut. She closed her eyes and prayed.

The rowboat came alongside the ship and a rope ladder dropped down next to them. The pirates clambered up the ladder, as agile and quick as monkeys. One of them, the big red-haired man, hoisted Beckett over his shoulder and climbed up easily despite the extra weight.

Then it was Isobel's turn. She stood, and when Sir Harry tried to play the gallant gentleman and assist her, she shook him off, wishing her eyes were daggers. Apparently it had some effect, because Sir Harry allowed her to climb up by herself.

When Isobel reached the top of the rope ladder, the red-haired pirate pulled her aboard the ship with thick arms and set her down on the deck.

Her eyes searched for Beckett and she caught sight of him being dragged down below. She whirled around to face Sir Harry, asking desperately, "Where are they taking him?"

"To the brig, my dear," he replied. "Don't worry, no harm will come to your husband until I am good and ready to inflict it."

"Please, leave him out of this," she begged. "It's me you want, and now you have me. You don't need Beckett. Let him go."

"Ah, but I don't have you, yet, precious one," Sir Harry pointed out. "I cannot make you my wife while your husband still lives. So I intend to see that you are widowed before this voyage is over. Then we shall retire to Hampton Park, and live out our lives in perfect happiness."

"That is what you think these twisted plans will bring you—happiness?" Isobel asked, incredulous. "How can a man without a heart ever be happy?"

"Make no mistake," Sir Harry answered, "I have one, and it beats only for you, Isobel. You'll understand that one day."

As she stared at Sir Harry in disgust, another man approached them. He possessed a fierceness and an effortless air of command, which made Isobel assume he was the captain. Though he only looked to be in his forties, his hair was white as snow. He wore it tied back in a blood red ribbon.

He held a cat curled in one arm and Isobel recognized the animal at once—Captain Black!

But how had the cat come to be here?

"You must be Lady Ravenwood," the man said.

"Yes, I am the Countess of Ravenwood," she replied.

"I am Captain Worthington" he said, "and this is my ship, *the Revenge*."

"I've heard of you," she replied. "Forgive me, Captain, if I am less than delighted about our meeting under such circumstances. And would you please explain how you have come to be in possession of my cat, sir?"

"Firstly, Madam," Worthington answered, "he is *my* cat, as I'm sure you know. Be assured, I am most grateful to you for taking care of him. When I paid a visit to Ravenwood Hall earlier today, I found him living like a king."

Isobel's stomach knotted in fear as she thought of Josephine and the others at Ravenwood Hall. "Was anyone hurt while you were absconding with Captain Black?" she demanded.

"No, no," he said, shaking his head as if the idea were ludicrous. "They did not even know that I was there."

He seemed to notice Sir Harry then and regarded his scratched face with raised eyebrows. "Had a little trouble did you?" He asked, then turned back to Isobel. "I applaud your efforts, madam."

Sir Harry stood taller, eyes narrowing as he said, "A man must not be afraid to shed a little blood in order to get what he wants, Captain."

"Especially if what he wants is what shed the blood in the first place, eh?" Worthington observed.

"It does seem that my little kitten has claws," Sir Harry said, grabbing Isobel's arm and pulling her next to him. "But they shall soon be trimmed. It is nothing I cannot handle."

"Undoubtedly," Worthington said with a humorless smile. "We have calm seas, Sir Harry. I'm sure you'll find the seasickness that plagued you on the voyage over will be less of a nuisance—for the time being."

Sir Harry snarled, "I told you, Captain, it was the food."

"Ah, yes," Worthington replied. "So you did."

Isobel felt somehow reassured by this exchange. It seemed that Captain Worthington had no love for Sir Harry, either.

"I would like to go below now, Captain," Sir Harry said.

"As you can see, I'm in need of a change of clothes. I shall leave Lady Ravenwood in your care for a few moments, if you think you can manage her?"

He whispered in Isobel's ear, "Behave now, my darling. I'm sure Captain Worthington will not be so indulgent of your antics as I."

She stared straight ahead until he released her arm, then watched with relief as Sir Harry disappeared below.

Worthington turned to Isobel, saying calmly, "Lady Ravenwood, you strike me as an intelligent young woman, so let us come to an understanding. I am a businessman. I work for profit, nothing more. If—let's say—a sack of coffee beans fell overboard, no one on this ship would bother to fish it out of the water. You are a piece of cargo that I am being paid to transport. My crew and I have as little interest in you as we would in a sack of coffee beans."

He adjusted the cat in his arms and continued, "So if at any time, you are considering trying your luck with the sharks, be warned, no one from my ship will come to your rescue. Of course, if Sir Harry wants to play the hero, he is welcome to it."

"It would almost be worth it to have Sir Harry gobbled by sharks, too," Isobel replied. "Oh, what does it matter? The truth is, I would welcome such a fate, compared to the one that awaits me."

"With Lennox?" he asked.

"He will murder my husband, and force me to be his bride," Isobel said, bitterly. "I have already seen him commit murder, once. He is a madman."

"Then I am sorry for you," the captain replied.

"Are you?" she demanded. "Yet you will allow him to do this? Have you no conscience?"

"You ask a pirate if he has a conscience, madam?" he said, coolly. "Then I truly am sorry for you. Sir Harry has promised me a substantial sum for your passage back to England. It is none of my business what he does with his goods when he arrives."

"I'll wager this isn't the first time you've transported human cargo, is it, Captain?" she challenged.

"No, it isn't," he replied, unfazed. "And it won't be the last."

"I'm not surprised. You likely did so under Captain Black." She stepped closer to the pirate and reached out to stroke the cat in his arms. "Captain Mayfield told me much about you and your former captain—wild stories of obeah, and strange ceremonies of transfiguration. Josephine, our housekeeper at Ravenwood Hall also told me many stories of her own. Of course, they must be whimsy. We all know that such transformations are not possible. But if they were... Ah, well, I'm sure Josephine was just spinning stories. Don't you think?"

She saw something flicker in Captain Worthington's eyes, then quickly disappear. Worthington held the cat closer and regarded Isobel with a thoughtful expression. "I would like to hear these stories, Lady Ravenwood. Captain Black is quite legendary in these islands. And he is just a silly cat, after all."

Captain Black meowed sharply and looked up at Worthington, batting a paw at the man's chin.

"Silly, indeed," Isobel muttered.

Worthington looked unamused, saying, "We shall continue the conversation over dinner. And you must tell me more of these 'folk-tales' regarding Captain Black."

Isobel nodded, wondering how she could use the stories about Captain Black to her advantage. If there was a way, she would find it. Captain Black might help her and Beckett, yet.

"Ah, Sir Harry has returned," Worthington said. "I

shall leave you under his care. I shall see you both tonight at my table for dinner. Until then, Lady Ravenwood."

He strode across the deck with Captain Black peeking at her over his shoulder.

Surely, having Captain Black here was a good omen. She'd seen the look in Worthington's eyes. Had it been one of fear? The man was a pirate and the captain of this ship. What could he possibly be afraid of?

But he'd given her a weapon, however small. And hadn't David slain Goliath with a rock the size of an egg?

It was obvious that Worthington thought she knew something rather important about Captain Black and the mystery surrounding his fate. She had to find a way to use the stories to her advantage.

And she had to find a way to see Beckett—to save Beckett.

Or she would die trying.

CHAPTER TWENTY

Beckett moaned as he struggled to move.

Ugh. Why was the room rocking so? What was that smell? And why did his entire body hurt?

He opened his eyes.

Dear Lord, I've gone blind...

He opened and closed them a few times, his eyes adjusting to the dark. Then he remembered.

Isobel.

He sat up and tried to get to his feet, but fell back down. He knew what the pain in his side meant.

Broken ribs.

Oh, bugger.

Beckett lay on his good side and clenched his teeth in frustration. He ignored the pain and struggled at the bonds that held his hands behind his back. It was fruitless. He was trussed up like a Christmas goose. Beckett felt a knot of white-hotanger harden in his gut.

Where was Isobel? If Sir Harry had hurt her, had even touched a hair on her head...just the thought of it made Beckett growl in fury.

He had to do something or he would go mad.

Beckett heard scuttling across the floor, and knew it was a rat. Well, who had he expected to meet in the hold of a pirate ship, the Prince of Wales? He would have laughed at the idea if the situation wasn't so serious.

Trying to ignore the pain in his side, Beckett thought back to the Battle of Salamanca during the war. He and his men had been cut off from the main force by a legion of French dragoons. His colonel had panicked and led half the battalion to their deaths.

Beckett had taken command then, leading the remaining men to safety by keeping a cool head and refusing to give in to the enemy.

He would do the same now.

The first thing he had to do was escape from this cell.

The second was to find a way for himself and Isobel to off this ship.

And the third was to kill Sir Harry Lennox. Of course, the second and third items might change order, depending on the circumstances.

This situation obviously proved the validity of Isobel's previous claims regarding Sir Harry. Everything she'd said was true.

Beckett stared at the dingy floor in the murky darkness. He decided not to contemplate the origins of the sticky substance that covered it, for it smelled worse than the back end of an ox. This cell would be his home for a little while. He'd lived through worse things in the war.

The sound of keys rattled outside the door, and Beckett sat up, wincing from the pain in his side. Warm yellow light streamed into the cell and momentarily blinded him. He squinted, trying to focus on the looming shadow in the doorway.

"Lord Ravenwood," said Sir Harry Lennox, stepping into the cell. "So glad you're awake."

A large red-haired pirate blocked the entire door with his towering form.

"Your accommodations are comfortable, Ravenwood?" Sir Harry asked, glancing about the brig.

"Quite," Beckett answered, fighting the urge to attack the weasel before him. It would be no use while he was injured and with "Redbeard" standing just feet away. He'd learned during the war to pick his battles carefully.

It was apparent Sir Harry had some despicable plan in mind, and it was not killing him—not just yet. Lennox would have simply thrown Beckett over the side by now if he wasn't saving him for something else.

"Your wife's accommodations are very different, you'll be pleased to know," Lennox said. "Not like this dunghole. But what else could I provide for a thief like yourself?"

"Thief?" Beckett asked. "I suppose I'm somehow responsible for stealing my wife and myself, then?"

"I have only recovered what is mine, Ravenwood. You'd do well to remember that."

"Isobel is not yours," Beckett answered. "She will never be yours."

"Oh?" Sir Harry smiled easily. "How do you know that I haven't made her mine already?"

Beckett refused to take the bait, replying, "Because there are not enough marks on your face, and you can still walk. If you had tried to possess my wife, I daresay you'd be much the worse for wear. Though I applaud her for the gash she gave your cheek back on the island."

Sir Harry self-consciously raised his hand to the fresh wound on his face and stared down at Beckett darkly. "Don't worry, Ravenwood. I do plan to tame the little cat, and take much enjoyment from it."

"Do you?" Beckett said. "It's obvious that you do not

know my wife, sir. She is tenacious as a terrier. I don't doubt she will have you for luncheon."

"Brave words from a man who is destined to spend his last days in a the belly of a ship," Sir Harry pronounced. "We'll see how brave you are on the day of your execution, Lord Ravenwood."

"Have you a date in mind," Beckett asked. "Do be good enough to let me know so I can have my clothes in order. I wouldn't want to swing in anything other than the latest fashion."

Sir Harry said smugly, "Who says I'm going to hang you?"

"Well, a hanging may be unimaginative," Beckett began, "yet it does hold a certain amount of drama, as well as being easy. I thought it would suit a coward like you perfectly. Just think of it. The yard-arm extended over the water, my hair blowing in the wind, all your pirate cronies assembled on deck waiting to watch me gasp my last. Sounds like nothing more than a boring play at Drury Lane."

"I can assure you, Ravenwood, your execution will be anything but boring," Sir Harry threatened.

"You have your work cut out for you, Lennox," Beckett replied flatly. "I'm afraid fighting against Napoleon has made me ever so hard to impress."

Sir Harry adjusted his cuffs, saying, "Then I shall do my best to entertain you, my lord. And Isobel, of course, as she will be present to watch your long, painful death. You may spend the rest of the voyage in this miserable cell, with nothing else but that prospect to occupy your thoughts. That, and wondering which part of Isobel's body I have my hands on at any given moment. Good day, Ravenwood."

Beckett clenched his teeth and fought the urge to hurl

himself at Sir Harry. But with his hands tied behind his back, the gesture would be useless. Instead, he watched the slimy coward take his leave, followed by Redbeard. The cell was again plunged into darkness and Beckett heard the key turn in the lock.

He sat back and leaned his head against the wall, fighting the awful knot of dread that had balled itself in his stomach.

Isobel.

The sight of her face swirled in his mind. His heart tightened painfully at the memory, and of the awful things he'd said to her on the beach.

What a wretched excuse for a husband he was.

He had sworn to protect Isobel, had given her his word. And he had been unable to keep it. Now she was in danger and he was locked in the brig, wounded and unable to help her.

God only knew what Sir Harry planned.

The very thought of him touching Isobel made Beckett want to rip the heavy oak door from its hinges.

He'd kept his head during Sir Harry's visit, but at what cost? Should he have tried to escape just now, no matter how unlikely the odds?

Yet, even if Beckett had somehow succeeded in killing Sir Harry and Redbeard, what would happen to Isobel if he himself were killed? He doubted that the pirate captain, whoever he was, would return Isobel safely to England.

No, he had to stay alive until he was better able to fight. Then he would get both himself and Isobel to safety. Or at the very least, Isobel.

All of a sudden there was a lump in his throat. He breathed deeply to try to get rid of it, but it didn't work.

His mind filled itself with images of her laughing merrily at a shared joke; covered in dirt, but radiant and indomitable as they'd fought the fire together; panting and helpless in his arms as he'd made love to her for the first time.

Like a slap in the face, the realization of such feelings stung him. How ironic that he'd denied having any feelings for her at all, only hours before on the beach.

Was all this to be torn away from him?

Could he allow his true bride to be taken from him forever because of the wickedness of a madman?

No.

Not as long as there was breath in his body. Because there was something he had to tell Isobel.

Something very important.

CHAPTER TWENTY-ONE

In the week that passed on the pirate ship *Revenge*, Isobel had not been able to see Beckett even once.

She had tried on two occasions. Once, she'd feigned sickness and headed back to her cabin alone, but the man with the red beard had found her in another part of the ship. He hadn't said anything; he'd merely taken her arm, gently but firmly, and returned her to the deck.

The second time, she had attempted to convince a burly pirate that he would guarantee himself a place in heaven if he assisted the cause of true love. That hadn't worked either.

She was allowed a semblance of freedom, however, after proving on the first day she wasn't going to throw herself overboard. And since a sudden seasickness kept Sir Harry cabin-bound, she'd been put in Captain Worthington's charge. He was usually too busy running the ship to take much notice of her.

At least she had a companion in Captain Black. Though he spent a fair amount of time sitting on Worthington's shoulder, her old feline friend would seek her out as well, always appearing when her heart was darkest with worry.

He would purr and nuzzle his face against her neck, and gaze at her with knowing green eyes. Once, when a teardrop escaped and trickled down her cheek, the cat had reached up and gently touched her face with his paw.

Who had ever heard of a cat who wiped away your tears? she'd thought.

To keep her mind occupied and her sanity intact, Isobel had taken to sitting up on deck, drawing. Captain Worthington had generously provided paper for her. But today she was finding it especially hard to concentrate.

As Captain Black lounged beside her, Isobel tried not to think about Beckett, or if she would ever see him alive again. She would stay calm, and not think about what might be happening to him in the hold of the ship.

Perhaps nothing was happening to him.

Perhaps he was already dead.

As for Sir Harry, from Captain Worthington's account the man was green to the gills—just as he'd been on the trip across.

Good. She hoped it was fatal.

Surprisingly, she hadn't encountered much trouble from the pirate crew. Though she had noticed some leering glances and muttered comments, Isobel always noticed that a glance from Captain Worthington or his first mate stopped the sailors cold. The men were too busy working most of the time to take much notice of her, anyway, and she thanked God for it.

Isobel began sketching without really knowing what she was doing, but soon a face emerged before her. It was no surprise to see Beckett staring back out at her. Something shone from the eyes on the page. Hope? Love? Was it hers or his?

Her hand faltered and she inadvertently slashed a mark across the image she had just sketched.

Immediately, her heart throbbed with pain as she regarded the ruined picture in her lap.

A terrible fear struck her. Would she ever touch Beckett's face again? Would she ever feel the heat of his blue eyes as they looked at her as only he did? Would she feel his mouth on hers or his strong hands caressing her body once more?

She looked out at the ocean surrounding her—the same color as Beckett's unforgettable eyes. She had drowned in their depths long ago, and would not be sorry now.

If the price of loving Beckett left her with a broken heart, she would accept it. And if being Sir Harry's whore would save Beckett's life, she would do it gladly.

There must be a way to convince Sir Harry to spare her husband's life. She would sign over the deed to Hampton Park. She would tell Sir Harry there was more money hidden away somewhere, anything to buy Beckett some time.

But perhaps he would try to play the hero and refuse to leave without her, even if she won him the chance. Yes, she could see that happening. Beckett might not love her, but he would never leave her to a fate with Sir Harry in order to save himself.

She stared at the skyline and shook her head. None of this would be happening if she hadn't run away that night. Beckett would never have found her, or taken her in, or made her his wife. Now, she was back where she'd started—doomed to a life as Sir Harry's plaything.

But the man she loved would be killed because of her.

Isobel turned her head toward approaching voices from the lower deck. It seemed to be a good time to return to her cabin. She picked up her pencils and started to leave, but stopped as she heard whispering.

"I tell ye, we must move tonight, McGregor!" the whispered voice said forcefully.

Something told her to hide then, and she crouched behind the crate on which she'd been sitting.

As if sensing the tension in the air, Captain Black made himself scarce. Isobel listened to the pirates' hushed conversation and held her breath.

"I 'aven't got enough men yet," a gruff voice replied. "I needs a few more days, still."

"In a few more days it'll be past the turn," the man replied. "I told Brinkman we'd be in Jamaica to pick up the cargo next week, see? If we don't move now we'll not make it in time!"

"Styles, 'ave ye gone daft, man?" McGregor hissed. "If we move without enough men, neither of us will make it to Jamaica. Now, d'ye want control of the ship, or don't ye?"

"Of course I do, ye dung-head!"

"Then ye'll have to trust me," MacGregor said. "Just a few more days, and we'll 'ave most o' the men on our side then. It'll be much easier to slit the cap'n's throat if 'is lackeys are with us."

"Alright, then," Styles said. "But don't disappoint me. I want Worthington's 'ead on a platter. And that little miss 'e's been protectin' will fetch a nice price in Kingston...after we've all had a few turns with her, o' course."

Isobel's blood turned icy cold.

Was there no end to her woes?

"I'll do what I can tonight," McGregor said. "Meet me in the galley after, grub n'grog. I'll know more then."

"The sooner, the better," Styles replied. "Shite, someone's comin'!"

Isobel heard their footsteps scramble away, but could

only crouch numbly behind the crate as she contemplated her bleak future. The situation was going from bad to worse, rather quickly.

There was only one thing to do.

She had to reach Beckett. He might know how to turn this situation to their advantage. And if he didn't, it might be the last time she would ever see him.

Isobel peeked over the crate and, seeing that it was safe to move, quickly grabbed her pencils and stood. Purposefully, she walked across the deck toward the doorway that led down to the sleeping quarters.

"I think I'll retire to my cabin, now," she said to no one in particular. The pirates there ignored her as she walked past.

She searched the deck for Captain Worthington, but didn't see him. The red-bearded first mate seemed to be in command at the moment. That meant Worthington was in his quarters, working on charts, or counting gold coins, or doing whatever pirate captains did.

"Yes, I am tired," Isobel continued saying to the air. "I think I shall have a long nap."

She reached the doorway and yawned loudly before she went through. As she'd become used to the steep stairway, she descended it as quickly as a monkey. There companionway was deserted.

She went to her cabin and left her papers and pencils on the small table, then peeked out the door. It was still clear.

Quickly and silently, Isobel scuttled down the companionway. She went in the opposite direction she'd tried before, hoping that this was the way to the brig. Her heart thumped hard in her breast as she went deeper and deeper into the bowels of the ship.

As she came around one corner she saw a big, burly

man fiddling with some keys near a door. Ducking back, she waited and listened.

"Damn. I needs me pipe," the pirate said to himself. "Been too long without a smoke."

Isobel heard him shifting around on his feet, snorting and clearing his throat.

"Now, be a good chap and behave yerself while ol' Williams is gone," he said. "A man has to have his pipe now and again, or like as go mad, eh?"

Chap?

Could he see her? Isobel wondered.

"So right, Mr. Williams," a voice replied. "Be a good fellow and fetch me back a cigar, won't you?"

It sounded like Beckett!

Williams laughed. "Yer a right funny one, ye is, m'lord. Tell ye what. I'll have an extra smoke in yer honor. 'Ow's that, eh?"

"Take your time, my good man," Beckett said. "We both know I'm not going anywhere."

"I shall, sir," Williams said, chuckling. "And not a word o' this to the cap'n, now. Wouldn't look good if he thought we was becomin' friends, eh? Might toss me overboard, he might. An' I needs this job."

"Don't worry, Mr. Williams," Beckett answered. "If the captain comes by, I shall do my best to quake in fear at the mention of your name."

"Right good of ye, sir. I'll be off then." Williams turned with a snort, and headed towards where Isobel stood at the end of the passage.

She looked frantically for a place to hide, but there was none. She backed up all the way into a set of stairs. There was no place to go!

Just then Isobel saw a small crevice next to the stairs...she thought she might be able to squeeze in there.

It was risky, though. If she got stuck and Mr. Williams found her, what explanation would she have for being wedged between the stairs and the bulkhead?

She heard the man's heavy footsteps approaching, and knew it was now or never. Isobel squeezed herself sideways against the narrow opening and wiggled an arm through. It was going to be tight.

He was getting closer. She could hear him approaching around the corner. She closed her eyes—though what good that would do she didn't know—sucked in her stomach, and shoved.

Like a pearl through a button-hole, she popped through the opening. Isobel crouched down in the shadows just as Williams's foot touched the first step. He clomped up the stairs with heavy feet, and soon disappeared out of sight.

Isobel breathed a sigh of relief and quickly went about squeezing back out of the opening. There was no time to lose.

She peeked around the corner again and breathed a sigh of relief when she saw the passageway was still empty. Beckett was just a few feet away. Isobel crept closer as silently as a cat. She reached the sturdy oak door and saw a small square window near the top. It was blocked with sturdy iron bars.

"Beckett!" she whispered. "Beckett, it's me, Isobel."

His head popped up in the opening like a Jack-in-the-box, and Isobel felt tears come to her eyes.

"Isobel?" She saw the disbelief in his eyes as he looked down at her.

Her hands flew up to the bars and Beckett's fingers threaded through to twine with hers. The touch of his skin sent a jolt of happiness through her body. She was laughing and crying all at once.

"I didn't know if you were still alive," she said. "Oh, Beckett!"

"Are you alright, my darling?" Beckett demanded. "Lennox, has he—"

"Sir Harry has a terrible case of seasickness," she explained. "He's been in his cabin most of the time, and other than that, he hasn't had the strength to do much more than scowl. I'm quite well."

Beckett closed his eyes in relief, then looked at her with that fiery gaze that made her heart skip. "I've been going mad with worry," he said.

"So have I," she said, clasping his hand through the bars. "Are you alright?"

"I had some broken ribs," he said, "but they're on the mend. It's too bad Williams didn't leave his key. Don't suppose you feel like breaking down the door, do you my dear?"

"If only I could," Isobel replied. Promise me you won't try anything foolish, Beckett."

"I will try anything if it will get us out of here."

"Well, that is the least of our problems now, it seems," she said, worriedly.

"What do you mean?" Beckett asked.

She took a deep breath, and explained, "I overheard two men talking just now about a mutiny that is going to take place very soon. They plan to kill Captain Worthington, and I can only imagine what they mean to do to us."

"Damnation!" Beckett cursed. "If we didn't have bad luck, we'd have no luck at all. Where is the captain now?"

"I haven't seen him about," she answered. "I assume he's in his quarters."

"You must go and warn him, Isobel," he said. "It's too risky to hope we could escape in the midst of a mutiny. I'll give odds that he won't believe you at first. He'll think you're trying to help me or yourself escape. But you must find some way to convince him. Do you understand?"

"I can if it means our lives," she replied. "Oh, Beckett, I am so sorry you've been mixed up in this. If only you hadn't taken me home that night. If only—"

"Stop right there, Isobel," he said. "I have no regrets. Why, just look at us—here we are, meeting all kinds of interesting people on board this lovely ship. I daresay the *ton* will be terribly jealous when they find out we have sailed on a real pirate ship, and survived. I imagine the Prince of Wales will have us to dinner just to hear the tale."

Isobel laughed, though tears dampened her eyes.

Beckett's his eyes glowing with emotion as he said, "It will be alright, Isobel. I promise. Now find Worthington."

Isobel reluctantly pulled away, unwilling to give up even one more moment with him. She finally turned to go down the companionway, but stopped. This could be the last moment they ever saw each other alive....

She pressed herself against the heavy door, wishing it was Beckett's body she clung to instead of the barrier that separated them. "I have to tell you something," she said. "I can't leave you here, not knowing if I'll ever have the chance again. And I know you don't want to hear it, but I must."

"No, Isobel," he replied. "This won't be the last time we have together. I promise. You must believe me."

"I'm afraid of losing you!" she said desperately.

"You won't lose me, Isobel. And I won't lose you—not to Sir Harry Lennox. As long as there is breath in my body, I won't."

"Beckett, I love you." Her voice was no more than a whisper. "Even though you don't want it to be true. Even though I don't want it to be true. And I don't care if you don't want to hear it. I love you more than life itself. So you better take care, do you hear? Don't take any foolish chances with my husband's life. I want him in one piece when this is over."

"You must go now, Isobel," he commanded. "We're running out of time."

She nodded. A numbing coldness washed through her heart. She turned away, slipping around the corner. She paused for a moment and stood with her back against the bulkhead before she continued. Hidden from Beckett's sight, she felt her heart aching, as if the love and pain inside would overflow and burst it open like the banks of a swollen river.

He still didn't love her.

Even now, when their lives were in such danger, when they might never see each other again, he'd said nothing of love.

It shouldn't matter. Not now. But it did.

She swallowed and steeled herself against the tears that threatened to fall. She had no time for them now. She had a mutiny to stop.

CHAPTER TWENTY-TWO

Isobel walked purposefully down the companion-way, taking deep breaths and trying to calm herself. But she didn't know if it was from the danger she was facing or from the scene with Beckett.

How she had wanted to believe that he loved her! And she had foolishly thought he would answer her declaration of love with one of his own.

She had to clear her head of such notions. Now was not the time to lament her unrequited passion. Beckett had made his feelings plain on the beach. And if they did get out of this together, she could not expect anything more from him.

She came around the corner, seeing the dark, sturdy door to the captain's quarters. As usual, there was a fearsome looking brute standing guard outside. Apparently, Worthington's trust went only so far—and rightly so.

She took a deep breath, and walked up to the guard, saying firmly, "I need to see the captain, if you please."

The big man looked at her, unimpressed. "'E's not to be disturbed."

"It is of the utmost importance," she insisted.

The man moved his face close to hers, and the strong smell of his unwashed body penetrated her nostrils. The stubble on his face almost scraped her cheek as he spoke again, slowly and quietly. "I said, 'e's not to be disturbed...didn't I?"

Isobel tried avert her gaze from the rotten, jagged teeth that sparsely filled his mouth. "Good sir, I must see the captain," she said, again. "If you will not knock on the door, then I shall."

The big man blocked Isobel's approach and grabbed her outstretched arm, holding a wicked-looking dagger just inches in front of her face.

"Ye see this, Miss?" he asked.

Isobel nodded mutely.

"Well, the cap'n, see, 'e tol' me to put it through the heart of anyone who come near that door, there. An' I would hate to dirty yer lovely dress." He pushed her away but held the dagger up threateningly. "Now, ye be a good lass, and shag off, before me and me dagger poke holes in ye."

Oh, dear...this was not going at all well.

"I shall return later, then," Isobel said with as much haughtiness as she could muster. "And if the captain emerges, please tell him that I must speak to him right away."

The man grinned at her as if she had just asked him to perform Hamlet in its entirety.

"'Course, Miss," he said. "I'll do that."

Frowning at her failure to talk her way past the guard, Isobel turned on her heel and made her way down the narrow passageway. Not knowing what else to do, she headed back to her quarters.

Fighting the urge to return to Beckett's cell, Isobel

forced herself back to her room. She would wait a quarter of an hour or so, then try again. Feeling terribly powerless, she sat on a chair and looked around the room, as if the answer to her troubles might be lurking somewhere.

Her eyes came to rest on the tray that held her luncheon dishes. Usually, it was removed right away, but someone had neglected his duties and hadn't picked it up.

Isobel looked at the plate. It was made of porcelain, and looked quite old and dingy. But perhaps it could be more than that. She wanted to laugh at herself for not thinking of it before.

She picked it up and hit it against the side of the table. The plate broke into a few pieces that fell to the floor, and consequently broke into more. Reaching down, Isobel picked up one that was long and sharp, like an oddly shaped knife. She ripped some of her underskirt and wrapped it around the end, making a handle to grip. At any rate, the cloth would protect her hand from the jagged edge.

Lifting her skirt, she tucked the makeshift weapon into the laces that wrapped around the top of her boot. She arranged it as best she could, and hoped she wouldn't inadvertently stab herself in the foot.

She picked up the rest of the broken plate and hid the pieces under the lumpy straw mattress of her bunk. Armed as well as she could be, Isobel set out on her mission once again.

As she neared the captain's quarters, she noticed that the man who had previously stood guard outside was nowhere to be seen. Instead of reassuring her about any chance of seeing Captain Worthington, instinct told her this would be worse.

Isobel slowed her pace, listening for any sound beyond

the door, when a big dirty hand clamped over her mouth and yanked her around the corner.

"And where d'ye think yer goin', Missy?" a voice rasped in her ear. Isobel grimaced at the stench of the man's breath. Strong, beefy arms held her easily and pressed her back against a solid chest.

Isobel kicked and thrashed about in the man's iron-hard arms. The pirate only laughed and squeezed her tighter.

This couldn't be happening.

Not now—when Beckett's life depended on her reaching Captain Worthington.

Using all the willpower she could muster, Isobel sank her teeth into the meaty hand that covered her mouth and bit as hard as she could.

The pirate bellowed and tried to pry her mouth open with his other hand, but Isobel's jaws held tight. She tasted blood in her mouth, but refused to let the revolting hand go.

The pirate's hand curled around her neck, and she felt his fingers dig into her flesh.

"Let go, ye bloody bitch!" the man hissed.

"Leave off, Murray!" another voice said. "No marks on 'er skin, remember? Styles will have yer tongue cut out if ye bruise er."

"To 'ell with Styles! Help me get 'er off," Murray groaned.

The two men struggled to pry Isobel's jaws apart. When they finally succeeded, both regarded her warily. Isobel could feel the warm wet blood running down her chin, and knew she must look quite a sight indeed.

"Look what she to me, Dobbin!" Murray held out his wounded hand as gore dripped from it onto the floor.

"You should have the surgeon look at it," Isobel said,

spitting out some of the blood in her mouth. "While I was on Barbados I contracted a rare disease—Caribbean parrot fever!"

It was a bold-faced lie.

There was no such disease as far as she knew.

Nonetheless, it had the desired effect.

Murray's face turned white and he looked at Dobbin accusingly. "Why didn't you grab 'er? Now I've got 'Caribbean parrot fever'!"

"Gag 'er, and put 'er in the galley," Dobbin ordered. "That should keep the baggage out o' trouble for a time."

"You gag 'er, Dobbin! I've had me fill o' bein' her dinner, thank you very much," Murry said. "The little bitch can take a bite out o' you."

"Hold 'er hands then, and I'll gag 'er."

The men roughly turned Isobel around, and Murray pulled her arms back painfully as Dobbin approached.

Isobel glared at the man, saying, "Fever symptoms can be hideous. It won't be long now."

She saw a flicker of fear in the pirate's eyes and felt a small thrill of victory.

Dobbin bent down and ripped off a piece of her skirt, then stood, twisting it into a coil. Slowly, he brought the gag to her face.

Isobel shook her head like a terrier, but he managed to get it between her teeth and tied it tightly around her head in a secure knot.

She heard another tear of her skirt and soon her hands were bound behind her back, as well. At least Dobbin hadn't seen the porcelain knife in her boot when he'd ripped her dress.

Roughly, the men dragged Isobel down the narrow passageway and into the galley. Pots and pans hung from the low ceiling, along with various ladles and other cooking utensils, which all clanged together as the ship rocked.

A galley with no cook?

So, the mutiny had begun.

The pirates dragged her over to the table, pushed her down into a sitting position on the floor, then bound her hands to the table leg. Of course, being on a ship, the table legs were nailed to the floor. She wasn't going anywhere.

Isobel glared up at the pirates, truly wishing that looks could kill. Strangely, the overwhelming emotion she felt was anger, not fear. But that would most likely change when the reality and hopelessness of the situation set in.

What would happen to her—to Beckett? She hoped that Sir Harry Lennox would be consigned to eternal Hell for this.

"She should stay out of harm's way in 'ere," Dobbin pronounced. "If a pot doesn't fall on 'er head!"

"Per'aps we should take a pot to 'er noggin and knock 'er out now," Murray said, nursing his wounded hand. "I don't trust 'er."

Isobel tried to calm her fears as she pictured Murray taking a skillet to her head.

"I don't think so," Dobbin answered. "Might make her go daft, see? It would lower 'er price in Kingston."

"And she's not daft already?" Murray asked, looking unconvinced. "Said she 'ad parrot fever after all. Her an' me both, now."

"Ah, quit yer cryin'," Dobbin said. "Our job's done 'ere. McGregor will be wantin' us, up on deck. Come on."

The two men took a last look at Isobel and closed the door behind them.

Isobel struggled against her bonds but it was of no use.

Frustration made her want to scream. But the sound

she made came out like a muffled mewling and that made her fume in aggravation even more.

Hearing an odd squeaking noise, she twisted her head but could not see anything.

Then she saw it.

A little gray mouse scuttled straight toward her across the rough plank floor.

After fighting bloodthirsty pirates, Isobel wouldn't have thought she could still be frightened by a mouse.

Not so.

And now she would spend her last moments being terrorized by one. How fitting.

She recoiled as the tiny rodent scurried in front of her. It began to sniff around the edge of her skirt, which was soiled with spilled food and drink from the floor of the galley.

Then, with an other-worldly growl, a cat sprang from the shadows.

Captain Black!

He truly was her knight in furry armor.

The mouse squeaked and scuttled across the floor in a blur of grey fur. Captain Black darted after the poor creature, and though it had surely been about to nibble her to death, Isobel feared for the rodent's life.

Just as Captain Black was about to pounce, the mouse disappeared through an opening in the planked flooring. The cat meowed and batted at the mouse-hole with his paws, unwilling to give up the chase.

Reluctantly, it seemed, Captain Black abandoned his hunt and returned to her side.

Oh, I wish you could help me, she thought, looking at the cat in desperation.

The cat meowed at her loudly, as if saying, *What are you waiting for, a cat to set you free? Get on with it.*

The feline was right, Isobel thought. She had to find a way out if this. No one was going to come to her rescue, and Beckett's life depended on her.

She wriggled around and tried to reach the makeshift weapon she'd hidden in her boot. But she couldn't touch it.

Captain Black meowed at her again, encouraging her.

I can do this, she thought. *I just need to think.*

The galley table was nailed to the floor, so she couldn't drag it or flip it over. But a thought took hold. If only she could change her position so that she could reach the weapon in her boot....

She tried to move, but her bonds were tight. However, the pirates had ripped them from her underskirt—which was made of cotton. And cotton could stretch.

Isobel winced in pain as she pulled against the bonds. Heavens but they had tied them tightly! Yet she refused to give up. She stretched and pulled against them as hard as she could.

Captain Black meowed at her again, as if to say, *Now you've got it!*

It was tiring work, especially in such an awkward position, but Isobel kept on. Soon, she felt the cotton bonds loosening, just a little.

It was enough.

She maneuvered into a kneeling position and slowly slid her bound wrists up the leg of the table. With a little more wriggling, she was able to reach down and grab the jagged piece of porcelain stowed in the side of her boot.

"Meow!" Captain Black intoned.

Even with the gag still in her mouth, Isobel grinned.

Captain Black was right, she was almost there. *Don't give up now!*

She squirmed and stretched, turning the weapon in her

fingers until it rested against the cotton strips. Slowly, so she didn't lose her grip on the jagged porcelain blade, Isobel pushed it back and forth against her bonds, like a saw against a sapling. It seemed fruitless at first, but then she felt one of the strips weakening, then the fibers began to pull apart.

Isobel felt a thrilling surge of victory as she finally freed herself from her bonds. She reached behind her head to untie her gag, and turned to thank her valiant friend.

"Thank you for helping me, Captain Black," she said. "I shall have to give you a very large fish for this. Captain Mayfield was right—you are watching out for me, aren't you?"

The cat meowed as to confirm the idea.

Grabbing a skillet, Isobel scrambled to the door.

There was not a moment to waste.

Both hers and Beckett's lives depended on it.

CHAPTER TWENTY-THREE

The ship held an eerie silence as Isobel walked quietly towards the captain's quarters. Captain Black bolted down the companionway and disappeared from sight.

Isobel had no idea where Sir Harry would be in all this, but with any luck he would be mortally wounded during the melee. She only hoped Beckett was still safe in his cell.

As Isobel approached the door to Captain Worthington's cabin, she heard snarling voices from within. Taking a deep breath for courage, she crouched down in front of the door and peeped through the keyhole.

What she saw made her gasp.

Captain Worthington sat tied to a chair. The pirate she knew as Styles held the tip of his saber dangerously close to Worthington's throat.

Oh, he couldn't be killed now. Worthington's death would make things much worse for her and Beckett.

She had to do something...anything!

Isobel knocked on the door, then wondered what exactly she was going to do when it opened.

She heard footsteps approaching and stood back.

"Who is it?" a raspy voice asked.

Isobel used the gruffest voice that she could muster. "Message for Styles," she croaked.

She heard a grunt from behind the door. Taking a deep breath, she crouched and held her skillet ready.

The door opened and a large, ugly head popped out.

With all her strength, Isobel swung the skillet, smashing it into the pirate's face.

Perhaps she should have used her makeshift knife, but the truth of the matter was that she hadn't felt quite up to stabbing someone. The skillet produced the desired effect, however, as the large pirate crumpled in a heap across the door's threshold.

Isobel peeked around the door and saw Styles pause for a split-second.

It gave Worthington the chance he needed. His boot flew up and connected with Styles's crotch. The man let out a bellow and dropped his saber, his hands covering his injured privates. Worthington kicked the saber into a corner as Isobel dashed in. There was no one else in the room.

"Hurry up and untie me!" Worthington commanded.

Isobel dropped the skillet and ran over to cut the captain's bonds with her little knife.

Styles quickly recovered. Like a wounded bull, the pain seemed to fuel his anger.

Isobel cut as fast as she could, but the ropes were thick and her silly piece of porcelain was not very sharp.

Styles approached slowly, his eyes blazing like a madman's as he pulled out a long thin dagger from his boot. He fingered it idly.

"Per'aps I won't sell ye, little whore," he said. "I shall carve ye up and feed ye to the sharks...after I've done with him."

Isobel worked frantically on the last rope, and as Styles neared, she finally cut through it.

Worthington sprang up like a panther. He easily dodged Styles's lunge and landed a few well-placed punches in his opponent's ribs.

Then the captain's leg shot up and he kicked the dagger out of Styles's hand. Worthington swung his boot around to land in the mutineer's stomach.

But Styles was far from beaten, and in hand-to-hand combat, he did some damage to Worthington, as well. Both men stared at each other, out of breath, waiting for their opponent's next move.

Isobel glanced down and saw Styles's dagger by the wall. She scurried to retrieve it. As the men locked in a deadly embrace, Isobel jumped out of the way, crouching behind a leather wing back chair. The men crashed backwards onto a table, sending books and papers flying in all directions. The two rolled over it and onto the floor.

There was a shattering of glass and Isobel peeked from around the chair. Worthington lay pinned to the floor, and Styles hovered over him with a broken bottle, poised above the captain's face.

Isobel sent the dagger sliding towards the captain, and prayed that Worthington would be able to reach it in time. It bounced off the captain's thigh and he struggled mightily to make a grab for it, but with Styles above him it was near to impossible.

A heavy barometer rolled across the floor. Isobel picked it up, took aim, and launched it at the back of Styles's head.

It was just the advantage Worthington needed. In an instant, Styles was not only stunned by the hastily thrown projectile, he was on his back with Worthington hovering over him, a dagger pressed dangerously against his throat.

"Didn't anyone ever tell you that mutiny can be very bad for your health?" Worthington growled.

Isobel shuddered as the captain pushed the blade home.

She turned around, shutting her eyes, and covering her ears. Death was not something she wanted to witness again, even that of an enemy. She heard muffled groans and gurgles, and in a moment Worthington grabbed Isobel's arm and lifted her to her feet.

He wiped the blade against his pant leg and said, "My, my—you are truly full of surprises, Lady Ravenwood. And how did you know to come here, may I ask?"

Isobel gulped, feeling a new uneasiness spreading through her gut. Would Worthington think she'd a hand in this?

"I heard some men plotting against you," she explained. "When I tried to warn you, they tied me up and left me in the galley. I escaped and came here—just in time, it seems."

"It was very brave of you to attempt such a thing," Captain Worthington said, seriously.

"Bravery had nothing to do with it, sir," Isobel replied. "I heard them saying they were going to sell me in the Kingston market—after getting to know my acquaintance better, of course. If you were killed, my fate would have been sealed."

Worthington folded his arms across his chest, saying, "Quite so. What else did you hear? Did Styles have any accomplices you could name?"

"Yes—a man named McGregor was recruiting the men against you," Isobel answered. "He wanted to wait. He said he needed time to get more men on their side, but Styles insisted they move now. And the men who tied me up in the galley were named Dobbin and Murray. That's all I know for certain."

Worthington nodded grimly, saying, "McGregor—I should have known he would be involved." He studied her for a moment, and asked, "Is that blood on your chin, my lady?"

"I bit Mr. Murray," she said.

To her surprise, he laughed. "Good for you! Though I'm sure he tasted terrible."

"He did, at that," she agreed.

"Now, we must leave," the captain said. "I must gather my men and stop this mutiny before it starts."

Worthington led her to the door, and they quickly entered the narrow passageway.

They stopped in front of Isobel's cabin, and Worthington opened the door.

"You must stay here while my men and I sort out this business, my lady," he said. "I will lock you in so no harm will come to you."

"But my husband," Isobel said, "will he be safe in the brig?"

"He will be, for the time being," he said, opening the door and pushing Isobel inside. "Until we meet again, madam."

"Wait—" Isobel protested, but the door slammed in her face. She heard the key turn in the lock and she pounded at the door with her hand. "Oh!"

Frustration boiled inside her, though she knew the captain was right. This was probably the safest place for her at them moment.

She sat on her bunk and in a futile gesture, covered her heart with her hands, trying to keep it from bursting with pain.

Oh, Beckett...will I ever see you again?

She heard shouts and bodies crashing on deck above her head and ducked instinctively, as if they might fall through on top of her. The clanging steel of sabers rang through the ceiling planks, along with the sounds of death.

Fear clutched at her heart with its cold, icy fingers. She curled her knees up to her chest and prayed.

Beckett paced around in his cell. He was finding it more and more difficult to keep his mind occupied. And more and more difficult to keep his hopes up.

Isobel.

He had failed her.

Not knowing what was happening to her was its own form of torture.

So far he'd been unable to swipe the key from his guard's belt. And there had been more than one guard, lately. That meant trying to overtake one or both of them would be virtually impossible. He wanted to avoid physical combat—not only would his chances of victory be slim without a weapon, the noise of a fight would undoubtedly bring reinforcements.

During the war, he'd learned that timing was everything. He had to wait for the right time to strike. But each day that passed meant one more that Isobel might be suffering at the hands of Sir Harry Lennox.

Still, bad odds usually guaranteed failure. If he made a premature attempt and got himself killed before he could rescue Isobel, they'd both be as good as dead.

And he'd discovered something important while locked up in this cell.

He wanted to spend the rest of his life with Isobel.

It had never been any use denying the truth.

He loved her.

There it was.

Earlier, when Isobel had come to his cell, he'd been so close to saying it then, but he hadn't. He hadn't known how.

Those three little words had held him prisoner far better than this cell ever would. But he had escaped them. He was no longer in their power. Now, they were in his power. The most important words in the English language were no longer a thing of fear, but of freedom.

And now, looking back, he wondered what he had been so afraid of. Losing himself? Believing in something that could not possibly be true? But the alternative had been closing his heart to the most powerful gift of all.

He thought of Cordelia then. Of how he'd thought himself in love with her. But that hadn't been love. It had been a feeling that masqueraded as love, which had been quite convincing—like drinking cheap wine and being told it was champagne. You could only know the difference when you'd tasted the real thing.

And Beckett *had* tasted the real thing. Now that he knew the difference, he'd never go back to shoddy imitations. Like cheap wine, imitation love left one feeling quite sick and empty inside.

His thoughts went to Isobel, of their confrontation on the beach just before Sir Harry had snatched them. The things she'd said about her heart being full of him, about not being able to remove him from there—he understood, now.

She was inside his heart as surely as the blood that pumped there and gave him life.

He wanted to see Isobel, to tell her of his discovery. He grabbed the bars in the window and though he knew it was no use, he shook them, as if that would have any effect. He peered out and tried to see down the passageway. His guard was absent, and there was no one else about.

The ship seemed unusually quiet. He hoped that meant the mutiny hadn't yet started. He stretched up again and tried to see if his guard was asleep on the floor, but no one was there.

Then Beckett heard the familiar sound of Williams's heavy footsteps coming down the passageway. He heard the man whistling a jaunty tune as he approached.

Williams's large round face appeared in the window.

"Brought ye some dinner, m'lord," the man said.

Beckett heard the sound of the key in the lock and was about to thank the man, when Williams made a strange gasp. A look of surprise came over his face and he fell forward against the door, regarding Beckett in confusion. Then he slid down out of sight.

"There, take that, Williams, ye old bugger!" a voice hissed.

Another voice said, "Ye sure we was s'posed to kill him?"

"O' course I'm sure, ye cork-brained git!" the first man said. "Come on, now, there's more to be done before this day is out."

Beckett flattened himself against the wall beside the door, waiting for it to open.

It didn't.

He heard quick footsteps echo down the passageway until they were gone. Then came the sounds of scuffling on the deck above...the sounds of close combat, of men yelling, and metal blades clashing.

Gads, the mutiny had begun.

A chill of fear ran up his spine as he thought of Isobel.

Had she been able to warn Worthington? Where was she in all of this?

In anger and frustration, he grabbed the bars of the little window as he had before and pushed and pulled against them. Surprisingly, the door opened.

He jumped back, waiting to see who had opened it. But no one appeared. The door just creaked open slowly, gently inviting him into the passageway, and freedom.

Beckett peeked around the door and saw the key sticking out of the lock. There was no one else about, and he hopped over Williams who lay crumpled on the floor. Beckett crouched down and turned the pirate over. He was dead.

"My condolences, Mr. Williams," Beckett said, removing a long dagger from the man's boot. "I don't think you'll be needing this anymore. But I most certainly will."

With that, Beckett turned and trotted down the hall. There seemed to be no one at all below-deck—at least on this end of the ship. But he would be ready if he encountered any resistance.

He turned another corner, hoping to find Isobel's quarters, and instead looked straight into the black eyes of Sir Harry Lennox.

Chapter Twenty-Four

"Ravenwood," Sir Harry hissed, stepping back. "I must say, I'm surprised to find you here. I was just coming to see you. To see you *die,* that is. Thank you for saving me the walk."

Sir Harry slashed out with his dagger as Beckett quickly side-stepped the move.

"You bastard!" Beckett growled, his anger blazing. He hated this man with absolute clarity.

Sir Harry snarled and slashed at him, but Beckett nicked him on the wrist with a return cut.

Good. He wanted Lennox to bleed a bit before he died.

Beckett had fought men like this before—men without much training, but dangerous as a wounded beast. Such men could be goaded into making a mistake.

Sir Harry smiled as he prepared to strike again, saying, "When Isobel is my wife, Ravenwood, she'll pay for every drop of blood you make me spill."

"Isobel will never be your wife, Lennox," Beckett said, flatly.

Sir Harry's expression darkened as he lashed out again with his dagger, nicking Beckett's elbow.

Beckett ignored the minimal pain, though Lennox seemed overly pleased by the blow. Beckett would let the man tire himself out a bit before he attacked in earnest.

Sir Harry's eyes glittered maliciously, as he said, "You stole my bride, Ravenwood. I swore I'd make you pay for defiling what was mine."

"I beg to differ with you there, on both counts," Beckett replied, slashing his opponent's thigh, who gave a groan. "Isobel was never yours, Lennox. But she is mine. We love each other, you see. That's something you'll never understand."

Beckett heard a muffled voice shouting from down the passageway, and pounding on a door. He thought he heard his name.

"Isobel?" he shouted, deflecting Sir Harry's dagger once more.

"Beckett!" Isobel answered.

"Yes, it's your beloved husband, Isobel," Sir Harry shouted over his shoulder. "Say your good-byes, my dear, and listen to him die!"

"No!" she cried.

Sir Harry attacked like a mad bull. Beckett moved quickly, landing a hard kick in his opponent's groin. This was a dagger fight, and he doubted Lennox would observe any gentlemanly rules of conduct.

Sir Harry doubled over in pain, but managed to keep his weapon out in front of him. Beckett kicked again, and knocked the dagger from his enemy's grip. In a moment, he was pulling Lennox up by the scruff of his neck and placing the tip of his own knife to the base of the man's throat.

"I can't say that I'm sorry to do this," Beckett said, preparing to deliver the killing stroke.

"But I can," a voice said from behind him.

Beckett recognized the sound of a pistol being cocked near his head. He felt the cold tip of the barrel against his skull, and cursed.

"Worthington!" Lennox croaked, "It's about time."

"My apologies, Sir Harry," the captain said, stepping around Beckett and taking the dagger from his hand. "Had a bit of a mutiny to take care of, which Lady Ravenwood was good enough to warn me about. It is because of her that I didn't shoot you dead just now, Ravenwood."

"Let me see her," Beckett said, staring down the barrel of Worthington's pistol.

The man was flanked by a crew of loyal pirates.

"I'm afraid that would be unwise," Worthington answered. "Your wife is safe in her quarters, and that is where she will stay."

"Not for long," Sir Harry said, smiling.

Beckett made a lunge for him but was stopped by Worthington's men. "If you touch even a hair on her head, Lennox, I'll hunt you down like the dog you are!" he growled.

"Too late," Sir Harry said with a satisfied grin.

Beckett struggled anew, but Worthington stepped between them, sheathing his pistol in his belt. "Be assured, Ravenwood, your wife will remain unharmed while she is on my ship. I owe her that, at least." He nodded to his henchmen, and said, "Take Lord Ravenwood back to his cell."

One of the pirates pointed a pistol at Beckett's head, then yanked him back down the passageway.

Beckett struggled against them as they headed back to his cell, but he knew it was useless. He would not be able to escape now, that was certain. At least Worthington had promised to keep Isobel safe for the duration of the voyage. That would give him more time.

Soon, they were at the door to his cell, and the pirates pushed him in. The door creaked loudly behind him and he was back in the familiar darkness. How long had he been out of this mean little room—twenty, thirty minutes? Surely, it had been the world's shortest escape.

Beckett heard the key turn in the lock and the muffled sound of men dragging Williams's body down the passageway. He turned around and slammed his fists against the wall.

"Isobel!" he yelled into the darkness, though he knew it was useless.

Sir Harry had won this round.

But Beckett was not about to give up—not by a long shot.

The wind whipped Isobel's hair mercilessly around her face. She pushed it behind her ears for the hundredth time, and wondered why she attempted to put it up each day.

She pulled her shawl close around her. The wind had gotten colder the closer they got to England. And now they were almost there.

Isobel looked out across the horizon, seeing land loom in the distance. She tried desperately to fight the despair that had been growing in her heart steadily since yesterday. Their voyage was almost over, and Sir Harry had promised to make her a widow before they reached shore.

She had been unable to see Beckett after the attempted mutiny. Worthington had come to her quarters with Sir Harry in tow, to thank her for warning him.

She had begged to be able to see her husband, then, but

the pirate captain refused. All he would say was that Beckett was in good health. Her only consolation was that he'd assured Isobel of her personal safety while on board his ship. Judging by his purposeful glance at Sir Harry, she knew that meant safety from him.

Isobel turned, and when she saw Sir Harry approaching across the deck, turned back toward the water. There was no use in trying to get away from him. He would merely follow her. At least up here, she would be under the protection of Captain Worthington.

"You should not spend so much time in the sun, my dear," Sir Harry said. "It will darken your freckles."

Isobel refused to look at him, replying, "Then I shall stay out in it all day, if only to displease you."

He chuckled, but there was no warmth in it. "Still bent on defying me at every turn, I see. That's alright. You'll learn soon enough. And I shall relish teaching you."

Sir Harry lifted his hand to her face and tried to stroke her cheek, but Isobel jerked her head away as if his hand were a burning iron. She glared at him, wishing the power of her hatred could kill.

"The fire in your eyes excites me, Isobel," he said dangerously. "It will make taming you even more enjoyable."

Isobel turned and faced him squarely. "You shall not extinguish the fire in me, Sir Harry. If you try, you'll be burned."

Sir Harry's eyes darkened and he came closer to her, bending his face down near hers, as he said, "You are so like your mother, Isobel, in countenance, as well as in spirit." He reached into his jacket pocket and pulled out something small. Smiling tenderly, Sir Harry held it up in front of Isobel's face.

Isobel's stomach twisted into a hideous knot when she saw that it was a miniature portrait of her mother. "What are you doing with that?" she demanded.

"I first set my sights on her, you know," Sir Harry explained. "Since your father inherited the family fortune that should have been mine, I planned to reclaim control of it through his wife...or shall I say, his *widow*."

"What are you saying?" Isobel asked, as cold fear coiled in the pit of her stomach.

Sir Harry gave a reptilian smile. "You remember the highwaymen who attacked your parents' carriage that night? I sent them," he said simply.

His voice was like a dull blade cutting open Isobel's heart with excruciating slowness. She shook her head. No, this couldn't be true!

"Shall I tell you more?" Sir Harry inquired, his voice mocking. "The plan was for the highwaymen to stop the carriage, rob it, and in the process shoot that inconvenient husband of hers—your father. Which they did. But your mother attacked one of them. During the struggle, the pistol went off. Everything would have gone according to plan if it hadn't been for your mother's stupid actions. I would have married her and we all would have lived happily ever after at Hampton Park."

"You monster!" Isobel cried. She clawed at his face, but she was no match for the man's strength. He easily grabbed her wrists and crushed them together with one hand.

"Unlike your mother, you are not going to foil my plans," he said.

"I hate you!" Isobel struggled against him. "You have taken everything that I have ever loved away from me! My parents, my guardian, and now my husband—a man that I love more than life itself."

Isobel raised her chin and stared defiantly into his coal-black eyes, seeing the displeasure there.

"But there is one thing you can never take away from me, Sir Harry," she said, "and that is love. The love that my parents gave me and I gave them, the love I feel for Beckett, and the love we've shared as man and wife. Those are moments you will never know. And they are mine—forever."

Sir Harry released her and sneered, "Cherish them, Isobel. Cherish your precious moments of love. You're right—they are yours, forever. *Just as you are mine.*"

He turned to go, but Isobel grabbed at his sleeve. "Please, let Beckett go. If it's me that you want, then no one else need suffer. I will go with you willingly, but please, please set my husband free. I beg you to do him no harm. He is innocent in all of this."

"Innocent, you say?" Sir Harry spat. "Ravenwood has taken your purity, Isobel. He has defiled my bride, and for that he will pay very dearly." He pointed up at the masts. "Tomorrow, he shall swing from the yardarm."

"No! No, please!" Isobel cried, shaking her head.

"Oh yes, and you shall watch it!" he answered, darkly. "Tomorrow at dawn, Isobel, your dear husband will be executed."

Dear Lord, Sir Harry truly was a madman.

He meant to make her a widow, and witness her husband's murder.

And Isobel had no idea how to stop it.

CHAPTER TWENTY-FIVE

Beckett squinted at the bright light that came into the brig from the doorway. He shielded his eyes and made out a tall figure standing in the doorway. It was Redbeard.

"Up an' at 'em, m'lord. Cap'n wants to see ye on deck, now," the pirate said.

"What's the occasion?" Beckett asked groggily.

"Oh, there's to be a hangin'," Redbeard replied. "Some say it's to be yours."

Beckett rose to his feet. "Mine, eh? Too bad. I always thought a hanging to be a damned inconvenient way to start the day."

Redbeard laughed, saying good naturedly, "To be sure, m'lord, to be sure. Now, don't you be givin' me no trouble, an' I'll make sure yer face stays pretty 'til ye put it through the noose, alright?"

Beckett said, "Very kind of you—ah, what is your name, if I may ask?"

"Josiah Cox, sir. First mate."

"Well, Mister Cox, it has been nice knowing you," Beckett replied.

"Been lovely knowin' ye, too, sir," Cox said. "Now, if ye don't mind, they're waitin' for ye."

Beckett stepped through the door, squinting at the light. As he walked down the passageway, his mind raced, and his heart—damn the bloody thing—pounded in his chest.

This was undoubtedly his last chance to save Isobel and himself. He would have to keep his head, find an opportunity, and grab it. It would be bloody difficult surrounded by armed pirates, but there was no choice. He had to succeed.

So many memories of Isobel whirled before him. Some he could see, and some he could only feel. They all seemed to flow together and blend into one, like the ever-changing colors of a sunset.

The silkiness of her skin, her warm cocoa-brown eyes, kissing her neck that night in the Whitcomb garden, the sound of her gasping beneath him as they made love for the first time.... The images all swirled together in his head and his heart.

Would Isobel be up on deck to watch him hang? If Sir Harry had his way, she would most certainly be there.

Beckett steeled himself as he ascended the stairs. He would find out soon enough.

"Ah, I see the guest of honor has arrived," Sir Harry said, with a thin smile.

"Beckett!" Isobel cried. Instinctively she tried to move toward him, but Sir Harry's strong hand clamped down on her shoulder and held her firm.

"Now, now, my dear," Sir Harry said. "You must stand back in order to appreciate the view."

Isobel stared helplessly at Beckett, feeling her heart ache in her chest at the sight of him. He met her gaze with his own, and though his face was pale, unshaven and thin, the intensity in his eyes touched her soul.

Dear God, help us!

Isobel turned toward Worthington, who stood nearby, and wrenched herself free from Sir Harrys grip. She ran to the captain's side, sank down onto her knees and grabbed his hand, pressing her lips to it. Tears dampened her face as she looked up into the wolf-gray eyes of the pirate lord.

"Please, I beg of you, don't let him do this!," Isobel pleaded. "Don't let him kill my husband. I would do anything to save his life. This is your ship. You can stop this."

Worthington looked down at her and pulled her to her feet. For a moment, she thought she'd seen something flicker in his eyes—compassion, or sympathy perhaps. But it only lasted a moment before it was gone.

"I am sorry, Madam," he replied coldly. "I can do nothing to help you."

"You mean you won't do anything!" Isobel spat. "You are a coward, sir—of the first order. I'm sure you are the only pirate in the world who is afraid to stand up to the likes of Sir Harry Lennox."

"I am not afraid of anything, madam," Worthington replied, raising an eyebrow in warning. "Except of course, ruining my reputation—which I have no intention of doing by interfering with a paying customer. Not for you, not for your husband."

"Then I will pray for your soul, Captain, for it is surely destined for hell," she replied.

"You do that," Worthington said, unfazed. He gave the order to the men holding Beckett. "String him up."

Isobel looked about in desperation. Could no one help her?

Captain Black crouched on the nearby railing. His green eyes watched her, calmly.

"Wait," Sir Harry said.

As he walked toward her, Isobel thought he reminded her of a snake...so smooth, so dark and menacing.

"Perhaps my future bride has a point," he said. "I am, after all, not without some feeling. I see no reason why you shouldn't be allowed to say goodbye to your first husband, Isobel. I know I would enjoy seeing it. The tears, the final kiss...oh, I do love romance."

Isobel stared at him, horrified, but unable to resist the promise of kissing Beckett for one last time. She nodded mutely.

"Shall we, then?" Sir Harry grabbed her arm and yanked her toward where Beckett stood, surrounded by pirates.

Sir Harry pulled her up in front of Beckett, so she stood just out of reach. Her eyes devoured the sight of him, trying to memorize every line, every curve of Beckett's face. She tried to get closer to him, but Sir Harry jerked her back.

"But you said we could have one last kiss," Isobel pleaded.

"I lied," Sir Harry said.

"Get your hands off her, you bastard," Beckett growled.

"You mean these hands, Ravenwood?" Sir Harry asked, sliding his palms over Isobel's shoulders as he pulled her back against him. "You mean, the ones that are going to be undressing your little wife on our wedding night, while you rot in hell?"

Beckett thrashed against the pirates who held him.

"I won't let him hurt you, Isobel—I promise you that!"

Beckett said. "Whatever happens, I'll come for you. Do you believe me?"

Isobel nodded, "I love you, Beckett."

"String him up!" Sir Harry ordered, dragging Isobel away while her husband struggled against his guards.

"Beckett!" Isobel cried out over her shoulder, trying to see him.

"Isobel," his muffled voice answered, drowned out by the scuffle.

"Get him up there, now!" Sir Harry barked.

Isobel watched in horror as the pirates dragged Beckett toward the side of the boat, where the noose hung off the yard-arm and swung mockingly in the breeze.

Isobel stood transfixed, unable to speak. She wanted to turn her face away from the scene she was about to witness, but she couldn't abandon Beckett.

"For goodness' sake, Ravenwood," Sir Harry complained, "at least have the decency to put your head in the noose like a gentleman."

Something snapped in Isobel, then. White hot anger filled her veins and she shoved Sir Harry as hard as she could, catching him off-guard. He stumbled sideways and fell against one of the heavy cannons, clutching his arm and yowling in pain as he landed on the deck.

She spun around to do more damage, but as she turned, Isobel's heart leapt at what she saw.

Beckett was breaking free of his captors!

While two of Worthington's men tried to force his head through the noose, Beckett grabbed one of their daggers. It now flashed before him, glinting in the early morning light as he fought against the remaining guard.

But the tide was turning yet again.

Soon five, then six armed pirates swarmed around Beckett. Isobel gasped as Beckett climbed up the rigging like a monkey, his dagger swishing through the air behind him as the cutthroats clambered after him in pursuit. The clanging of blade on blade rang out from above and made an eerie music for this strange dance.

"Damnation!" Sir Harry growled from beside Isobel, cradling his injured arm as he watched the action high above, along with the rest of those on deck.

Isobel ignored him. Her heart, her entire being was too fixed on the deadly ballet going on above to pay Sir Harry any attention now.

Beckett stopped climbing, desperately fighting off the closest of the pirates. He kicked out and the man went flying off the rigging, falling to the deck below. The pirate landed with a great thud, then lay inert. Another pirate closed in on Beckett and their blades clashed anew.

Then, Beckett ducked to avoid a blow and lost his hold, falling through the air. Isobel screamed as he hit the water.

Isobel ran to the side, joined by the entire crew. Frantically, she scanned the water for sign of him, but saw nothing.

"Beckett! Beckett!" she cried.

A hand grabbed her arm and tried to pull her away, but she fought against it.

"Where is he?" she said desperately. "I can't see him!"

Worthington's voice spoke from behind her, and she realized it was his hand that gripped her arm. He peered over the side down into the water.

"He's gone, my lady," the captain answered.

"No!" Isobel shook her head, refusing to believe.

"A fall from that height...," Worthington explained, "he went straight down. Or broke his neck when he hit the water. Your husband is dead."

"No. I don't believe it" Isobel said. "I won't believe it!"

Worthington shook his head. "He is gone, madam."

"Well, I certainly hope so," Sir Harry said, finally. "Though I must say, I am not pleased with the way it went. I wanted to watch Ravenwood dance at the end of that rope. But, as you say, Worthington, dead is dead. Now, we can be married, my dear."

Isobel, unable to speak, turned and looked out at the deep water that surrounded the boat.

The idea that Beckett was gone—it was too painful to even think about. Instead, she would stare out at the water, looking for a glimpse of him. She would not think about Sir Harry or his diabolical plans.

The truth was, she didn't care anymore. If Beckett was dead, then so was her heart. Sir Harry could do whatever he wanted to her, and none of it would matter.

But she wouldn't think about that now. She couldn't.

She wiped away the tears that stained her face. The thought of losing Beckett forever chilled her so completely, she began to shake, her teeth chattering noisily. She had lost so much already...how could she bear to have lost the only man she would ever love, as well?

Not knowing what else to do, Isobel stared down into the cold blue water and prayed.

CHAPTER TWENTY-SIX

Isobel stood on the deck, watching the pirates preparing to drop anchor. The gulls overhead seemed to be speaking for her as they cried out in a haunting lament to the skies above.

It was fitting music for this day.

The *Revenge* bustled with activity as it prepared to unload both its passengers and its smuggled cargo. It had hidden itself in a secluded cove that would have been dangerous for any other ship to enter. But it was obviously a spot well-known to the pirate crew.

Feeling a presence nearby, Isobel turned to see the cool stare of Captain Worthington regarding her. He held Captain Black in one arm and extended the hand of the other. She made no move to take it.

He raised a brow, acknowledging the snub. "Though you may not believe it, I wish you well, Lady Ravenwood," he said. "You would have made a splendid pirate, I think. If you are ever in need of employment, perhaps I could find a place for you on my ship."

"Is that intended as a compliment?" she asked.

"It was, indeed," Worthington replied.

"If you truly want me as a member of your crew, throw Sir Harry overboard," Isobel said. "Then I'll be happy to join you."

Worthington chuckled, saying, "A noble attempt, my lady, but double-crossing my paying customers would have a negative effect on my business."

"Ah, yes, your business," she said. "Forgive me if I see my husband's life as rather more important than any financial transaction could be."

He stroked Captain Black's fur, and replied, "I am a pirate, after all. It's what I do. And though I know circumstances have made it difficult for us to be friends at the moment, I admire your indomitable spirit. You have the survival instincts of a fox, Lady Ravenwood. You're clever, and you know when to stay hidden and when to run."

"Sometimes the fox gets caught," she said.

"True," he answered. "But whatever happens, the fox never gives up. That is how it escapes the hunters."

"Are you suggesting I can do the same?" she asked, confused by Worthington's amiable advice. What was he getting at?

"I am suggesting, dear lady, that you can do anything you put your mind to," Worthington said.

Isobel she gazed out over the forbidding sea, and said, "If only that were true, yet none of us have the power to turn back time. If I did, I find a way to save my husband's life. Yet such a thing is impossible."

"Is it?" he asked.

She regarded him quizzically. "You are talking about the fantastical, Captain. Such a power does not exist."

"My lady," he continued, "I have sailed the world over many times, and in my travels, I have seen many strange, mystical things—things that defied explanation, or things that should not exist. For instance, there are those who say mermaids are a figment of the imagination, yet I have seen them in these very waters."

"Mermaids?" she asked. "Indeed, Captain."

What game was he playing at now? The man was becoming as mad as Sir Harry Lennox.

"There are many stories of mermaids here in Diamond Cove," he replied, "and *mermen*, too. I should keep my eyes open, if I were you, Lady Ravenwood. One never knows what one might find in these waters."

What was the man trying to say? Was he trying to give her false hope? Or did he know something about Beckett's fate?

Sir Harry appeared on deck, fussing with the lapels of coat. As he approached Isobel and Worthington, she felt her stomach sink like a stone.

This was it, then.

"Coaching my bride-to-be in the tricks of your pirate trade, Worthington?" Sir Harry asked crossly.

"Oh no, Lennox, she needs no coaching from me," the captain replied with a mocking smile.

"You think to laugh at me, do you?" Sir Harry said, grabbing Isobel's arm and pulling her roughly beside him. "Believe me, Captain, I will have the last laugh...on all of you."

Captain Black hissed at Sir Harry, but Worthington held the animal fast. Startled, Sir Harry took a step back.

Worthington stared him down, saying, "To quote Mr. Shakespeare, 'A fool thinks himself to be wise, but a wise man knows himself to be a fool.' I wish you luck, Sir Harry, as you will most likely need it."

With that, the man turned away and walked to the open cargo hold to oversee the unloading of smuggled goods into their landing boats.

Sir Harry glared after the pirate captain, then turned his attention to Isobel.

He pulled her close to him so that her breasts were pressed uncomfortably against his chest. Instinctively, she turned her head away from his leering face, but he grabbed her chin and forced her to meet his dark, dangerous eyes.

"I shall be your husband now, as I was meant to be," he said. "You will see that no man could ever love you as much as I do, Isobel. Soon...you will see exactly how much I love you."

He pulled her head towards his and she tried to squirm away, but he was too strong, and his vile lips covered hers as he forcibly kissed her. Isobel felt bile rising in her throat.

What would she do? How would she fight him off when they reached Hampton Park and he tried to claim her body?

"That was only a taste, my love," Sir Harry said, releasing her. "I shall show you much more tonight in our chamber. After you've been taught a lesson for cuckolding me, of course." He touched her cheek. "Until tonight, then."

Cold fear washed over her heart in icy waves as she pondered her fate with Sir Harry. She would be his prisoner...he would use and abuse her in any way he wanted.

As Sir Harry led her toward the side of the ship, a gull swooped down from above, having apparently decided to use Sir Harry's head for target practice. Lennox stood stunned for a few moments, then scowling, he gingerly reached up a hand to investigate what had landed on his head. His face seemed to curl inward as he grimaced in distaste.

"Bloody hell!" Sir Harry howled. "Damned ignorant bastards, those disgusting birds." He pulled out his handkerchief to mop at his head.

Isobel found herself laughing, along with the pirate crew. The scene lifted her spirits, as surely the gull had been sent by the Lord Himself to give her a sign.

"Alright, the theatricals are over," Sir Harry said, crossly. "Isobel, get down that ladder and into the boat. It's time to get off this bloody scow."

Captain Worthington sent Lennox a withering look.

With no other choice, Isobel took a deep breath and descended the ladder. If she hoped Worthington would intervene at the last moment, she was disappointed.

Stepping into the boat, Isobel sat silently while Sir Harry descended the rope ladder. The two pirates he had hired sat in the middle, each one holding an oar. Soon, her abductor took his seat and the boat began to move through the water towards shore.

For a moment, she had the urge to jump overboard and try to swim to shore herself. She knew it would be impossible—the men would be able to pick her up very quickly, if she didn't drown first.

No, she would not go willingly to her death. She must stay alive. There might be an opportunity for escape after they reached Hampton Park. She had grown up there, and knew all sorts of hidden passages that she doubted Sir Harry would. One way or another, she would escape this madman.

Until then, she would think of nothing but Beckett.

Hampton Park loomed dark and foreboding in the distance. The yellow moon hung low and eerily above the house as the carriage rattled over the bumpy road. This was certainly not the homecoming Isobel had hoped for.

She regarded Sir Harry across from her in the dark cab. He stared at her, and she saw his eyes flash in the dim light from the lanterns that bobbed outside the windows.

The man looked like the devil himself.

Dear Lord, was this truly happening?

Would this blackguard finally be victorious in his utter destruction of her and her family? Obviously, Sir Harry thought so. He'd sent word ahead to rouse the parson from his sleep to be ready to marry them when they arrived. Then they would finally enjoy their wedding night, he'd sneered.

Just the thought of it made her sick with fear. How could she let Sir Harry touch her as Beckett had done? How would she survive something so horrible, with the memories of her husband's sweet touch swirling in her head and mocking her as this villain defiled her body?

Sir Harry leaned forward and took her face in his hands. Isobel stiffened, trying to keep calm, but the touch of his skin made her want to retch. He brought his face closer, trying to cover her mouth with his own. Isobel struggled against him, pounding his chest with her fists in a vain attempt at freedom.

"Stop it, Isobel!" Sir Harry barked. "You can't escape, do you understand? You are mine, now. Ravenwood is dead. Forget him."

"I can't forget him," she cried. "I won't!"

"Yes you will, little wife," he said, maliciously. "I will drive his memory from your head and your heart. I will drive him out of your body with my own. Beginning tonight."

Sir Harry pulled at his neck cloth and untied the elaborate bow. "It seems you need to be trussed up, my dear. I suppose it's just as well that you develop a liking for such things now."

He yanked her arms in front of her, easily binding her wrists with the strong silk. Isobel struggled, but it was futile. He was much too strong for her.

"There," Sir Harry huffed. "Now, you shall stay put until we reach Hampton Park. And no more nonsense, Isobel. Make no mistake, you will learn to obey me."

Isobel kept her face turned away from him and stared out the window. Her heart ached unbearably, her stomach seized in dread. Escape would be impossible, now. He would be watching her every move.

She heard a little thump on the roof of the carriage, and then a faint yowling sound. Were they to be attacked by creatures of the night as well? Nothing would surprise her on this terrible journey.

How could she face a life as Sir Harry's plaything? How could she bear the brutality that he would surely inflict on her for his own corrupt pleasure? If she knew Beckett was alive, she could endure any suffering, if there was any chance they would be reunited.

But without that hope, what was there to live for? No one had seen Beckett resurface after he'd fallen into the water. Everyone considered him dead.

Part of her refused to believe that he was really gone. Was it just a refusal to accept her grief, or could Beckett be alive? Could he have made it to shore on his own after falling from the rigging?

Or was her bleak fate with Sir Harry making her fall into madness?

CHAPTER TWENTY-SEVEN

Beckett sat on the damp ground, thankful that his trousers had already been ruined from his plunge into the ocean. It was one less thing he had to worry about.

After the pirates had fished him out of the water, they'd landed their rowboat on shore and held him prisoner there. He'd been looking down the barrel of a pistol for at least a half-hour, since. None of the pirates would tell him why they'd rescued him, only that he would be wise not to give them any trouble.

Since the odds were against him, he obeyed their orders—for the present. The fact remained that his wife was in the clutches of a despicable villain and that he was determined to rescue her.

Not even an armed band of pirates would keep him from doing that.

Another boat appeared out of the darkness. As it neared shore, the pirates leaped out and dragged the boat up onto the sand.

Beckett watched as the men approached. Instantly, he recognized the white-haired captain at the fore.

"Lord Ravenwood," Captain Worthington said, his teeth glinting in the golden moonlight, "may I be the first to congratulate you on cheating the Grim Reaper."

"Thank you, Captain," Beckett said. "I'm rather delighted by it, myself. I must thank your men here for fishing me out of the drink and keeping me company. And while I would love to stay and chat, I'm afraid I have rather important business to attend to."

"As do I, my lord," Worthington replied. "Some of it concerns you, and of course your lovely wife."

"Save your breath," Beckett warned. "If you plan to kill me now, I wish you luck. Your men may have me outnumbered, but I will most certainly be taking you with me."

"My dear Lord Ravenwood, you misunderstand," the captain said smoothly. "I came to offer my help, for a price of course." He motioned for the pirate guarding Beckett to lower his pistol.

Beckett stood slowly, considering the man's words. "Go on."

"My crew and I would be happy to help rescue Lady Ravenwood," he said, "in exchange for a generous reward."

"Why the change of heart?" Beckett asked. "You were willing enough to let me hang. Now you want to play the gallant hero?"

"Lennox hired me to do a job," he replied. "It was nothing personal, I assure you. Now that I have fulfilled my obligations to him, I am free to offer my services to whomever can pay."

Beckett considered the man's offer. It would certainly be useful to have Worthington and his men along. Money was no object for him, at least now.

"You have a deal, Worthington," Beckett said. "Shall we

say, a thousand pounds to your bankers after we safely retrieve my wife?"

They stepped forward and sealed their agreement with a firm handshake.

"Pleasure doing business with you," Worthington said with a nod. "I have a carriage waiting up the road, and the horses are fresh. We'll be at Hampton Park before long, I'll wager."

"Lennox will be surprised to see you again," Beckett said, following Worthington to the roadway. "Not to mention *me*."

"So he should," Worthington said, chuckling. "He's an odious excuse for a man."

"He is, at that," Beckett agreed, getting into the waiting carriage. "Now let's go and stop him before he puts his odious hands upon my wife."

"Just stand there and perform the marriage, you idiot!" Sir Harry snapped at the parson, who seemed a trifle uneasy about the scene unfolding in the huge drawing room.

"Please!" Isobel implored. "You must help me. I am here against my will. I do not wish to marry this man!"

The little cleric eyed Isobel with uncertainty, then addressed her captor. "Forgive me, Sir Harry, but it would seem that the bride is voicing some objection."

"Don't listen to her, Parson," Sir Harry said, dismissively. "She is nervous, that's all."

"I'm not nervous," Isobel protested. "I'm mortally opposed to being in the same room with this man, let alone becoming his wife. I'd rather be fed to an ill-tempered tiger."

The parson frowned.

"A lovers quarrel," Sir Harry explained.

"It is not a lover's quarrel, sir," Isobel countered. "He has me here against my will." She raised her wrists so the parson could see her bonds.

"Oh, my," he said, glancing at Sir Harry. "It is most unusual for the bride to be bound in such a way, my good man. Most unusual, indeed."

Sir Harry glared at the parson with a dangerous expression, and said, "My fiancee has just suffered a great loss. She has been beside herself with grief. The doctor has ordered her to be bound thus for her own protection."

"That is not true!" Isobel cried.

"You see?" Sir Harry said. "She is beside herself, as I explained. Not that it is any of your concern. I wish to marry the girl, to bring some joy back into her life. Surely, you will allow me to do that by marrying us sometime between now and the next century?"

"Oh, yes." The parson nodded, still seeming unsure. "Of course. The poor girl. Where was I, then?"

"You weren't anywhere!" Sir Harry spat. "You haven't even started."

"Oh...of course. Now, let's see," the parson said, slowly turning the pages.

Isobel looked away. It was no use. This country preacher would not help her. He would do as Sir Harry ordered, no matter what she said.

"Oh, give me that, you buffoon!" Sir Harry said, grabbing the book and flipping through the pages. "Here! Now, read it."

The two pirates Sir Harry hired stood by the wall, acting as witnesses. Stranger bridesmaids she had never seen.

As Isobel waited for the parson to say the words that would seal her fate, she absently looked around the drawing room. This place, where she had enjoyed so many quiet evenings with her parents, would now be the setting of a nightmare.

Suddenly, something caught her eye in the corner of the room...a movement in the shadows. Was she imagining things?

"Ahem," the parson said, clearing his throat. "Dearly beloved, we are gathered here, today..."

The parson stared at something behind them, his expression changing quickly from confusion to fearful disbelief.

"Oh, what on earth is the matter, now?" Sir Harry demanded.

"How unkind of you," a familiar voice said from the doorway, "not to invite a man to his wife's wedding."

Isobel turned, slowly.

Beckett.

Alive!

And standing in the doorway with Worthington and his pirates.

"You!" Sir Harry hissed, staring in shock.

"Yes, me, Lennox," Beckett said, stepping fully into the room, his powerful frame poised for action. "Very much alive, and very intent on reclaiming my wife, if you please. And even if you don't please."

Isobel felt life pouring back into her heart, coursing through her veins in a flood of joy.

Beckett was alive! And though it seemed impossible, he had come for her as he'd promised.

Isobel moved toward her husband, but Sir Harry grabbed her arm and whirled her in front of him. He whipped something off the table beside them. With one hand, he covered her mouth and with the other he held a letter-opener poised to stab her throat.

Beckett aimed a pistol at her tormentor, regarding him with ice-blue eyes. "Let her go, Lennox."

Sir Harry backed toward the wall, taking Isobel with him.

"I said release her," her husband ordered, his voice commanding. "There's nowhere for you to go, Lennox. There is only one exit to this room and as you can see, it has been blocked. You're surrounded and outnumbered. You can't win."

Sir Harry's mouth curved into a menacing grin as he said, "I may be surrounded and outnumbered, Ravenwood, but I'm still going to win. If I can't have Isobel, no one will—including you!"

Sir Harry pushed back against the wall and the secret door opened. He pulled Isobel through and shut the portal behind them, bolting it quickly. They were plunged into pitch blackness.

Isobel heard pounding on the door and Beckett's muffled voice fading away as Sir Harry dragged her through the dark, narrow corridor. She struggled and kicked at him but he grabbed the bonds that tied her wrists and pulled her behind him. Isobel was forced to keep up or be dragged across the ground.

"You've lost, Sir Harry. Do you hear?" Isobel said, trying to catch her breath. "You've lost!"

He stopped short and Isobel slammed into him. In the pitch blackness, she heard his awful, menacing voice as his hand encircled her throat. He pushed her up against the wall.

"I have lost nothing!" he spat. "It is not yet over, I assure you. Just because your husband has risen from the grave doesn't mean he can't go back there just as quickly. The detestable man is like a cat with nine lives! But I assure you, my darling bride, his luck is about to run out."

Isobel gasped as she felt something furry move past her leg. A rat? Oh, what did it matter when she was in the hands of a madman?

Sir Harry took hold of her bonds again.

A strange, otherworldly cry echoed through the passageway, and Sir Harry yelled in surprise.

Isobel shrank back against the wall, paralyzed with fear.

But something was attacking Sir Harry. He cried out for help, and she heard his arms flapping uselessly as he tried to fight off his assailant.

Isobel could hear the mysterious presence hissing as it bounced off the walls near her. But it never touched her—it only seemed to want Sir Harry. He screamed pitifully for mercy. From the sound of it he was being ripped to shreds.

The attack continued. Sir Harry cried out, each sound more desperate than the last. Finally, she heard him sink to the ground, whimpering like a wounded animal, and the assault was over.

Would she be next?

Isobel stood against the wall, unable to move.

"Isobel?" she heard Beckett's muffled voice call from far away.

"Here! I'm here, Beckett!" she cried.

"I'm coming, Isobel," he said, the sound of his voice growing closer.

She only hoped the ferocious creature wouldn't attack her before Beckett arrived. To be safe, she crept further away from where Sir Harry lay.

Light bounced across the floor, her eyes searching the shadows. And then—

Beckett.

His strong arms circled around her and held her close, finally putting an end to the nightmare.

Isobel heard boots trample by in the dark corridor and

knew it was the pirates going to see to Sir Harry. But she didn't care.

She didn't care about anything but this moment, and this man, and the love that threatened to burst her heart open with its beautiful power.

"I—I feared you were dead," she whispered, as tears filled her eyes.

Beckett held her in front of him, and she stared through the lamplight into the brightest, bluest, most beautiful eyes she had ever seen.

"I would have been as good as dead, if I hadn't found you again, Isobel," he said.

Beckett's warm mouth covered hers and he kissed her with such fierce passion, Isobel wondered fleetingly if they might shock the pirates. But she didn't care.

She was in the arms of the man she loved, and nothing else mattered.

Nothing ever would.

"Ahem," someone said.

Beckett broke the kiss and they both looked at Worthington, who stood with arms folded and an amused grin on his face. "My apologies for interrupting your reunion, Ravenwood. My lady. But there is something I think you should see," he said, moving to where Sir Harry was lying.

They came closer, and Isobel couldn't stop a gasp from escaping her.

Sir Harry lay on his side, seemingly unconscious. His clothes were torn and bloodstains marred his shirt. His face and hands were covered in scratches and cuts, all of them bleeding. It looked as if someone had taken a knife to him.

Behind him, sitting just in the shadows, was a cat...calmly cleaning its paws.

"Captain Black," Isobel exclaimed. "But how?"

Beckett shook his head, saying, "I'm certainly glad he turned up, though I have no idea how he did."

"He must have hitched a ride on Lennox's carriage," Worthington said. "After all, that cat does have a fondness for you, Lady Ravenwood."

At that, Captain Black looked up at his audience. His green eyes glowed, and as he walked toward Isobel, she could see bloodstains on some of the white patches of his fur. He stopped at her feet and meowed up at her. Isobel lifted him in her arms and snuggled him close.

"Captain Mayfield was right—you did protect me," Isobel said, scratching his ears in gratitude. The cat purred and closed his eyes.

"Thanks for looking after her, old boy," Beckett said, reaching over and stroked the cat, too.

Isobel looked down at Sir Harry, then at Worthington. "Is he—?"

"Dead?" Worthington replied. "No, the silly sap just fainted from the shock of it all. His wounds, while painful, are unfortunately not fatal. Still, he'll have some nice scars. Ought to fit right in with the lads at Newgate. I have connections that will ensure Sir Harry is taken into custody. I must admit, I never liked the man."

"Yet you did his bidding onboard ship," Isobel countered. "You kidnapped us because of him!"

"That I did, Lady Ravenwood," the captain agreed, "but as I explained to you, it was a business transaction. I had nothing personal against you or your husband. That is why I helped him to rescue you now."

"Another business transaction?" Isobel asked, warily.

"Yes, Isobel," Beckett said.

"And what was the price?"

Beckett looked at her with a serious expression. "A thousand pounds. I thought it quite steep, myself—"

"What?" Isobel exclaimed.

Beckett pulled her close, saying, "I'm teasing. I would have given up my entire fortune, my dear, if that was what Worthington had asked."

"Damn me," Worthington said, chuckling, "if only I'd known! Ah, well, I still made a tidy profit. It should cover the ships repairs."

He reached for Captain Black, and Isobel reluctantly handed him over.

"Now, you and your husband must be tired," Worthington said. "You should get yourselves home. I and my men will take care of everything here, including Sir Harry."

"But this is Isobel's family home," Beckett said, regarding her with concerned eyes. "Perhaps you want to stay here for the night?"

"No, Beckett, it is ours, now," she replied. "But I don't want to stay here. Let us go to Covington Place."

Beckett kissed the top of her head. "I would like that very much indeed. My wife and I are going home. Might I hire two of your men to drive us?" he asked Worthington.

The captain shook Beckett's hand, saying, "Of course. Mr. Evandale and Mr. Martin will be happy to escort you. Best of luck to you, Ravenwood. My lady." He kissed Isobel's hand.

Isobel took one last look at Captain Black, then she and Beckett headed out of the passageway. Soon they were rumbling down the road, away from Sir Harry and the nightmare that had almost come to pass.

But the nightmare wasn't over yet. There was still the false murder charge hanging over her head in London. Would Palmerston proceed with prosecuting her?

Oh, she couldn't think about that, now. She wouldn't think about it!

Beckett was alive. He was beside her, warm and strong and alive. She would let nothing else spoil this moment.

Beckett tipped her chin up towards him. His face looked unbearably handsome in the yellow moonlight.

"Tell me something, wife," he whispered.

"Yes?" She thrilled at the sound of his husky voice.

"Have you ever made love in a carriage?"

CHAPTER TWENTY-EIGHT

Beckett knelt on the floor of the carriage before her, his eyes glowing like jewels. His hands reached up and slid her dress down over her shoulders.

Slowly, with exquisite control, he ran his hands over her naked breasts. Isobel heard her own intake of breath as he caressed her with deft fingers.

His touch was maddeningly light as his fingertips drew circles around the sensitive pink tips. With each thumb, he teased the hard peaks until Isobel heard herself gasping. And all the while, she stared at him, at this beautiful man's face with blue eyes that seared her like the heat of the sun.

Suddenly, his hands moved to the hem of her skirt. Beckett stopped for a moment, and the wicked promise in his eyes was almost too much for Isobel to bear. He smiled and pushed her skirt up over her knees. His hands explored her thighs, and Isobel arched her back and spread her legs, wanting so much for him to touch her. He pulled off her undergarments and threw them over his shoulder.

Beckett leaned forward and captured her mouth in a burning kiss while his hands stroked between her legs. Isobel felt herself becoming slick with heat, and when his fingers went inside her she moaned and gripped his shoulder.

"I want to worship you," he whispered in her ear, and it sent shivers down her spine.

Beckett knelt back and dipped his head to kiss her inner thigh. He teased her with lips and tongue, and she jolted as his warm, wet tongue delved between her legs.

He raised his head and looked up at her. "It's alright, Isobel. Just lie back and let your husband love you."

His words sent a bittersweet pain through her heart.

The man she loved had come back to her alive...but would he, *could* he ever love her in return? He had told her before that such emotion was impossible for him.

If only she could keep her feelings at bay when he made love to her, and accept their coupling as pure physical sensation. But that was much more difficult than it seemed.

She closed her eyes as his mouth pleasured her. The sensation was so exquisite, so intense, she could never have imagined such beautiful wickedness. It was frighteningly intimate, almost too much to bear. But she would let him take her down this unknown road, for she was powerless to do anything else.

Beckett moved his mouth with a smooth rhythm, Isobel's breath quickened. Warmth spread through her body with maddening slowness, like cream travelling through coffee.

She spread her legs wider, her hands reaching down and holding his head as he worked her with his tongue. He lifted her legs over his shoulders. Isobel heard herself gasping. It sounded as if she were in terrible pain, so desperate was her response.

Two of his fingers slipped inside her and she thought she would lose her mind—the double pleasure was unbearable. She wanted to beg him to stop, but words were impossible.

Isobel moaned loudly and rocked her hips against his hand and mouth. Her head thrashed from side to side against the back of the seat. She bit her lip to keep from screaming.

Then, a mind-numbing pleasure passed through every fiber of her body. She felt it everywhere, in her legs, her arms, even her fingertips. It emptied her and yet filled her completely.

Beckett pulled his head away and she regarded him through half-lidded eyes. He unfastened his trousers and slid them down over his hips. Then he reached forward and lifted her towards him. He sat back on the opposite seat and lowered her down onto the hardness between his legs.

Instinctively, she wrapped her legs around his waist. His hands cupped her buttocks, his mouth joining with hers as their bodies moved together.

Isobel circled her arms around his neck as he pumped into her. She closed her eyes and threw her head back as the pleasure of him filled her completely. Then she felt it coming again, that speeding, heady flood that would wash her away so completely.

Beckett groaned and pounded into her with a blinding rhythm. He moaned as he gripped her buttocks and thrust harder.

Isobel felt lightness overtake her—as though she were weightless and couldn't feel her body anymore. She cried out, bursting through glorious waves of pleasure yet again.

Beckett groaned and crushed her to him, burying his face in her shoulder as he, too, found release.

They remained that way for awhile, unable to move. Then Beckett kissed her sweetly, tenderly, and looked into her eyes. He brushed the stray hair away from her eyes and stroked her face.

"You never answered my question, Isobel," he said.

"What question?" she asked, dazedly.

"Have you ever made love in a carriage?"

She smiled, and said, "Oh, yes—I have."

"And how was it?" he pressed.

"Absolutely incredible," she answered, truthfully.

"I must say, that is good news," Beckett said. "Perhaps you'll want to go for more carriage rides, all about London. Perhaps we'll go through Hyde Park at five o'clock on a Saturday, and draw the curtains."

"We couldn't!" she said, giggling.

"We couldn't draw the curtains?" he asked. "Wicked woman. Then everyone would see."

"No," she replied, though she knew he was teasing her. "We couldn't do *that* riding around Hyde Park...could we?"

Beckett pulled her to him and kissed her so passionately, she thought he might make love to her again, right there.

"We shall see," he said. "Now, we should get ourselves dressed. We'll be entering the outskirts of London soon. And while I am entranced with your current state of dishabille, I'm afraid I'd rather not share the sight with Hartley when he opens the door."

Isobel laughed as he threw her undergarments at her head. When she was once again presentable, Isobel sat back on the seat and Beckett joined her. He encircled her with his arms and she leaned her head back against his chest. Though she hadn't meant to, relief and happiness overwhelmed her and she promptly dozed off.

Isobel rolled over and pulled the covers higher over her

head, refusing to let the troubles of the world disturb her. She was certain that she could stay in this bed forever. It was so warm and soft. And yet, there was a niggling feeling in the back of her mind. Where was she?

Isobel sat upright in the bed and realized she was naked. Oh, yes. She was in Beckett's bed in the townhouse in Covington Place, exactly where this adventure had started.

But she didn't remember coming into the town-house, let alone Beckett's bedroom. The last thing she remembered, she'd started to doze off in her husband's arms as they neared London. Could she have been asleep all this time?

A knock sounded at the door, and Isobel pulled the sheet up to cover her naked breasts. A pair of bright blue eyes peeked around the door. They belonged to the most handsome man she had ever seen. Her heart did a flip-flop, and she smiled as her husband entered the room. Close on his heels was the most handsome dog she had ever seen.

"Monty!" She held her arms out to the dog as he bounded over to the bed, his great pink tongue lolling in his excited rush to see her. The shaggy brown dog skidded to a halt just before crashing into the bed, and plunked his rump down obediently, resting his chin on the coverlet.

"Good heavens, wife, I could have had Hartley with me instead of Monty," he said, pointing at her naked shoulders and cringed in mock horror.

"But you didn't," Isobel replied, scratching the dog's ears as the animal gazed at her with a look of unadulterated devotion. "Besides, I seem to have a strange habit of waking in your bed, wearing not even a stitch of clothing. Have I been asleep since the carriage?"

Beckett sat next to her on the other side of the bed and

leaned over to kiss her as he absently fondled a breast. "Yes. I carried you in and put you to bed. Rather like the first night we met. Only last night I climbed in beside you in a most premeditated manner. Then I joined you in dreamland. It's no wonder we slept so soundly. We'd had a bit of an exhausting day, I think."

"Oh, Beckett, is it true?" she asked. "Is Sir Harry really out of our lives?"

"Yes, Isobel," he replied. "I promise that no one will ever hurt you or take you away from me again."

"But what about Lord Palmerston?"

He put his hand to her lips, saying, "We shall talk about that later. Now you must get dressed. Alfred is due at any moment. Unless you prefer to entertain guests in all your natural glory."

"I shall reserve such wicked pleasures for my husband only," she said, flirtatiously.

He grinned, saying, "Perhaps I shall take you up on it tonight. I must confess, I have an urge to see you play the piano-forte thus."

Isobel laughed and pushed him away.

A knock sounded at the door, followed by Hartley's voice. "Lord Weston downstairs to see you, m'lord."

"Yes, Hartley, I'll be down directly," Beckett answered, ring from the bed and heading for the door. Monty obediently followed. "Come down as soon as you're dressed. Oh, and there's something I've been meaning to tell you. Remind me, will you?"

Isobel nodded and watched them leave. She wondered at his words. Whatever he had to say to her, she would find out soon enough.

Isobel threw the covers back and walked to the washstand. Quickly she bathed and dressed. She chose a simple gown the same blue as Beckett's eyes. And as she headed downstairs, she thought to herself, there was one subject she would not bring up.

Since they'd been reunited, she'd been careful not to speak of love. Certainly, they had made love in the carriage, and they had made love before—but it was only the physical relations between husband and wife. She would not confuse it with real love.

It was enough, Isobel had decided, that she loved him. Though she would not speak of it, she would know that in her heart. And Beckett had an affection for her, even if he couldn't truly love her.

She had so much to be thankful for. Beckett was alive, and Sir Harry was out of their lives. That alone was more than she could have hoped for, only a day ago.

Descending the staircase, she felt as she had on that first morning, hearing Beckett and Alfred talking and joking in the salon, and Caesar squawking noisily along with them. But, no—then she had been afraid. This time, she had nothing to fear.

Isobel entered the salon, and Alfred quickly crossed the room to greet her. Opening his arms, he embraced Isobel and kissed her cheek.

"My dearest Lady Ravenwood, Beckett has been telling me about your adventure," he said. "I must say, I can scarcely believe it."

"Believe it! Believe it!" Caesar shrieked from his cage.

"Oh, Caesar—really," Beckett admonished.

Monty barked his own disapproval at his feathered friend. Isobel laughed as the bird ignored his master and squawking.

"Nor can I, Alfred," she answered. "Only yesterday, I was Sir Harry's prisoner and I feared that Beckett was dead. Now I am here at my husband's side where I belong."

"And what of Sir Harry?" Alfred asked. "As I was telling Beckett, I acquired heaps of incriminating evidence against him while you were in Barbados. Blackmail, bribery, smuggling, swindling—I'm afraid the man is as dirty as a dung-heap. Where is he? Has he been taken off to the magistrate?"

"No," Beckett replied, reaching for a note on the table. "This came while you were sleeping, my dear. I thought you and Alfred would like to hear it."

Beckett opened it and began to read aloud as Isobel looked on.

"Lord Ravenwood,

I write to you as the Revenge prepares to set sail for Jamaica. I hope you and your wife are well.

Sir Harry Lennox is dead. He was shot while trying to escape from Newgate. Fortunately, no one else was hurt in the escape attempt.

While he was in my custody, I was able to "persuade" Lennox to make a full confession regarding the murder of Edward Langley, the kidnapping of both you and your wife, and his manipulation of Lord Palmerston; a signed copy of which is attached. I will keep the other copy in a very safe place.

With Sir Harry's death, you and your wife are finally free.

Sincerely Yours,
Captain Richard Worthington
P.S. Captain Black sends his regards."

Isobel let out her breath, though she hadn't realized she'd been holding it in.

Beckett pulled her close and kissed the back of her hand. "You're safe, my dear. Lennox can never hurt you again."

Alfred reached for the letter. He looked over the confession and seemed satisfied, then said, "Now that Lennox is dead, I should think the trumped-up murder charge against Isobel will be dropped."

"I daresay it will," Beckett agreed. "He was the one pulling Lord Palmerston's strings. I'm sure Palmerston wouldn't want it known he'd accepted a bribe from Lennox in the matter."

Alfred turned to Isobel, asking, "And what do you think, my dear lady? Do you think that justice has been served?"

"Sir Harry was responsible for my parent's deaths," she said, "for the death of my guardian, and he almost took Beckett away from me. Sir Harry has earned his fate, and he has occupied more than enough time in my life. I have no more room for him—only for happiness."

Beckett regarded her proudly.

"A remarkable woman you married, Beckett," Alfred said, smiling. "No doubt about it. Oh, and I have news about someone else who won't be bothering you anymore. Cordelia."

Beckett's eyebrows rose in question.

"She's gone and married Sir Montague Tate," Alfred explained.

"Tate—why, he must be close to sixty!" Beckett said, surprised.

"He is. But Sir Montague must be in good health for he and Cordelia were—" he looked at Isobel "—forgive me, my dear, but they were caught in a disastrously close embrace at Lady Ashbrook's ball not two weeks past. I must take some responsibility, as I was the one who misinformed her about Tate's fortune. You see, Cordelia had set her cap for the Marquess of Rutledge, who, as you know, is enormously rich, and also a very good friend of mine. What could I do? I simply had to intervene."

Alfred continued, "Apparently Cordelia was beside herself after the fiasco with Tate. But what could be done? Her father wisely forced the match. They were married in a little church in Huxley Lane, and removed to Sir Montague's modest—meaning terribly small—estate in Shropshire. Can you imagine Cordelia in Shropshire with all those sheep?"

Beckett shook his head, but smiled. "No, but I wish Cordelia and Sir Montague well in their marriage. As Isobel said, we must let go of the past. Let only happiness into our hearts."

Isobel agreed. Yes, she could let go of the past. She could let go of the need to be loved by Beckett. She would let only the happiness of loving him every day into her heart, and that would be enough.

It would have to be.

CHAPTER TWENTY-NINE

Isobel stood in the doorway as Alfred prepared to leave. He and Beckett had enjoyed their morning together, and she had enjoyed watching them reunited. They were like brothers, and it warmed her heart to see her husband so happy.

"Well, I'm off," Alfred said, adjusting his hat so that it sat at precisely the perfect angle upon his head. "Now, you must promise to come for a visit. Great Aunt Withypoll is up from Broomely Park and she is driving me 'round the bend. Say you'll come. I am not averse to begging, you know."

Beckett chuckled and patted his friend on the back. "Don't worry, Alfred. We would be overjoyed to see the dear lady. I think she and Isobel will get along famously. Tomorrow evening, then."

"Splendid!" Alfred said, beaming. He bent to kiss Isobel's hand. "Until tomorrow, madam."

"Goodbye, Alfred."

The door closed behind him, leaving Beckett and Isobel alone. For a moment silence hung heavily between them, and they looked at each other as if not knowing what to say. An uneasiness gnawed at Isobel's heart and she knew she couldn't ignore it.

As they walked back into the salon, she took a deep breath and said, "You asked me to remind you that there was something you wanted to tell me."

"Oh, yes—I'm glad you reminded me," Beckett said, steering her toward the sofa. "It is quite an important matter, you see. I am convinced it will have a profound effect on our future as husband and wife."

They sat down and Isobel stared at her hands folded in her lap, braced herself for the worst.

Dear Lord, was he going to tell her he wanted to live apart? After all they'd been through?

She had to prepare herself for such a thing. If that was what Beckett wanted, she would go back to Hampton Park and live out her days there alone.

"Isobel—" Beckett gently lifted her chin up so that she looked into his eyes.

Oh, how could she bear it?

"What I want to say is," he began, "well, I have been trying to make something plain to you for quite some time, now. I tried to tell you when you came to my cell on the ship, but I was a bloody coward and I couldn't say it properly. Then I tried to say it on the deck just before they were going to hang me, but as you know, I was very rudely interrupted. But it is important, and though it is difficult to say—"

"Oh, don't say it, please," she whispered, closing her eyes. She supposed she wasn't as strong as she thought.

"Don't say it?" Beckett said, sounding perplexed. "But I really feel that I must, my dear."

"Oh, please, I beg you not to. For my sake," she replied.

"But it is for your sake that I want to say it," Beckett insisted. "And for my sake that I must. I assure you, this is much more difficult for me than it is for you, Isobel."

"I doubt it," she muttered.

Beckett touched her shoulders, turning her toward him.

Reluctantly she faced her husband, looking into the depths of his eyes as he shook her slightly.

"Isobel, you are making it increasingly impossible to tell you that I love you," he said, finally.

She stared at him in shock.

"You what?" she asked, unsure that she heard the words correctly.

He smiled at her, his eyes shining with emotion as he said, "*I love you.* That is what I've been trying to say. I love you! Irrefutably, indisputably, and most conclusively. There. What do you have to say to that?"

Isobel didn't bother trying to hold back the tears that filled her eyes. They were tears of love.

Irrefutably, and indisputably.

"Oh, Beckett!" She threw her arms around his neck and laughed and cried and hugged him tightly as he hugged her back. "I love you, too."

"I must say that I had my suspicions," he said, teasing.

She pulled away and whacked his arm, but they were both laughing. Then, he touched his lips to hers in a kiss that echoed his words, and she felt both of them flowing into it—sharing their love with open hearts.

Beckett broke the kiss and stroked her face. His eyes glowed warm and clear like the Bajan sea. "I have loved you far longer than I knew, Isobel," he explained. "I was simply too afraid of feeling anything so deep, so frighteningly pure. I'd been burnt by the flame of love with Cordelia. It seemed foolish to play with fire after that."

He continued, "But when I was in that cell, I had an

epiphany. I realized that I had been fighting a losing battle with my heart. That was why it ached so unbearably when I thought of losing you. I realized true love is a prize reserved for those willing to give themselves to it with an open heart. And I speak from experience."

"I believe I was fighting the same battle myself," she said, "knowing that I loved you more than life, and trying to convince my heart to change its mind about the matter. As you discovered, it was a fruitless attempt."

Beckett pulled her close in his arms. "Well, I, for one, am glad."

"Oh, Beckett, I'm the happiest woman on Earth!"

"Well, that's good, because I am the happiest man on earth," he replied. "And it is only fitting that the happiest man and the happiest woman should be married to each other. Now, let me take you to bed, and show you exactly how much I love you."

Isobel smiled at his devilish grin and sparkling eyes, saying, "Beckett, it's almost noon!"

He stood and swept her up into his arms, and she squealed and kicked half-heartedly.

"I know what time it is, my dear," he answered. "And by my calculations, we can make love for over three hours before Martha rings the bell for tea."

Beckett bent his head and kissed her with passion. "Unless, of course, you'd prefer that carriage ride around Hyde Park...."

Dear Reader,

Thank you for reading SEDUCING THE BRIDE, book one in the *Brides of Mayfair* series. I hope you enjoyed it and will pick up book two as well, which is Alfred's story. He has quite an interesting time when he meets his match late one night in the London Theatre District. I had a great time writing his story, and you can read on for an excerpt and more information about it.

After Alfred's story, the next book in the series is HIS COURTESAN BRIDE, and a description of that book follows as well. If you would like to be notified about future releases in this series, as well as special events and giveaways, please visit my website at www.michellemcmaster.com and sign up for my mailing list. I would love to send news to you.

I also encourage you to follow me on Bookbub at www.bookbub.com/authors/michelle-mcmaster to learn about temporary 99 cent sales on ebooks from my backlist. Just click the blue follow button, and Bookbub will send you an email to let you know.

Lastly, if you enjoy the thriller genre, please check out my *Watch Me* series, which I write under the pen name of Avery Holt. I have a separate website for my Avery novels, and you can visit Avery's website at www.averyholt.com.

Once again, thank you for reading one of my novels.

Until next time!

Michelle McMaster

Other Books in the *Brides of Mayfair Series*

TAMING THE BRIDE

BOOK TWO

The last thing Prudence Atwater wants is a husband, for her sole purpose in life is to run The Atwater Finishing School for Young Ladies. But her beloved institution is not just *any* finishing school, for secretly, her ambition is to rescue unfortunates from the streets, even if it means dressing up as a streetwalker herself in order to infiltrate their world. What she doesn't count on one memorable night outside Drury Lane is to be propositioned by a devilishly handsome nobleman who leaves her breathless...

After a night at the theater, Lord Alfred Weston is surprised to find himself engaged in a most titillating conversation with a strangely intriguing and intelligent light-skirt. The moment ends in a heated kiss, followed by an inconvenient turn of events that leaves him desperate to track down the cheeky tart who caused him to wind up in the *Times*. Imagine his surprise when he discovers that by day, she is a bookish, innocent school-marm!

Like Prudence, Alfred has no interest in the shackles of marriage, but this strikingly beautiful and recklessly independent young woman arouses his passions—and his frustrations—at every turn. Alfred vows to have her in his bed, and to do that he must find a way to tame her.

"Filled with a colorful cast of characters and laugh-out-loud moments, the story of Lord Weston and the incomparable Miss Prudence Atwater is an enjoyable, entertaining, and deliciously sexy Regency romp."

– USA Today bestselling author, Julianne MacLean

HIS COURTESAN BRIDE

BOOK THREE

When Miss Serena Ransom is caught in a scandalous embrace with Lord Kane at a Mayfair ball, her reputation is destroyed and her future looks grim. But when she joins The Courtesan Club, conceived by the famous courtesan, Lady Night, Serena begins a new life and vows to take charge of her own destiny as never before. Serena is a celebrity, and London's most powerful men are competing to become her lover and protector.

Everything is falling into place, except for the one man who threatens everything—Darius Manning, the Earl of Kane.

Serena stirred Darius's passions as no other woman ever had. Even as he kissed her that night at the Mayfair ball, he knew he could never make her his wife, for he was pledged to another. Now, years later, Darius is free at last and cannot forget the passionate, auburn-haired miss that still fires his blood. The wealthy Lord Kane makes Serena an offer she can't refuse, to share his bed as his exclusive courtesan.

But as Darius and Serena begin a journey of unbound pleasure together, they soon learn that the most dangerous emotion of all isn't passion, or desire... but love.

Read on for an excerpt from TAMING THE BRIDE...

Enjoy an excerpt from

TAMING
the BRIDE

BRIDES *of* MAYFAIR SERIES – BOOK 2

MICHELLE MCMASTER

CHAPTER 1

London, 1816

"There, Miss—" Dolly said as she yanked Prudence's plunging neckline quite decidedly lower, "ye looks just like a proper Drury Lane trollop. Sort o' like me when I was plyin' the trade."

"I do look most convincing, thanks to your expert touch, Dolly," Prudence replied, assessing her reflection in the mirror.

She had done this so many times, yet still the sight of herself thus dressed—or *undressed*, as it were—still surprised her, to say the least. Thanks to Dolly's ministrations, Prudence's breasts swelled enticingly over the tight, red satin bodice, like cream-puffs rising out of a pan. Her skirts were hiked up to expose a generous length of her thigh, which was clad in a scandalous striped silk stocking. Her flame-colored hair, usually held captive in a severe knot, now fell wildly about her shoulders in a tangle of curls.

She looked like a harlot.

Which was exactly what she wanted to look like.

She wondered if she would she ever get used to it. But what choice did she have?

Dolly bent down to tuck Prudence's skirts up around

the red satin garter that hugged the top of her thigh. "That red hair o' yours naturally draws the eye," she pronounced, "and when they see this shapely leg—ye'll be stealin' all the gents away from the proper lightskirts, or my name ain't Dolly Simms."

Apparently satisfied with her handiwork, Dolly regarded Prudence with a serious expression. "But miss, are ye sure ye should be doin' this? A young lady like ye walkin' the streets—well, it don't seem right, it don't. Ye should be settin' at the fire with yer needlepoint, not dressin' up like a tart and lurkin' about London at night."

"I like to think of it as more of a treasure hunt," Prudence said, patting her friend's arm. "And I have Mungo with me for protection. How else am I to find more students to keep you company at the Atwater Finishing School for Young Ladies? Why, you and I would never have met if I didn't make a habit of walking the streets."

"That may be true, miss, but for ye to be puttin' yerself in danger for the likes o' us—"

"The 'likes' of who?" Prudence said, cocking an eyebrow. "There are only *ladies* at the Atwater School, Dolly—no 'likes' of anyone at all. And there is no danger. None that I can't handle, at any rate."

Dolly laughed. "If ye say so, miss."

"I do, Dolly," she confirmed. "Danger or no danger, it is our duty to help those who are not as fortunate as ourselves. That is what Papa taught me—that education is the great equalizer of society. With the Atwater Finishing School for Young Ladies, I intend to take as many unfortunate girls off the street as I can, and give them a quality education. It is what Papa would have wanted to do himself, if he had lived longer."

"Lud!" Dolly exclaimed. "What would 'e say if 'e saw ye now—lookin' like a such a lewd hussy? I daresay 'e wouldn't let ye go about town in such a manner, no matter what ye say."

Prudence felt a lump form in her throat and promptly swallowed it. "He would understand the necessity of such actions," she said, quietly. "I'm sure he would."

Dolly put an arm around Prudence's shoulder and gave a gentle squeeze. "An' so 'e would. Yer father must 'ave been quite a man indeed. Raised a right fine lady, so 'e did—and ye just a girl when yer poor mother died. She'd be proud of such a courageous daughter, I'll reckon."

Dolly smiled warmly at her. "I remember the night ye come across me, miss...rainin' as 'ard as it was, and ye tryin' t' pass ye'self off as a lightskirt. Ye looked like a drowned rat, so ye did. If ye 'adn't taken me home with ye, well it don't bear thinkin' about. I 'adn't eaten for days, and there was no work that night. Probably would o' died if it 'adn't been for ye. And now thanks to ye, I've got a real job as a housekeeper. I thank ye miss—ye and Lady Weston both."

Prudence fastened the clasps on some cheap-looking earbobs and said, "I shudder to think of our patroness's reaction to knowing I was dressed like this, out on the streets myself. Lady Weston might very well pull her support from the Atwater School, and we need her funds to stay afloat. We must strive to keep my nocturnal adventures a secret from the dear old lady."

"Not t' worry, miss," Dolly replied. "I've told a few white lies in me time. I can tell a few more."

"Thank you, Dolly. Now, be a dear and tell Mungo that I will be down in a few moments."

Dolly nodded and left Prudence alone in her bedchamber.

Prudence applied the finishing touch to her costume, fastening a custom-made garter around her thigh. It held a sheath and a sharp little dagger which Mungo assured her would do considerable damage if need be.

It was Mungo who had crafted the garter for her out of leather, and he who had shown her how to defend herself with a blade. So far, she had never had to use the skills the former pirate had taught her. Settling her skirts to conceal the weapon, she hoped she never would.

Looking at the clock, Prudence threw her cloak over her shoulders and headed downstairs. It was almost time for the theater to let out. And that was when most of the customers would come by, looking for a little more entertainment after they'd enjoyed a conventional performance. The streetwalkers would be waiting for them in their usual places. And Prudence would be waiting for the streetwalkers.

"Ah, Miss Atwater," Mungo said, stooping his towering form to bow as she entered the salon. "Ye look delightful this evening."

"Delightful?" Dolly said, quizzically. "She don't look delightful. She looks a disgrace, just as she should." She fussed with Prudence's hair and adjusted the violet silk cloak about her shoulders. "There. Every harlot should be so lucky."

"Thank you for all your help, Dolly," Prudence said, smiling at her friend. "But Mungo, we must make haste. The theater will be letting out. Have you the carriage ready?"

"Yes, Miss. And 'ave you that little dagger I give ye?"

Prudence patted her thigh. "Right here, Mungo."

"But ye won't need t' use it with ol' Mungo around," he said, smiling a gap-toothed grin. "I still got a few pirate tricks in me yet, miss, never fear."

"What would I do without you, Mungo? And you, Dolly—" Prudence asked.

"Probably some more lady-like things than this," Dolly muttered.

Prudence chuckled and took Mungo's offered arm. "Alas, duty calls. Don't wait up."

"But ye knows I always do, miss," Dolly answered.

Mungo opened the door to the carriage and handed Prudence in. Soon they were on their way, and the clip-clop of the horse's hooves echoed down the dark cobblestone street. As she stared out the window, Prudence thought of the task that lay ahead of her this evening.

How many girls could she reach tonight? And how many would she never have the chance to help at all? It was the latter thought that sent a chill to the pit of her stomach.

Prudence had to show these unfortunate women that there was a better way...that there was hope. She had already done so successfully with almost a dozen girls. She hoped to add to their number tonight.

The carriage stopped down the lonely street where it usually did. She heard Mungo hop down from the top and then the door swung open, his big strong hand reaching in to help her out. He spoke a few words to the driver instructing him to wait. Then they headed down the dark narrow lane towards the Theater District.

"Why does ye go t' all this trouble, miss?" Mungo asked. "For a bunch o' whores? I mean, I think it's lovely, ye dressin' up an' all, but why don't I just swipe a few for ye? Save a lot o' time, it would."

"No, Mungo," she replied. "They must come to the school of their own free will. Kidnapping these girls would do no good. They'd simply run away.

One thing my father taught me was that you can't force happiness on a person. They must reach for it themselves."

Prudence motioned for them to stop behind a leafy oak. The light from a nearby gaslamp fell in a dappled pattern across Mungo's face and made him look even more terrifying than usual. Prudence wanted to laugh, for in truth Mungo Church was as gentle and faithful as an old dog, though he liked to play the roaring lion. Tonight, she would need the lion's protection as she went on the hunt.

"I see a few girls across the street, there," Prudence said. "I'll stand here for awhile and make my way over to them. You may keep watch from behind this tree, Mungo, but keep well-hidden. No one must see that you are with me. If I need help, I'll scream."

Mungo nodded and folded his arms across his chest. "I'll be beside ye before the first scream can pass yer lips, miss."

"Wish me luck," she said, turning toward the street.

"Good luck, then," he said and gave her a nod.

Prudence walked to the corner, pushing up her breasts as if they were feather pillows that needed to be fluffed. She shook her hair and arranged it over her shoulders. Then she pinched her cheeks to make them rosy, though she didn't know what good it would do in the dark.

She stood for awhile, keeping to the shadows as she watched the passersby amble down the street. A few gentlemen walked by, some looking at her with leering grins, and some ignoring her completely.

Soon a dark-haired young girl appeared on the next corner. She eyed Prudence warily from the shadows, like a frightened alley-cat looking for food. Her clothes were shabby, much shabbier than Prudence's costume, and her face looked gaunt and smudged with dirt. She couldn't have been older than sixteen.

Prudence wondered how long the girl had been coming to this corner. Weeks? Months? A sick feeling swam in her gut. But as the girl made eye contact again, Prudence felt the rush of promise in her heart. This could be the Atwater School's next student.

Prudence began to stroll toward the girl non-chalantly, as if she were simply looking for a better spot to peddle her wares.

But something made her stop.

She felt a presence near her, quite close, in fact. Whoever it was, she would have to handle it like an experienced streetwalker or risk destroying her disguise. Hadn't she done it before?

Forcing her nerves to stay calm, she turned slowly.

A man leaned back against the wrought-iron fence. He seemed to be lounging there, as if in a favorite club, with his arms folded easily across his chest and his glossy boots crossed at the ankles.

He was dressed in a fashionably cut frock coat, which looked almost black in the lamplight. His neck cloth was tied in the latest fashion and his shiny beaver hat perched at the perfect angle upon his head. Dark curly hair framed a face that could only be described as devilishly handsome.

Prudence realized that he was grinning at her. And in the shadows, his eyes—which seemed to be as black as the night around them—sparkled mischievously.

"Without appearing to be bold," the man said in a languid voice, "may

I ask what it is you are doing?"

Prudence winked at him and shifted her shoulders. Trying to emulate Dolly's cockney accent, she said, "Just plyin' the trade, Guvna. And not ta worry—I likes 'em bold."

He chuckled, saying, "Do you, now? I must say I find that surprising."

"Ye shouldn't be surprised, sir," she replied. "I mean, me bein' a trollop an all."

"And yet I am," he said, smiling and standing away from the fence, "for you look about as much like a trollop as I do."

"Oh, Guvna!" Prudence exclaimed, feigning injury. "Yer hurtin' me feelin's, now. Be assured, sir, that I am a trollop. Of the first order."

With a sweeping bow, he said, "My apologies, madam. I am mistaken. I did not mean to insinuate that you were anything less than Drury Lane's most experienced, most highly regarded, most sought after trollop in recent history."

Prudence glanced over at the girl she'd been watching on the next corner. She was ambling down the street, presumably to find a better location.

Prudence would have to move fast or risk losing her.

She smiled again at the man. "So right, sir—so right. Ye've hit the nail on the 'ead. And now, I must go join me friend, there. Good evenin'."

She made to turn away, but the man's voice stopped her, though why it should, she didn't know. Perhaps it was the velvety smoothness of it, or the complete confidence of his tone that made her freeze as if suddenly rooted to the spot.

"But you have not given me a chance to ask for the pleasure of your company this evening. And I would so enjoy the pleasure of your company, little flower."

The man stepped 'round and stood directly in front of her, blocking her path. He reached out to touch a tendril of her hair, and for a reason Prudence couldn't fathom, she let him.

"You see," he continued, gently twirling the hair around his finger, "I know your secret, Lady Trollop."

Prudence swallowed. "My secret?"

He stepped closer. *Oh, where was Mungo? And why wasn't she calling for his help?*

But all Prudence could do was stare at this dark stranger who stood so close to her and curled her hair about his finger as if it was the most natural thing in the world for him to do.

"Right away, it was obvious to me that you did not belong here," he began. "And it took a few moments to understand why. But now that I do, I wish to help you."

"You do?" Prudence said, confused.

"Yes, my sweet." He touched her face lightly with the back of his knuckles. The intimate sensation of his warm skin brushing against hers was shocking, yet exquisite.

"You see, now that I know the truth," he said softly, "I've decided I would like nothing more than to oblige you by being your *first paying customer.*"

Short Story Collections by Michelle McMaster

SUMMER PASSIONS

Seasons of Love Volume 1
Three Delicious Regency Short Stories

"A lady should enjoy those hot summer nights..."

For three lovely ladies in Regency England, the long, hot summer holds the opportunity for decadent pleasures, wicked pursuits, and forbidden passion.

CUPID'S DART

The Marquess of St. Clair has long been a thorn in Daphne Summerville's side. But when she is forced to act as his nursemaid after a bizarre accident, Daphne discovers that the Notorious Marquess has sensual talents she never knew existed.

LADY ASHTON TAKES A LOVER

Lady Ashton's friends finally convince her to take a lover for the summer. At a wicked masquerade ball, she meets a mysterious man who fires her passions and turns her world completely upside down, threatening all she holds dear.

THE WEDDING PARTY

Jilted by her intended, Lady Althea Ramsay calls in a favor from her brother's friend, the Duke of Wakefield. He will pose as her fiancé at a society wedding which the odious man will be attending. But Althea soon discovers that playing a part can set real desires burning in the human heart.

Autumn Desires

Seasons of Love Volume II

When autumn leaves start to fall, passions burn like fire...

The second volume in the delightful SEASONS OF LOVE quartet features three unforgettable Regency heroines in three delectable, entertaining short stories.

The Taming of Miss Carew

Helena "the Hellion" Carew takes pride in speaking her mind, even if it sends most eligible bachelors packing. When her father loses his estate—and Helena—in a card game, she meets the brutish Lord Adrian Rutherford, the one man who has a chance at taming her.

Branded

Abandoned by her husband, Lady Alexandra Trent lives a quiet life in the countryside with her young son, trying desperately to forget the man who left her heart in tatters. But when Brandon returns, he awakens dangerous desires and makes a shocking demand of his wife.

Thief of Hearts

Olivia and Jack are two of London's most notorious jewel thieves. Skilled and passionate lovers, they take each other to the heights of physical pleasure, yet keep their true feelings secret. As they prepare for their next heist, Olivia discovers something about Jack that could change their lives forever.

About the Author

MICHELLE MCMASTER loves writing about dashing heroes and spunky heroines in her historical romances, and is known for humorous dialogue and memorable characters. Michelle holds a degree in English Literature from Dalhousie University, Nova Scotia. She enjoys traveling, reading, quilting, and gardening. She lives on the east coast of Canada with her husband and their two dogs, a Nova Scotia Duck Tolling Retriever and a Border Collie mix. Please visit her website at www.MichelleMcMaster.com for more information about her novels and to sign up for her email newsletter to stay informed about future new releases.

If you enjoy fast paced thrillers, Michelle McMaster also writes under the pen name Avery Holt. Check out her website at www.AveryHolt.com and look for her exciting *Watch Me* series.

29028209R00171

Made in the USA
Columbia, SC
19 October 2018